PATRICK THOMAS

PADWOLF PUBLISHING INC.
WWW.PADWOLF.COM
www.facebook.com/Padwolf

WWW.PATTHOMAS.NET
www.facebook.com/PatrickThomasAuthor
WWW.MURPHYS-LORE.COM

MURPHY'S LORE AFTER HOURS™: THE MUG LIFE

© 2019 Patrick Thomas

COVER ART BY PATRICK THOMAS

BOOK EDITED BY JOHN L. FRENCH

Short Fuse was originally published in The Stories in Between: A Between Books Anthology edited by Greg Schauer (and Dan Clyne won a contest to be tuckerized in the story.)

The Gargler's Game was originally published in Dragon's Lure edited by Danielle Ackley-McPhail

Sad Daye was originally published in Terrorbelle The Unconquered

Iron Bars was originally published as Terrorbelle at the Alamo in Time Capsule edited by Edward J. McFadden III

Be Careful was originally published in Hellfire Lounge 3: Jinn Rummy edited by R. Allen Leider

ISBN: 13 digit 978-1-890096-84-7   10 digit 1-890096-84-9

Printed in the USA First Printing

Evil walks the Earth in many forms, but so do those who oppose it. Protecting the innocent & seeking justice, they fight to beat back the darkness. Their names are legend or soon shall be. Welcome To Murphy's Lore After Hours.

PRAISE FOR THE MURPHY'S LORE SERIES:

"MIX GAIMAN'S AMERICAN GODS & ROBINSON'S CALLIHAN'S CROSSTIME SALOON ON PRACHETT'S DISCWORLD AND YOU GET AN IDEA OF PATRICK THOMAS' MURPHY'S LORE." -David Sherman, author of STARFIST and DEMONTECH

"ENTERTAINING, INVENTIVE AND DELIGHTFULLY CREEPY." -JONATHAN MABERRY, Bram Stoker Award Winning Author and bestselling author of Rot & Ruin, V-Wars and ZOMBIE CSU

"A GIFTED AND INTELLIGENT WRITER...UNIGUE AND ENTERTAINING STORIES." -EDWARD DOUGLAS, MIDNIGHT SYNDICATE, Director of THE DEAD MATTER

"UNIQUE BLEND OF FANTASY/HORROR/HUMOR... HORROR FANS WILL LOVE THE CAST OF WEIRD CHARACTERS... IS ALWAYS A FAST FUN READ & A PLACE YOU'LL WANT TO VISIT AGAIN." -Nick Cato, THE HORROR FICTION REVIEW

"JOIN HEX, PADDY & THE GANG IN THEIR RACE TO UNDO THE FUTURE IN FOOLS' DAY, PART OF HIS COMIC MURPHY'S LORE SERIES."   -PUBLISHER'S WEEKLY

"WANT TO LEAVE YOUR LIFE BEHIND? THEN FOLLOW ME TO BULFINCHE'S PUB... THE CLIENTELE WILL NEVER CEASE TO AMAZE YOU." -Michael Laimo, PIRATE WRITINGS

"HERE MAGIC IS THE NORM... MURPHY'S LORE OFFERS THE READER A LOOK AT THE WORLD BEYOND." -Alan Zimmerman, THE NEW YORK PRESS

"A DELICIOUS COCKTAIL OF HUMOR, FANTASY & HEART WITH A DASH OF SUSPENSE THAT YOU WON'T BE ABLE TO PUT DOWN... MOST OF THE TALES MIX LAUGH-OUT LOUD BITS WITH SERIOUS CONSEQUENCES, BUT THE MOST AMAZING PART IS HOW AUTHOR PATRICK THOMAS BLENDS REAL-WORLD ISSUES AND THE MAGICAL PATRONS WITHOUT BEING TRITE, MAUDLIN OR PREDICTABLE."   -Beth Hannan Rimmels, THE LONG ISLAND VOICE

"SUCCESSFULLY COMBINES HORROR AND COMEDY... A DIFFICULT THING TO DO AND THOMAS DOES IT WITH FLYING COLORS. I RECOMMEND THIS BOOK HIGHLY AND... LOOK FORWARD TO SEE MORE OF THIS SERIES."   –D.W. Jones, BLOOD MOON RISING

"THE CHARACTERS ARE ENGAGING AND AMUSING...THE PLOTLINES ARE CREATIVE AND ENTERTAINING." -Sara Sutterfield Winn, GREEN MAN REVIEW

"DON'T EVER THINK TO PRESUME THAT YOU KNOW WHAT'S COMING NEXT. THE STORIES ARE FUNNY... ENTERTAINING. ....LINGER IN THE MIND FOR AGES AFTER YOU'VE READ THEM... A SOLID GROUNDING IN THE MULTIPLICITY OF HISTORY, RELIGION AND MYTH OF THE HUMAN RACE... WHENEVER A RAINBOW BEACON LEADS A TROUBLED SOUL TO THE DOOR OF BULFINCHE'S, HE, SHE OR IT WILL ALWAYS FIND SURCEASE AND HELP... THE BEST THING ABOUT THESE STORIES IS THAT THEY ADDRESS SOCIAL ISSUES RIGHT ALONG SIDE THE WHIMSICAL ONES."   -Marianne Plumridge, INFINITY UK

"FUNNY, DRAMATIC, ACTION PACKED; " -Jon Minors, G-POP

"AN EXCITING TALE...SIMULTANEOUSLY HYSTERICAL & DOWNRIGHT CREEPY."   -Michael D. Pederson, N[th] DEGREE

BOOKS BY PATRICK THOMAS

The Murphy's Lore™ series
TALES FROM BULFINCHE'S PUB
FOOLS' DAY
THROUGH THE DRINKING GLASS
SHADOW OF THE WOLF
REDEMPTION ROAD
BARTENDER OF THE GODS

Murphy's Lore After Hours™
NIGHTCAPS
EMPTY GRAVES
THE MUG LIFE

Murphy's Lore Startenders™
STARTENDERS
CONSTELLATION PRIZE

Murphy's Lore After Hours™ Universe
Terrorbelle:
FAIRY WITH A GUN
FAIRY RIDES THE LIGHTNING
TERRORBELLE THE UNCONQUERED
Agent Karver:
RITES OF PASSAGE *(with John French)*
DEAD TO RITES
Hell's Detective:
LORE & DYSORDER
BULLETS & BRIMSTONE
(with John French)
THE CASE OF THE MOON MANIAC
(graphic novel with Blair Webb)
Hexcraft:
BY DARKNESS CURSED
BY INVOCATION ONLY
Soul for Hire:
GREATEST HITS

Xiles:
EXILE & ENTRANCE

Dear Cthulhu™ Series
HAVE A DARK DAY
GOOD ADVICE FOR BAD PEOPLE
CTHULHU KNOWS BEST
WHAT WOULD CTHULHU DO?
CTHULHU HAPPENS
CTHULHU EXPLAINS IT ALL

Mystic Investigators™ series
MYSTIC INVESTIGATORS
MEAN STREETS
ONCE MORE IN CRIME omnibus
by Patrick Thomas & Diane Raetz
SHADOWS & BRIMSTONES omnibus
by Patrick Thomas & John L. French

Playworlds:
AS THE GEARS TURN:
Tales of Steamworld

YA:
THE WILDSIDHE CHRONICLES
OMNIBUS *(contributing author)*

Anthologies as co-editor
NEW BLOOD *(with Diane Raetz)*
CAMELOT 13 *(with John French)*

THE JACK GARDNER MYSTERIES
THE ASSASSAINS' BALL *(with John French)*

Writing as Patrick T. Fibbs
UNDEAD KID DIARIES™:
OVER MY DEAD BODY
BABE B. BEAR MYSTERIES™:
BAD HAIR DAY
5 SILLY MONSTERS JUMPING ON
THE ZED: *an Ughaboos™ picture book*

This one's for Chester Thomas.
Miss you Dad.

TABLE OF CONTENTS

AN END TO PAIN

I have the greatest job in the world tending bar here at Bulfinche's Pub, but even at the NYC bar at the end of the rainbow, you can have a bad day.

For one thing, I woke up feeling like I've been hit by a truck. It wasn't a truck, it was our bouncer Hercules. Not that he was hitting me for no reason. He kept telling me it was for my own good. I know that makes me sound like I was in an abusive relationship but despite being the best job in the world, there are times at Bulfinche's Pub where my job leads to situations that go into dangerous territory and beyond.

Herc is a demigod, my boss Paddy Moran is a leprechaun. Dionysius, my fellow bartender, is the Greco-Roman God of wine, women, and song although not necessarily in that order. Fred our busboy and part-time bartender was a satyr who was stronger and faster than most people. Even our dishwasher Mathew was a runaway angel.

In the midst of all that power, I was just a human who's only exceptional talent was my sense of humor. Although there are those who would argue that.

Herc harped that I had to be in good shape and constantly practice my fighting and survival skills. Considering those skills have saved my life on more than one occasion, I stopped arguing with him a while ago.

Giving him a hard time, however, was another matter.

"Murphy, you look like you're hurt today," Hex said.

"I think I know how you feel on your bad days."

The magí was cursed. Hex can use any kind of magic and had the potential to be one of the most powerful people on the planet if he hadn't been cursed years ago so that using any kind of magic causes him pain.

"I doubt it," Hex said.

"I'd love to be able to feel just sore from working out," said Darren Willow.

I instantly regretted complaining. Having to see what happens to people like Darren is also what was what was really making my day bad. Six months ago, Darren was diagnosed with cancer. After three months of chemo and radiation, he thought he had it beat but then they found that the cancer had metastasized and spread to his brain, among other places. Darren wasn't long for this world. It was similar to how my late wife Elsie died and really hit home.

"Sorry for complaining," I said.

Darren chuckled but there was no humor in it. More of a social nicety. "Nothing to be sorry about Murphy. We've all got to play the hand we're dealt, although I wouldn't mind if life played by Bulfinche's poker rules.

Both Hex and I chuckled at that one. Ages ago the boss's late wife had found it shameful to see her husband and several of the staff and patrons cheat at cards and insisted they play by the rules. So Paddy changed the rules - players can cheat as much as they want as long as they don't get caught. If a player gets caught, they lose. It makes for some very interesting games. I once won a pot with seven aces, all of them hearts.

"To hell with this." Darren shoved his club soda with lime across the bar at me. "I want a real drink. Give me bourbon and make it a triple."

I hesitated. We tended to give most people what they wanted or needed, but it was a bartender's prerogative to refuse service if he thought there was a good enough reason. I wasn't sure there was but I needed to find out. "Won't that mess up your chemo?"

"Bah. It's already taken my hair, my strength, and my endurance."

"Then why go through it?" Hex said. He was actually a doctor with a specialty in psychiatry although he had done some time in an ER.

"Because the oncologist told me there was a 15% chance it might work and I may go down but I'm going out fighting. I got one week left and I don't think it's doing any good."

I looked over at Hermes at the end of the bar and he was actually sitting still for once. The god of travelers could move at speeds most people couldn't even dream of, but here in Bulfinche's Pub magic powers didn't work without the boss's dispensation so he got to move at the same speed as the rest of us. I caught his eye and Hermes shook his head. He had dispensation to use the healing aspects of his powers in the bar which included him being able to diagnose better than any MRI or CAT scan. I knew he had consulted on Darren's case but I also knew that even the god of physicians couldn't save everybody. I pointed with my nose towards the bourbon. Hermes gave me a quick nod.

I poured Darren out his drink and pushed it across the bar to him. He took a small sip, had a small coughing fit then took a second sip which seemed to stop the coughing. Then he sat staring at the drink which is when the door opened and Ixtab walked in. That made me nervous.

Ixtab was a mostly forgotten goddess from the Mayan Pantheon with a rather disturbing specialty. Besides being the queen of their underworld and protector of women in childbirth she was also the goddess of suicide. Ixtab wore a very unusual necklace that looked just like a hangman's noose, although when she was trying to pass as human it looked like a thick piece of jewelry.

Today wasn't one of the days when the forgotten gods could cross over without aid so I wondered how she had materialized in the mortal plane, although I had an idea.

Ixtab came over to my station.

The death goddess nodded to the magi. "Hex."

Hex nodded back. "Ixtab."

Next, she turned to me. "Hello, Murphy, my friend."

"Hello, Ixtab."

She leaned forward over the bar. I did the same and we kissed each other on the cheek. No, it wasn't a Godfather-like thing where she was setting me up to die. She's actually helped us catch a Gaizkin, a creature that causes people to commit suicide. She's actually a nice person. A lot of the death gods are once you get to know them, but due to their day jobs, let's just say they don't get invited to a lot of parties, even by their fellow deities.

"You know I'm always happy to see you but considering the day, I've got to ask if you're working," I whispered into her ear.

"I am."

Darren was still sitting there staring at his drink. My eyes darted towards him and the Mayan goddess of suicides nodded.

"Among others."

Before I could ask her to elaborate, the door slammed open and a portly man in his forties shoved two kids through the door. The boy might've been five or six, the girl seven. The kids' eyes were almost all pupils and they were trembling. Portly had what looked like a 38 revolver in his right hand.

Unfortunately, our bouncer Hercules wasn't in yet. Although our sparring session had left me tenderized like a hunk of meat, Herc had gone out carousing and ended up in Boston, quite a ways from Manhattan.

He'd called to let us know he was on his way but he wouldn't be back for over an hour. Hermes stood but I held up a hand and motioned him back down. If we been outside the bar Hermes would've already taken the gun and the children away from the guy but inside Bulfinche's he was no faster than the rest of us. I looked at Fred in the corner of the room and motioned with my eyes for him to go behind the guy.

I stepped out from behind the bar.

"You want help, Murphy?" Hex said.

I shook my head. "I got this."

All the employees here had their own style for handling situations like this. Mine was a bit different from the others but it always worked so far.

When I got to Portly I genuflected down on one knee in front of the kids.

"Hi, kids. Welcome to Bulfinche's Pub. I'm one of the bartenders here and my name's Murphy." I held my hand out to the little girl. "What yours?"

"Tiffany." She took my hand and I shook it in an exaggerated and silly manner while giving her a goofy smile.

I turned to the boy. "What about you?"

"Billy," he said in a voice barely above a whisper. I repeated the silly handshake and found the barrel of the gun pointed straight at my forehead.

"What the hell you think you're doing with my kids?" Portly said.

I stood up slowly and he kept the gun trained on a spot between my eyebrows.

"Watch the language, please. There are ladies and children present." I put my hands behind both children and slowly moved them so they were behind me.

"You have a death wish?"

"No, but I had to deal with one of those once." Involved a jinn turning a guy into a zombie. It wasn't pretty. "But I'm guessing you do."

What Portly suitably distracted by me, Fred sprinted, picked up both kids ran them over towards to the bar, putting them down next to Darren. Fred was probably the fastest of us inside the bar. He had special shoes that covered his hooves but his musculature gave them some serious running power even without magic.

"You better will damn well bring my kids back here…"

"Listen, Buddy, I already spoke to you about the language. Obviously, there's something wrong with you since you have a gun out in front of your kids but do you not understand English? We've got a bunch of people here at the bar who speak a lot of different languages, so if you need a translator, just ask."

Portly cocked the hammer back.

"Bring my kids back over here…" Darren stepped off his bar stool and stepped in front of the kids with his arms out to the side, ready to be a human shield if the need arose. It would have seemed odd to an outsider that Hermes, Hex, Ixtab, and the rest of the regulars didn't seem very nervous. The kids still seemed terrified.

"… Or I'll decorate this dump with your brains."

"I'm sorry but you just don't have authorization to do any redecorating. I'm afraid I'd have to see permission in writing from my boss before I can allow you to the paint anything in here. And brains really is never the way to go. They don't go on smooth, the lumps are very noticeable and between the gray matter mixing in with the white matter, it really doesn't go with anything."

Portly must not have been amused because he pulled the trigger. He was expecting the explosive noise of a gunshot but there was only a click. However, a loud noise came from me lunging forward with my head and hands towards his face and yelling loudly. "Bang!"

My actions startled him to the point where he lurched backwards and I was able to grab his wrist, bend it back and take the gun away. I tossed the weapon to Fred who opened up the cylinder, dumped the bullets into an empty beer pitcher and then placed the gun and the pitcher behind the bar.

"Why aren't you dead?" Portly said.

I held on to his wrist and bent it back more, causing him to drop to his knees. It was a surprisingly effective way to control somebody without doing permanent damage. Avoiding permanent damage was big on the boss's list of priorities.

"Guns don't work in here."

Another of the bar's special properties. Guns will work without Paddy's say so and to the best of my knowledge, he's never given any gun dispensation.

"On your feet."

Portly told me to go procreate with myself.

I bent his wrist back hard and he hit the floor face first. "I've already talked to you about language twice." Portly was whimpering in pain. "If there's a fourth time, you will regret it. Now get on your feet and walk over there."

As he stumbled to his feet and I guided him by his wrist over to his children. "Apologize to Tiffany and Billy."

Portly started with some more colorful language but before he could finish the phrase, I added bending his fingers to the mix.

"I'm sorry, kids."

"It's okay, Daddy," Tiffany said.

"No, it's not. No adult should ever harm a child, let alone a parent hurt their own kid," I said. "Fred, grab some coloring books and crayons for the kids."

The satyr reached behind the bar, got a stack of coloring books and a metal pail full of crayons and brought them over to a corner table. Hermes, Hex, and a bunch of the other adults in the room came over grabbed coloring books and joined the kids. It was an effort to both distract the kids and have some fun themselves.

That left me to deal with Portly.

"You want to explain to me exactly what was going on when came in here?"

"I don't have to tell you a damn…" Portly thought better of it. "…darn thing."

Even without her magic, Ixtab came across as a dangerous woman. With a sharp look and a raspy voice she said, "Answer the man."

Portly jumped back and bumped into the bar.

"Not that it's any of your business but my ex-wife is a bitc..." We really weren't that strict about language but I'd already started in on this guy so I cleared my throat and he swallowed hard. "She's an evil woman. She cheated on me but she got the house, full custody of the kids, and most of my money and half my pension. I had to move into a tiny little apartment and only see my kids every other weekend. It ain't right but the judge doesn't care and I don't have enough money left to pay a lawyer to fight it. She cheated on me, she destroyed her family, and she was given everything and there's nothing I can do about it. Nothing I can do to hurt her. Nothing except one thing."

I had to force myself not to punch this guy in the face. I let go of his hand so I wouldn't break his fingers. "Kill your own kids."

"And then kill yourself," Ixtab whispered.

Portly looked at the death goddess and saw something in her eyes that frightened him. He turned back toward me.

"Yeah. If I can't have them, why should she? I know there's no God or heaven because if there was then none of this would have happened. So I shoot myself and I don't have to go to jail. Besides those little b..." I cleared my throat again. "… Ingrates are already spending more time with her new boyfriend than they are with me. Their mother is even telling them to call him "Daddy'. What kind of a person does that?"

"A very mean one. But how do you get from there to killing your own flesh and blood? You could still try to be the best dad you could be, then when the kids are 12 they can choose who they want to live with," I said.

"She's got the house and I have a crappy apartment in a bad neighborhood. Who do you think they're going to pick? Plus, her new boyfriend's rich and has already bought each of them a big screen TV for their rooms. I have an old tube TV for my apartment. This is the only way I get to win."

"What kind of a man thinks murdering his kids and killing himself is a good solution, let alone a win?"

"One who suffered more pain than he can bear." I was surprised by the gentleness of Ixtab's voice.

"Now that you know my life story, give me back my gun and we'll be on our way."

"Sure and then I'll help push all three of you in front of the bus so you can save on the cost of the bullets."

"You can't do that. If I die, she still gets my life insurance policy, but from a suicide she won't get paid."

"It's not something that I usually have to explain, but I was being sarcastic. You're not getting the gun back. Or the kids. Or leaving here by yourself."

"You can't keep my kids. That's kidnapping."

"You said you only have custody's every other weekend. Today is a Tuesday. I think it's pretty safe to assume that you've already kidnapped them," I said.

"If you don't let me go, then you're kidnapping me."

"I think technically for kidnapping we'd have to take you somewhere. You came to us. I think the proper way to describe what we are doing is imprisoning you against your will. I really appreciate it if you got the crimes we're committing straight."

But that did leave me with a bit of a dilemma. Usually, in cases like this, Paddy was around and he made the call about what we did with somebody – whether it was teaching them a lesson or calling the cops.

Paddy was off visiting one of his kids in Orun Reres, a city in Faerie founded by Native Americans and escaped slaves that Paddy helped rescue with the Underground Railroad back in the days before the Civil War. It wasn't like I could just call him and ask him for his advice. And he had left me in charge which meant it was my responsibility, not something I could shirk off on Hermes or Fred.

Ixtab seemed to sense my dilemma.

"Murphy, if I may make a suggestion as to what should be done with William Senior here."

"Absolutely."

"William is not by nature an evil man. He has just been betrayed by the woman who'd sworn to love him for the rest of their lives. He has lost everything of value in his life. Can you imagine the pain he must be in to even consider doing something like this?"

"No, I can't." Although I did try. I tried to picture what it would've been like if my late wife Elsie had ever cheated on me and left me for another man. It probably would've left me a broken mess. Then oddly enough my mind pictured Terrorbelle dating the movie star who asked her out and found I was disturbed by that thought as well. Which was odd since we weren't together romantically and never had been.

"I think he needs help more than he needs punishment."

"What kind of help are you suggesting?"

"I think William should be committed to a psychiatric facility where he can go through counseling and given medication to help deal with his pain and his loss until such a time as he's not a danger to himself or those he loves."

"You think I will let you use my health insurance to put me away, then you're crazier than me. I'm out of here."

Portly walked toward the door. I moved to stop him but Ixtab grab hold of my hand in hers. Her fingers were ice cold.

"I got this, Murphy."

William ran out the door with Ixtab hot on his heels. He didn't get far before she got in front of him. And by that, I don't mean she ran faster than him. It was much more frightening than that. As soon as she hit the sidewalk outside of the bar's mystic null zone, the death goddess transformed. Her face became a skull, her clothes tore into rags and the noose necklace grew to become a thick rope whose noose end floated up in the air behind her and while the other end wrapped around her throat and she flew in front of him like she was being hung.

I watched through the barroom window as her skull then transformed into something that was probably going to give me nightmares. The noose snaked out and wrapped around his feet and lifted him up so he was hanging upside down in front of her so they looked into each other's eyes.

Outside of the bar, I've looked into the eyes of death gods and John Thanatos, Death himself. Let me tell you, no matter how nice they are, it is still a bone-chilling experience.

The pair exchanged words after which the noose threw William onto the ground. Portly ran back into the bar as Ixtab floated down to the sidewalk and followed him in, transformed back into her human aspect with smooth skin and a pretty dress. The noose was back to looking like jewelry.

"I've changed my mind. I'd like to be committed. Right away if possible," William said to me as his body trembled like a leaf in a storm.

"And?" Ixtab added in a whisper.

"And I will voluntarily sign a form relinquishing my custody of my children until Ixtab here says I can see them again."

"Hermes, I was hoping you might write something up for us?" Ixtab said.

"I'd be happy to." Hermes got a laptop from behind the bar and began typing swiftly. It wasn't supernaturally fast, but it was quick enough to make most typists jealous.

"Now go say goodbye to your children and tell them again that you're sorry, that you love them and that you will see them soon. If you try to do anything to hurt them…" Ixtab simply smiled and William shook so fiercely that he couldn't hold his arms still. Portly gulped and nodded then went over to where his children were coloring.

They were nice kids. They each gave him the pictures they had been coloring after he told him he was sick and he was going to go away to a hospital to get better.

"Murphy, I was hoping you could make two calls for me. Ringvue first." I nodded. That wasn't its real name, but it's what we called it. It was an asylum that dealt with problems of a supernatural nature. It was run by an archangel who played darn good trumpet.

"I'll give Gabe a call. Paddy has an account there so we'll make sure things are covered. And I'll call the kids' mother."

The death goddess smiled. "Which of course was my second request."

Ixtab moved to stand behind William as he sat to color his own page. In fact, he colored two and gave one to each of his children.

Gabe was able to send over an old-fashioned ambulance. An exceptionally tall man and woman in black scrubs walked in the door and over to me.

"Where is the patient?" the woman asked.

I pointed to William.

Ixtab put a hand on his shoulder. "William, it's time to go."

William nodded and pulled both his kids in for a hug and kissed them both on top of their heads. He walked to the pair in scrubs, then stopped and turned towards me.

"What I almost did is just starting to sink in. Thank you for stopping me."

"You're welcome," I said.

"I'm sorry I tried to shoot you. I hope you can forgive me."

"I'll make you a deal. You go to Ringvue and do the best you can to get better. If Ixtab says you're safe to be around your kids you'll have my forgiveness."

William nodded then turned towards the tall couple. The man took him by the elbow and the woman opened the door and brought him outside. The man got in the back of the padded ambulance and the woman got in front and drove them out of sight.

I ended up hanging two of the colored pages from Tiffany and Billy on the little fridge behind the bar. And of course, I ended hanging up a bunch more from the patrons who too.

Hermes took both kids in the blink of an eye back to their mother and did his best to explain what happened. He counseled her and pointed out how her actions had hurt her ex-husband but we have no idea if it did any good.

Darren came back to the bar where most of his drink was still sitting. He looked it up and took another sip and then put it back down.

"Not going to finish it?" I said.

"Nah. I've come this far with chemo. I only have another week of following the rules until then. After that, if this doesn't work, I'm coming in and getting rip-roaring drunk."

I nodded. "When you do, that night's drinks will be on me."

"Thanks, Murphy. I can't believe everything that happened here today. That idiot was willing to throw away his own life and that of two great kids like they were nothing and I'm doing everything I can to make mine last as long as possible. If this chemo doesn't work, they say the cancer will start attacking my brain and give me what will seem like strokes. I may not be able to walk, talk or take care of myself. It's just not right."

"No, it's not, but there are options." Ixtab placed a hand on his hand. "Do you mind if I walk you home so we can discuss them?"

"Sure."

I started to say something but Hermes had come around behind the bar and put a hand on my shoulder and shook his head.

"But I have to say something. Remind him that hope and happiness never die." It's what hung over the door to the bar written in Gaelic. It was basically our mantra.

"That's true, Murphy, but people do. And just because someone has hope doesn't mean that the hope will be realized. Darren is in for a very painful end with the potential of having his mind to be trapped inside a crippled body racked with pain."

Ixtab held open the door for Darren and waved goodbye. She didn't look happy. Neither did I as I waved back.

"But ending life isn't Paddy's way."

"True, but that's Paddy's life. And even he would recognize Darren's right to choose what's best for him. If there's any way of helping or saving him, I'd do it or get it done, but there's not. Ixtab is not going to force him to do anything. She's just going to give him some options. It'll be up to him to decide whether or not to take them."

I nodded. As bad as my day may have been, Darren's and William's were much worse. I've been at Bulfinche's Pub so long I just hated the times we couldn't change things.

Hermes walked out to the front of the bar and as he passed me, he held out my wallet. It was an ongoing struggle for years between us where Hermes pickpocketed my wallet constantly. He hadn't done it since I had managed to turn the tables on him a couple times. I think he was actually being nice by trying to take my mind off of things.

"You're slipping, Murphy. Didn't even notice me get your wallet," he said dropping on the bar in front of me.

"Oh, I noticed, but I was too busy getting yours to do anything about it." I held up his wallet and tossed it towards him. He laughed, nodded his head and tipped the rim of his baseball cap with the Bulfinche's shot of gold logo on it.

Which is when Hercules finally came in the door, walked around behind the bar and downed the entire pot from the coffee maker without pausing or somehow burning his mouth and throat.

"That's better. Sorry I'm late. Did I miss anything?"

"Just the usual," I said.

SHORT FUSE

I suppose there must be odder couples, but I hadn't seen one in a while. Jason Cervantes is an NYPD detective who tops out at about six foot six and that's when he's not in high heels. Bubba Sue is a gremlin from the South whose head wouldn't make it past the top of a yardstick in her best steel-toed boots.

Despite being on opposite ends of the height spectrum, the pair had been dating for a few weeks. I got my updates on the progression of the relationship when the pair visited Bulfinche's Pub where I tend bar. I didn't expect to see them at the mall, especially sitting on a bench making out as both are quite a ways removed from their teenaged years, but love and lust are a pair of splendid things.

Jason's back was to me and Bubba Sue was positioned on his lap, with her face stuck to his, but pointed in my general direction. I walked toward them, debating if passing by would be ruder than interrupting when Bubba Sue's eyes opened and she spotted me. The gremlin pulled her head back and looked at Jas. In an exaggeratedly childlike voice, she said, "Daddy, why do you always kiss me with your tongue like that?"

Jas's ears turned beet red as a mother with a child yanked her son away, beating a quick retreat from the odd couple.

"Young lady, is this cross-dressing man bothering you?" I said in a disguised voice. "Want me to call a cop?"

Without turning back to look, Jas reached in his pocket and flipped his badge at me. "Beat it, buddy. She's a short, but grown woman with a very twisted sense of humor."

"What a fake badge. Like the NYPD would let a cop dress in drag."

Actually, he got no end of grief for it, but there was a high-stakes bet involved so he toughed it out.

The muscles in Jas's jaw tightened and the color in his ears darkened. He stood up so fast that Bubba Sue practically plopped on the floor. He was in two-inch heels, which put him at an imposing height compared to my five foot ten.

Jas spun, realized it was me and sighed. "Hello, Murphy."

"Hi Jas, Bubba Sue," I said.

"Hiya Murph." Bubba Sue leapt off the floor, wrapped her legs around my rib cage and her hands around my shoulders, and planted a smack of a kiss on my lips.

We'd said hello many times before, so I knew what to do next. I cupped my hands together, she swung her right foot into the support, and back-flipped neatly away to land facing me. A tall man with bushy hair clapped as he passed by, and Bubba Sue took a bow.

"Why do I put up with this?" Jas said, but he had a smile on his face.

"Because I rock your world and women's clothes on a man don't phase me," Bubba Sue said. "So, Murph, what brings you to the mall?"

"The subway and a bus." Jas rolled his eyes but Bubba Sue's lips curled upward. "Terrorbelle's got a birthday coming up next week and I need a gift. What about you two?"

"Lingerie shopping," Bubba Sue said. "For both of us."

Jas gently smacked her shoulder and glared at her, but she only laughed.

"He gets to pick out one outfit for me if I get to pick out one for him. I'm thinking something with handcuffs and a cop hat."

"I have both at home," Jas said, his voice barely a whisper as his eyes darted back and forth as if looking out for anyone else he knew that he might want to hide from.

"Then maybe something with tassels," Bubba Sue said. "I'd like to see you get them going in two directions at once."

"I will if you will," Jas said.

"Deal."

We definitely had passed the point of too much information, so I started to excuse myself, but Bubba Sue spoke before I could.

"Murphy, you want to join us? I could help you pick something out for T-Belle's birthday if you like."

"We're friends," I said. "You don't buy lingerie for friends. I'd never buy a corset for Paddy."

"I'd pick something guaranteed to change that," Bubba Sue said with a conspiratorial wiggling of her eyebrows.

"With Paddy or T-belle?"

"Either."

"I'd pay to see you give Paddy a corset," Jas said. My leprechaun boss is a little uptight in some areas. The suggestion that he wear women's undergarments would undoubtedly be one of them, despite the fact that he's the one who made the cross-dressing bet with Jason.

"I'd pay to see him give one to Terrorbelle," Bubba Sue said. She wasn't doing Shakespeare but Bubba Sue was definitely doing a king-sized leer. "She'd probably break him in two saying thanks."

"She might at that," Jas said. Terrorbelle was equal parts ogre and pixie. Not only was she taller than me, but she was more than a little broader. T-Belle could lift me over her head with one hand without much effort. "But she'd make sure he went out with a smile on his face."

Terrorbelle's said as much herself, minus the breaking me in half part. It wasn't a step I was willing to take just yet but it wasn't seeming so farfetched to me anymore.

"I think I'll handle the gift giving on my own. You two have fun now," I said. "And leave me out of it. That means no gifts sent to Paddy with my name on them. I'd like to stay in one piece and employed, thank you."

"If we have to," Bubba Sue said. "By the way, Murph, do you know if they have locks on the dressing room doors?"

"I'm not sure, but they might have cameras." I was never a fan of the fact that dressing rooms monitor people trying on clothes. Most of the mirrors are two-way. Easy way to tell: Hold a pencil point up to the mirror. If it touches its reflection, chances are someone on the other side is watching you. I usually stick my tongue out to say hi.

"Tech I can handle," Bubba Sue said. It was the understatement of the week. Most gremlins can take apart tech, but Bubba Sue can also put it back together and make it do things its designers never imagined. I was peripherally involved once when she disarmed a nuclear missile while it was in flight. Disabling a surveillance camera would be as easy for her as mixing a martini was for me. "A camera would be great. I can get into their security system and make some copies of the footage. I hope you're not shy, Mr. Cervantes."

"I don't consider myself shy, but compared to you I might have to reevaluate that," Jas said.

"Of course, it won't matter if they don't have my size." Bubba Sue was tiny but exceptionally curvy, pretty much everywhere a woman should be. "Fortunately, they're supposed to have a little people section that is the best in the tri-state area. Not to mention a big and tall section for my boo here. Now that I've had time to think about it, I may select something in leather, spandex, and fishnets for him."

"That's a visual I'm going to have a hard time getting out of my mind," I said with a small shiver.

"Come in with us and I'll have him model for you. That'll cement the image forever."

"Yeah, in my nightmares," I said. "You coming by Bulfinche's later?"

"He's off until 11 AM tomorrow, so I doubt we'll be setting foot outside his apartment before ten."

"Again, that's more than I needed to know." I waved as they went into the lingerie store. Bubba Sue was skipping and Jas was half covering his face, but his pace was brisk.

I trekked up and down the mall searching for a gift, with no luck. As was I looping back past the lingerie shop, I was nearly knocked over by people running out. Never one to follow the crowd, even in cases where it is probably the best idea, I crept inside to see what was going on. I was working on the assumption that Bubba Sue had reverted to her trickster nature and was having the animated manikins do bizarre things to each other.

That would have been an improvement over what was going on.

The first thing I noticed was Jas in a cheerleader outfit and Bubba Sue spilling out of a leather corset and matching shorts. The next was the reason for the mass exodus.

Amid the racks of frivolous, mostly transparent clothing stood a brown-haired young woman in a heavy black trench coat. She wouldn't have been out of place at Bulfinche's Pub, as trench coats fit the mindset of some of the patrons and hid the unusual physical features of others. However, at the mall, on this warm a day, she stood out like a sore thumb. Even more unusual was the bomb she had strapped to her chest and the plastic cylinder in the palm of her left hand. And what stood out even more than a sore thumb was her actual thumb, the knuckle of which was white from pressing the top of the cylinder down like she was afraid to let it go.

Several people cowered behind the store's counter, afraid that the angry lady with the explosives might let go of the tube and go boom if they made a break for the door.

The exceptions were Jas, Bubba Sue and a man who was on his knees scowling. A second bomb was attached around his chest and neck. His predicament could have been the reason for his unhappy expression, but it looked too natural there for me to say for sure.

I pulled out my cell to call for backup. Jas saw me and shook his head no. I had no idea why. If Paddy could get a hold of Hermes, the god could be in and out with the bombs before anyone could blink. Still, Jas was a good cop, regardless of how ridiculous he currently looked. I knew he had a plan. I wondered if he had his gun hidden in one of his pom-poms. Or if the 'no' was just to discourage me from snapping a picture of him in his current outfit. Even for a man who wore women's clothing on a semi-regular basis, the cheerleader outfit was embarrassing.

The woman was yelling at the man to give her back what he stole. She hadn't noticed me, so I ducked down to hide in a clothes rack. It was already occupied by the gentleman who had applauded Bubba Sue's dismount. I waved. He waved back and offered me his hand.

"I'm Dan Clyne," he whispered.

"John Murphy." I hoped the woman's screaming would drown out our voices. "What's going on?"

"She's upset," Dan said. "He cheated on her and got her deported."

And upset she was. She was figuratively blowing her top. Hopefully, we'd figure out a way to stop her from doing it literally.

"The guy in the cheerleader outfit is a cop. The short woman can defuse a bomb." I hoped. It was tech after all. "I'm going to cause a distraction. Are you up for trying to get the people behind the counter out?"

"She'll see us," Dan said.

"I once had a job in this mall." Back when my late wife Elsie had been going through chemo, we had no insurance. Not unusual for a just-barely-not-starving artist and her even hungrier husband the writer. I worked as many jobs as I could handle to get extra money to try to cover her medical bills. It wasn't enough, but in this instance, my experience was coming in handy. "There are corridors behind all the stores. The back storeroom should have a door. Take everyone out that way."

"Are you going to be okay?"

"Sure," I said, not certain if it was a lie.

"Okay," Dan said, with not a squawk about the risk. Who says New Yorkers don't help others?

"Good luck," I whispered.

"You too."

I crawled out of the lingerie rack, staying low until I reached the opposite side of the store so Dan would have a better shot of getting the people out. I grabbed a slinky red teddy on a hanger and stood up.

"Excuse me, miss?" I said. "Do you have this in a 42 long?"

Bomb lady turned toward me, her expression making it clear she thought I was an idiot. I got that a lot. "I don't work here."

"That's good because I would have to question your taste for letting that woman wear that cheerleader outfit. It's not flattering." I put my hand alongside my face and stage-whispered, "Makes her look like a man."

"It is a man!"

"Well, it takes all types I suppose," I said. Dan had commando crawled his way over to the folks behind the counter. "No idea where I could find this in another size, then? Maybe in a nice plaid? It's my favorite color."

The woman turned toward me so I couldn't miss the explosives. As an added benefit, she couldn't see Dan ushering the people toward the storeroom.

"Miss, do you realize you have what looks like a bomb strapped to your chest?"

"Of course, you idiot," she said. "I put it there."

I'm an expert at annoying people. The majority of folks feel the need to correct me at length. I just had to keep her from noticing the hostage exodus, although she hardly seemed to be a professional or to have even thought this out very well. And maybe the correcting would also take her mind off any thoughts of detonation.

"Why?" I asked. "Is it the latest style? If you don't mind my saying, it's not a flattering look and simply not your color. A woman as pretty as yourself in a place like this could find dozens of much better outfits. I'd say you're an autumn. Maybe something in yellow?"

"You think I'm pretty?" The bomber brushed her hair behind her ear and actually smiled.

"Yes," I said. "Although the anger on your face and that bomb distract from it a bit."

"See, he thinks I'm pretty." She kicked the kneeling man in the thigh. He fell forward but oddly reached out to hold his hair. And not terribly good hair at that. "But that wasn't enough for you, was it?"

The man smirked. "Did I say you were pretty? Was I drunk at the time?"

She smacked him. "No, you said I was the sexiest, most beautiful woman you had ever met. But that didn't stop you from sleeping around, did it, Kev? I caught you and what did you do? First, you fired me. Then you used your factory security to take my purse, my money, credit cards, and driver's license. You ripped my engagement ring off my finger. When I started to cry, you wanted to get me to shut up so the rest of the workers didn't see the scene I was making, so you gave me a drink. Next thing I know I'm waking up on a deportation flight out of Kennedy on the way to Mexico City."

"You didn't have a job. No job means you couldn't stay in the country."

"I was born in this country, you idiot." Her face was turning crimson and two veins had popped out on her forehead. "I'm a citizen. I can't be deported."

Kev smirked again. "Obviously, you could."

"You drugged me then called your brother to get rid of me." She jabbed her index finger in front of his face like a dagger.

"Tilly," Kev said, "there's no way Mike would jeopardize his position at ICE to do something like that."

Tilly threw her head back and yelled that his statement was an oversized load of bovine excrement. Then she stomped away. Kev crossed his arms over his chest, looking very pleased with himself. Meanwhile, Dan was helping an older lady get out the back door.

"ICE?" I asked.

"U.S. Immigration and Customs Enforcement," Jas said. "Part of Homeland Security."

"Well, someone put me on that plane and faked the paperwork. I woke up on the flight and federal agents refused to believe I was an American citizen. They cuffed me and put me through Mexican customs with only the clothes on my back. I don't even speak Spanish! You have no idea what I had to do to get back into the US!"

"No," Kev said. "And neither do you. You're insane. That could never happen."

"Actually, it happens," Jas said. "The Vera Institute of Justice released a report that alleged there were at least 125 people in immigration detention centers who had valid U.S. citizenship claims. And several have turned out to be correct, so maybe she's telling the truth."

Kev's face wrinkled up and he stared at us in disbelief. "You are going to believe a stalker with a bomb over me?"

Bubba Sue and I looked at each other.

"Yep," she said.

"Pretty much," I said.

"See? You're going to get what's coming to you," Tilly said.

Kev tilted back his head and let rip some very impressive mocking laughter. I half expected him to bend forward and start rubbing his hands together like some bad villain. "You think the word of a domestic terrorist is going to hold up in court? Think again."

Tilly slapped him across the face.

Kev spat at her. "You whine a lot. You threatened me. I was just protecting myself. I'm not going to apologize for it. I had an affair? So what? All guys do it. I didn't owe you anything. As for the ring, I paid a lot of money for that rock. I wasn't going to let it go to waste on your dumpy hand. And I had put a lot of things in your name for tax purposes. I couldn't have you getting to the bank before I did. But I have no idea about this deportation thing." The smirk on his face said otherwise.

"Wow, you're such a great guy," I said.

Dan waved to me and quietly closed the storeroom door behind him.

"Mind your own business," Kev said.

"Nope. I think I'll mind yours for a while," I said. "I'll only charge you ten bucks an hour plus snacks." I put the teddy back on the rack. "Tilly, I understand your anger and the impulse to hurt Kev, but why hurt yourself?" I had just been through something like this at the bar but didn't have the same advantages this time.

"I loved him and he broke my heart. Have you ever had your heart broken?"

"Yes," I said.

"I doubt it was anything like mine," she said.

"No, his was worse," Bubba Sue said.

"You heard what he did to me," the woman snapped. "How could it be worse?"

"His wife, the woman he loved more than life itself, died."

Tilly looked at me. "Is that true?"

I nodded.

"How?"

"Leukemia. Elsie was my world. When she died, the most important parts of me felt like they died with her."

"You got over her?" she asked.

"Nope, but it got easier to be without her. I learned to live again. I found people and a job I love. These days I spend my time helping people, even if it's just by making them laugh. I'd like to help you too if you'll let me."

"Fine." Tilly put her free hand on her hip. "Go ahead. Make me laugh."

"Okay, but remember you asked for it." Being funny comes naturally to me, but being put on the spot does tend to make me a little nervous. Better not to think about it, so I took a deep breath and plunged forward. "Is that a bomb in your pocket or are you just happy to see me? After what Kev did to you, blowing him off makes sense, but blowing him up seems a little extreme. I mean look at him. If brains were dynamite, he couldn't blow his nose. I'm sure he's a real treasure. I'll help you bury him. I'm not sure what you ever saw in him. Is that a toupee or did a cat vomit a hairball on his head? He's so ugly—"

"Do you mind?" Kev self-consciously touched his hair and started to get up from his knees. Tilly kicked his legs out from under him and held up the dead man switch threateningly. Kev lay still.

"Do I mind that you not only screwed around on this nice woman but screwed her over so royally that she feels this is her only option? Yes, actually I do mind. And then deporting her on top of it?" I turned to Tilly. "Hell, this isn't the best way to get even. It's over too quick. Fogret the bomb. If you really want him to suffer, get a lawyer."

"Nobody will believe her cock and bull story about my brother somehow having her magically deported to another country. Where's the proof? I'll sue her for slander. My lawyers will bury her."

"My, you are dumb. Gravediggers bury people, not lawyers. I mean unless maybe they had a night job, but in my experience, there's not a lot of crossover between the two professions. Keep it up if you want to see who'll bury what's left of you." I pointed to the bomb he wore. "Not that it sounds like it would be that much of a tragedy for the world at large. I'm just thinking of the poor gravedigger. With no body to bury, how will he feed his family?"

"Tilly is a stupid tramp with a wild imagination," he said, "and got what she deserved. She can't even satisfy a man."

"How would you know who she can satisfy? Have you ever seen her with a real man? Not only are you the worst fiancé and boss ever, but you're a peeping tom as well. I bet you kick puppies, rip the wings off of flies, and have a flashy sports car to make up for personal deficiencies."

"Hey!" Kev grabbed his belt buckle. "I'll drop 'em right here."

"Please don't. I just ate," I said. "Just tell us what you drive."

Under his breath, he muttered, "A 'Vette."

"Bingo," I said.

Tilly smiled and gave the tiniest snort of a laugh.

"This is all a joke," he said. "She doesn't have the brains to make a bomb."

"I know how to use the Internet," Tilly said.

"Maybe, but you don't have the guts to blow me up."

"Actually, if she blows you up," I said, "she'll have all the guts she'll need. Of course, they'll be yours."

"This is all a desperate cry for attention, a ploy for me to take you back. Take the bomb off me and you can come home."

Tilly stood there, lowering her left hand and the switch. She was really thinking about it.

"Oh, no girlfriend, you aren't going back to that," Bubba Sue said. "He's something that doesn't deserve to be on the bottom of your shoe. You got off lucky."

Jas and I both looked at her. Sure, he was a nasty piece of work, but if this got the bombs off both of them, it was worth the deception. We could sort the rest out later.

"Lucky? What part of this is lucky?" Tilly tilted her head to accentuate her point.

"You could have married him first," Bubba Sue said.

"True," Tilly said.

"May I talk to these gentlemen alone for a second, dear?" Bubba Sue asked. Tilly looked at her nervously. "Don't worry. We aren't going yet. I personally wouldn't leave you alone with *him*."

Tilly seemed to be judging if Bubba Sue was on the level. "All right."

Bubba Sue motioned for us to join her by a rack of corsets.

"Nice outfit, Jas," I said. "NYPD has a cheer squad now?"

"No, but I'm working on it," Jas shot back. He turned to Bubba Sue. "Why didn't you let him convince her to kiss and make up so we could get the explosives?"

"Because the bombs are fakes," she said.

"You sure?" Jas asked.

Bubba Sue nodded. "Her dead man switch is the Nunchuk handle from a Wii with the wire cut off. The tubes are junk with some dollar-store electronics. There's no power source or explosives. It won't blow up. It can't. But there is a digital recorder in there. She's just trying to get a confession in a really bad way. I don't think she planned to hurt anybody. We need to get her some self-respect and make him pay at the same time."

"So I can call for help?" I said.

Bubba Sue nodded. "Jas was going with the NYPD playbook. With an unknown bomb, there should be no radio or cell signals because they could trigger the explosives. But hold off on the call. We can handle this ourselves."

"Then we need to do it fast," Jas said. "Someone has to have called 911. ESU…" Emergency Service Unit which includes SWAT. "…will probably be here soon, and I'd prefer to end this fast so nobody gets shot." He paused to look down at his cheer ensemble. "And I'd like to be out of this outfit before that happens."

"I'd like you to be out of it too," Bubba Sue gave him the once over and pinched his butt.

"Me too," I said, "but for a different reason. That short skirt really doesn't do anything for you."

"It does for me." Bubba Sue wiggled her eyebrows lasciviously then got serious. "We're all in agreement that Kev's the one deserving of punishment, not her?" We were. "I have a plan on how to do that. Jas, hang back. Murphy, you're with me."

"You're picking Murphy over me to deal with a hostage situation?" His voice went up half an octave. "I'm a trained and decorated detective."

"Yep, those pom-poms sure make great decorations," I said. "Have you considered a Christmas wreath as a necklace?"

Jas's hand shot out to point at me. "Murphy, this is serious."

"Which is why Murphy will be more helpful for what I have planned. He has more of a trickster mentality than you do. And he's survived multiple Fools' Days."

Every April 1st many tricksters of legend meet at Bulfinche's Pub to see who has pulled off the best prank of the day. It tends to get messy. I always make it out intact and even helped save the world once. Gives me trickster street cred.

"Here's my plan," Bubba Sue said.

It was a doozy.

"I like it, but can you pull it off?"

Bubba Sue grinned mischievously. "Can you?"

"I'll give it my best shot," I said. Bubba Sue told Jas to get dressed in his man clothes that he kept in his man bag, aka his purse, while she and I returned to the unhappy ex-couple.

"Tilly, can we speak for a moment, girl to girl?" Bubba Sue asked in a sweet Southern drawl. "I think you'll like what I have to say."

"Okay," Tilly said as the pair disappeared behind a rack.

I stepped over toward to the scumbag. "Quick, while she's not looking, let's get you out of here."

Kev was taken aback. "You've been insulting me since you got here and now you want to help me?"

"She has a bomb," I said. "You think I'm going to side with you?" Kev seemed to buy it. I helped him to his feet and slid off his jacket. Playing my hunch, I grabbed his hair and pulled. "And your toupee."

"Hey!" he yelled, making a grab for his stolen hair substitute.

I put the rug on my head and donned the coat. "Shh. I'll take your place and let you get away."

"But the bomb . . ."

"If you get far enough away, she won't be able to trigger it," I said, grabbing a brown wig with a style similar to Tilly's hairdo off a manikin, and a black silk robe from the rack. "Put these on so she won't recognize you if she spots you leaving. I'll stay here." I got on my knees next to him, put the man wig on my head and pulled the jacket on.

"Why would you do this for me?" he said.

"She can't blow me up unless she gets close enough, and I'll run before I let that happen. I just want to make sure you get what you deserve and who deserves to be blown up?"

He bought it, and without a word of thanks, put on the wig and robe and broke for the door. He had no clue that he looked a lot like the description of the female mall bomber with the brown hair and black trench coat.

Bubba Sue cut him off at the pass. She grabbed his robe and pulled him down, making him hold onto a metal rack to keep from falling. "Get down! You don't want her to see you."

"Let me go," Kev said, crawling like he was competing in a horse race until he was out in the mall proper, at which point he stood and ran.

"Glad to." Bubba Sue grinned, sprinkling talcum powder on the rack's metal bars. Then she placed pieces of scotch tape over the sweaty residue his hands left behind. She pulled each off and held them up to the light. "Beautiful."

Now came the tricky part. The mall had been evacuated and

police had cordoned off the building and were waiting on SWAT and the bomb squad. We wanted Kev to pay for his misdeeds, but we didn't want him to go down in a hail of bullets.

Bubba Sue hacked into the mall's security cameras so we could watch everything. Jas, now in guy clothes, hustled Tilly out the back corridor in a new outfit and ponytail, using his badge to get her past his fellow cops. He then went in the front door of the mall and met Kev coming out. Out of earshot, but in plain sight, he removed the so-called bomb, placed it on the floor and walked Kev out where he was promptly set upon and arrested by the waiting officers.

Kev protested his innocence, but couldn't produce any identification.

After years of being pick-pocketed by the god Hermes, I developed my own wallet lifting skills in self-defense. While not as good as the god of thieves, I could make a disrespectable living if I ever decided on a life of petty crime. Kev had been too concerned with the loss of his hair to notice my lifting his billfold.

When Kev got to the station they ran his prints and, lo and behold, he came up as a suspected terrorist. Considering Bubba Sue only got to the station a few minutes ahead of him, her planting the information with the lifted prints was impressive. Fortunately, gremlins have a gift for blending in, so none of New York's finest noticed her or what she was doing.

When his brother came to bail him out, they took him into custody and ran his prints also, because of the warning to look out for the brother of the terrorist. His prints came up a suspected terrorist match as well, but only because Bubba Sue had rigged the reader to have that response to the next inquiry.

Tilly lawyered up and got her life back. And ownership of the factory. Once they were in court, Kev and his brother had the questionable pleasure of learning that sometimes, the truth does not set you free. Posting an incriminating hacked video on YouTube that showed the brothers handing an unconscious Tilly over to ICE agents at Kennedy Airport didn't hurt either.

And best of all, I never had to see Jason in Bubba Sue's final choice of lingerie.

Hex was born a magi, a mage with the ability to use every kind of magic, but cursed with pain and worse for using his powers. Hex dares to stand between the innocent and the creatures of darkness – whether they be vampyres, Aztec gods, elder horrors, flesh-eating babies, mirror angels or the Devil himself. When facing those who make you curse the darkness, sometimes the only way to survive is to ask for help. The legend of the man you ask is called

HEXCRAFT

HELD FOR QUESTIONING

"If you just confess we could all go home that much sooner."

"I'm sorry, Detective Dumbass…"

"I've told you already, it's Dumas."

"Tomato, tomahto. Quite frankly, you just lied to me. If I were to confess to a crime, I wouldn't be going home. I'd be going to jail. It seems very ungentlemanly of you to try and trick me this way," I said, trying to get comfortable in a metal chair with my hands cuffed behind my back. I smiled at the mirror that took up most of one wall in the interrogation room.

"Listen, Robinson…"

"I told you, it's Mr. Hex."

"Tomato, tomahoto. Quite frankly, I'm surprised you aren't in jail already. I haven't seen a file this thick on *anybody* and I used to work in organized crime."

"So how organized are they exactly? Do you have a book to organize all your hits and extortion or have little plastic cubbies to put all your bullets, guns, and drugs?" I said. "And how exactly did you make the switch to law enforcement after being in organized crime? Were the benefits better? Did the mob not have dental?"

"You're hilarious. Keep talking. You're digging yourself a deeper and deeper hole. "

"Is that an organized crime thing? You make me dig my own grave and toss me in?"

"Shouldn't be too hard. Never is with guys like you who think they're so smart. All I've got to do is keep you talking and you'll say something that I can use to bury you with."

"You're right. No sense in fighting any longer. Shovel."

The detective tilted his head like a dog listening to a silent whistle. "Excuse me?"

"I just decided that you are absolutely right and said something that you can use to bury me with. I can add dynamite."

"Dynamite? Is that a terrorist threat?"

"Nope, but you could use it to make a big hole in the ground to bury me in."

"Listen, smart guy, we've got a giant H in a circle that looks like a weird bastardization of the anarchy symbol burned in a little old lady's forehead. What kind of a sick bastard does something like that to somebody's grandmother?"

I kept quiet. Cops tended to keep talking if you didn't. "She swore out a complaint that says you did it. I'm inclined to believe her."

"Why's that?"

"Because I when I came to pick you up for questioning, you were wearing a T-shirt with the same symbol."

Unfortunately, the cop had a point. The evidence did match up pretty good. But I wasn't about to admit that. This wasn't my first interrogation. I doubt it'll be my last.

"You have anything you want to say?"

"Backhoe."

"What the hell are you talking about now?"

"I came up with something else that you could use to bury me with. A backhoe would be a lot quicker than a shovel. Couple scoops and you'd be done. Probably safer for your back too."

"Listen, wise guy, I've got enough to book you right now for branding this poor lady, but I've got pages upon pages of notes listing events you're suspected to have been involved in. Stopping a subway train near a murder scene."

A mad Aztec God was manifesting on the mortal plane and I needed a way to get a bunch of people out of the line of fire quickly.

"A terrorist attack on a building in Jersey City."

Paddy Moran and his friends knocked down the building but I did alert them to some gang activity going on there.

"Dozens of suspected murders down in the village."

Most of those are probably vampires, but guys like Dumas don't believe in things they can't prove.

"You may be the single greatest threat to the citizens of New York City I've never even heard about."

"Then you mustn't get out much."

"If there's anything else you want to add…" I opened my mouth and the cop held up a hand. "…that doesn't involve digging a hole."

"It seems to me that you don't have a whole lot of evidence. What it sounds like you have a lot of stories. Stories are great fun, but they can be exaggerated or important details can be left out. They can even be totally made up. I've heard stories too, about how that brand is actually a symbol that someone evil has been given one warning, telling them that if they don't stop hurting others that things could end badly for them."

"How badly?" the cop asked.

"From the stories I've heard, quite badly. But in the same stories, the people who have those marks were usually in the process of trying to kill somebody. And they often have supernatural abilities which give them an unfair advantage against regular folks."

"So now you're telling me fairytales?"

"I think the genre would be better classified as urban fantasy, except for the fantasy part. Whether you believe it or not, the things that go bump in the night don't stop just because they get knocked down."

"Yes, the supernatural. I also see here in your record that you're a consultant for the DMA. Even had a badge on you when we booked you."

"I've done some work with the Department of Mystic Affairs. Why? Are you jealous because I work for federal law enforcement and you only work for the city? Is this all part of an interdepartmental rivalry that's gotten out of control?

"I verified your consultant status, but you're not a federal agent, not even for a fluff agency like the DMA."

Uncle Sam and I may not agree on a lot of things, but the Department of Mystic Affairs is about as far from a fluff agency is you can get, but guys like Dumas won't believe that until something supernatural has bitten them in the butt and they need help removing the teeth.

"Look, Detective Dumas, you're wasting your time here. The lady who swore out this complaint, Jean Cooper – she's not human."

Dumas laughed. "Oh, he's not? Then what is she? Vampyre?"

"No, but she can't come out in sunlight, which is why I'm guessing she filled out the complaint at night. Cooper is an ebu gogo. They can use glamours to look human."

"They use a fashion magazine?"

I rolled my eyes. "It's basically a type of spell that can make something look like something it's not, more often than not making something ugly look beautiful. Too bad you can't afford one on your salary, huh detective?"

"Keep it up, funny guy. You got a lot of nerve claiming the grandmother you attacked and branded is a monster. The only monster here is you."

"Actually in Nage, ebu means grandmother. Gogo translates closer to he who eats anything. In her case, people."

"So, if she's one of these cannibal grandmothers, how do you know?"

This guy is living in Manhattan and doesn't even believe in vampyres. No way am I going to try and explain to him what a □magí is. "I have certain gifts that most people don't."

Dumas laughed again. "Then how would a lowly civil servant like myself be able to tell?"

"Simple. Her natural glamour is rather weak and only covers her face and arms. The rest of her is covered in fur."

Dumas smirked. "How would you know Cooper has fur?"

"How do you know she doesn't?" I said.

"All this talk of cannibal people having fur sounds a little crazy. Maybe you don't belong in jail. Maybe you belong in Bellevue."

"An empty threat."

"Not so empty. Says in here you've already been committed numerous times."

"Not in years and I'd be able to use my professional opinion to trump yours."

"Oh yes, it does say here that you're a psychiatrist, but doesn't say where you work."

"I do some consulting here and there."

"You consult for the federal government, you consult as a doctor. Is there anyone you don't consult for?"

"Interesting, you equate two consulting jobs with consulting for everyone. It shows poor inference skills and perhaps some trauma when you were being potty trained. Detective Dumas, tell me about your mother."

"Nice try, Dr. Robinson, but I ask the questions here. Why did you brand Jane Cooper's face?"

"Look, Detective Dumas, you can cut the crap. We both know you jumped the gun when you arrested me for someone swearing out a complaint who had no witnesses. This is strictly a 'she said, he said' situation. Yes, I wear a T-shirt with the symbol that you say was branded into Cooper's head, but that's nothing more than circumstantial evidence. Maybe Cooper has self-destructive tendencies." I'd say she certainly does if she thinks siccing the cops on me was a good idea. "Maybe Cooper has it out for me so she did it to herself in hopes that the authorities would blame me for her self-inflicted wounds and send me to jail. Maybe you thought you'd get an easy collar by assuming I'd simply break. And I'm guessing you arrested me before you looked into my file and my other alleged activities. I've been nothing but courteous to a fellow law enforcement professional, but I insist that either you charge me so I can go to court and be proven not guilty so that I can get on with my life. Perhaps even contemplate a false arrest suit against you and the department. Or you can let me go. What's it going to be? Because I'm done talking and if your choice is not to let me go, the next words out of my life my mouth will involve you calling my lawyer, Mari Jenal."

That made Detective Dumas's brows rise then narrow. Mari Jenal is quite probably the best lawyer in the world and because of that, she charges an outrageous hourly rate. She owes me more than a few favors and her life on three occasions so I get free legal representation for anything up to a trial. If I ever go to trial, we'll have to negotiate.

A moment later there was a rapping on the mirror that we both were supposed to pretend was only a mirror, not a two-way glass with people watching us from the other side.

Dumas paused and looked down, listening to his earpiece. He glared, first at the mirror, then at me.

"Thank you for your time, Dr. Robinson. You're free to go."

Detective Dumas sat back down in his seat and smirked, knowing full well that my hands were handcuffed behind my back and that most people would need him to unlock the restraints before they can get up and go.

"So, to clarify, I'm free to go."

"That's what I said."

"Excellent." I stood up, my wrists unencumbered by any metal police jewelry which caused Dumas' eyes to open wide. I walked over to his side of the interrogation table and dropped the handcuffs in front of him. "I believe these are yours."

"Is that supposed to impress me?"

I shrugged. "Maybe a little." His pat down was thorough, but not overly so. I keep a small flat piece of metal attached to my rear belt loop. It's great for sliding in handcuffs to get them to open. I guess it wasn't that impressive. Anyone so inclined can learn how to do it by watching YouTube. "One thing I would like to impress on you is that Jane Cooper is dangerous. If she thinks I'm locked up in here, she's going to do something dangerous out there. Think about that."

I had come down hard on Dumas but that's just because it's my nature. My reading showed he was a hard ass, but he was a clean cop. He wasn't sure what to make of me, but at least he took me seriously enough to follow up with Cooper. He called the cannibal granny and asked her to come down to the police station to clarify a few parts of her statement during the daytime. Cooper said she couldn't because she didn't have a ride. Dumas offered to drive her but Cooper refused.

Detective Dumas showed up at Cooper's apartment in the late afternoon and knocked on the door. The ebu gogo opened the door a crack with the security chain on. "Detective Dumas, to what do I owe the pleasure?"

"I just wanted to clarify a few points of your complaint. May I come in?"

The monster hesitated. She didn't want to let a cop into her lair, but if she refused it would seem suspicious and would draw unwanted attention to herself.

"Okay, but only for a moment."

The creature who claimed to be Jane Cooper pulled the chain out and opened the door. Her apartment opened onto the hallway so there was no danger of direct sunlight. As Detective Dumas stepped inside, he realized there was no chance of that in the apartment either. Thick black drapes covered all the windows and the only lights came from the digital clocks on her cable box.

"Would you mind turning on a light?" Detective Dumas asked.

"Sorry, I have a headache and the lights hurt my eyes. So is Hex in jail?"

"He's not, I'm afraid."

"Why not?" Cooper growled in a very ungrannylike manner. It was hard to tell in the dark, but for a moment it seemed to Dumas like the old woman's face got longer and that she had sharp, pointy teeth.

"Unfortunately, in a case like this, it's one person's word versus another's. No one should have to endure someone else branding them like cattle, so I'd like to see this Hex go to jail, but I need more to get a conviction. What else can you tell me? Could there possibly be any witnesses you didn't mention the first time?"

Cooper paused and licked her lips. "No, there weren't. What kind of city are we living in where one man can get away with doing this to a little old lady?"

"I'm in total agreement with you, ma'am, which is why I'm following up. I just need some way to prove it was him. Look, I know you been through a traumatic event, so why don't you think about it for a couple days and see if something else doesn't come to you that could be used in court. Let me give you my card again so you can call me if you remember anything that would be pertinent to the case."

Detective Dumas reached into the side pocket of his suit and deftly pulled out a business card then oddly fumbled it so it dropped on the rug behind Cooper.

"Sorry about that." Dumas bent down to pick up the card, all the while turning his head to look beneath the robe Cooper was wearing. After grabbing the card, he got back up and took a step back.

"Why do you have furry legs?" Dumas asked.

"What? Now it's a crime for an old woman to stop shaving her legs?"

"That's not normal hair. It's thicker than my dog's coat. I think you better come down to the station with me."

Cooper let the granny glamour drop and rushed the detective faster than he could reach for his gun. The granny monster grabbed the cop by his jacket and threw him like she was shooting a basketball, smashing Dumas into the far wall. Her fingernails popped out like a cat's and I think the cannibal granny would have gutted Dumas if I hadn't kicked in her door.

"Jane Cooper, step away from the detective. I gave you your one warning to stop killing people. You're done."

Cooper leapt at me and I fired the Taser I was holding. Two needles shot out and I hit the trigger which sent a huge jolt of electricity across the wires. It knocked the ebu gogo to the rug. She was down but wouldn't be for long. I stepped around the cannibal granny, yanking her robe off as I passed then pulled her black curtains down.

The setting sun was right outside the window. Where sunbeams hit her bare skin, she started to smoke. The granny monster tried to crawl on feet and hands to the door but I hit the button on the Taser again. She hit the rug a second time, which gave the sunlight enough time to start a chemical reaction which cascaded through her entire body until it caught fire and she went up as brightly as magnesium flare and almost as quickly. Less than a minute later, nothing remained of the cannibal granny but a pile of ashes. I walked over and offered Dumas a hand. He took it and I pulled him up

The cop looked at the pile of ashes. "You killed her."

I shrugged. "Did I actually kill her or simply redecorate her apartment which allowed the sunlight to do the actual killing? I'm fairly certain redecorating isn't considered a felony, even in the fashion district. And I would ask you to consider that my actions ones prevented her from killing you."

Dumas leaned over and used his business card to sift through the ashes.

"That was the strangest thing I've ever seen. You did save my life, so I guess I should overlook your giving her a sunbath and kicking in her door, which *is* a crime. Besides I'm not sure there's enough here to be able to prove what happened to her. And without evidence, there is no way to get a conviction."

His business card finally got to the wires for the Taser. He stood up and took the device from my hand.

"Is this my Taser? You broke into my car and took it?"

I wasn't about to explain to him how my life was much easier if I didn't have to use magic because of my curse, so I tried to use mundane means whenever possible.

"It was just lying there and the door was unlocked."

"It was secured in the trunk next to my riot gear and a shotgun."

I smiled. "Tomato, tomahoto."

"How'd you even know taking the curtains down would work? What if she was smart enough to use the tinting they use on cars on her windows?"

"A good question. One, most of these killers think they are untouchable because nobody knows about them. And more importantly, I looked at the windows before I came to make sure."

"You're not a cop. Why are you doing this? No one is paying you or telling you to, right?"

I nodded. "It's what I do. I'm different that way. And a lot of other ways."

"Such as?"

"For one thing, I'm dating a penguin."

"A flightless waterfowl? Was she cursed?"

I laughed. "Not that kind of penguin. The nun kind."

Both of Detective Dumas' eyebrows rose up at that. "You're dating a nun?"

"You seem more upset by that than the idea of a bird."

"You saved my life, so I'm trying not to judge, but that just seems wrong."

"It would be. She *used* to be a nun. We hit it off so well and she liked me liked me so much she didn't take her final vows. Like Maria in the Sound of Music, only much less singing."

"Did you have to escape from Nazis?"

"No. Demons. And the CIA."

"Um. Right. Truthfully, I can't imagine anyone liking you that much," Dumas said.

Truth be told, neither could I but I wasn't complaining. Anna was the light of my life.

"On that note, if you have no more questions for me, Detective Dumas, I'll be on my way."

I was halfway to the door when he said, "Dr. Robinson…"

I turned and raised an eyebrow at him.

"Sorry, sorry. Mr. Hex, I didn't believe any of this stuff was real, but now I know I was wrong. It's my job to protect the people of the city and I can't do that if I don't know what I'm up against. Would you be willing to help teach me so I'm one of the people that do know about the monsters?"

Detective Dumas had basically said the magic words when he asked for my help. The only way I'm allowed to interfere in use magic because of a curse. Someone asked me to take care of Jane Cooper and stop her from killing people.

"Detective, I'd be happy to. The first thing you have to remember is not all monsters are the bad guys…"

Vince Argus made a deal with the Devil..
The power to avenge his slaughtered family
In exchange for his immortal soul.
For a price, he will end a life he deems deserving of killing.
The Devil will come for him, of that there is no doubt.
Until then, Argus lives by his own dark code of honor, a

SOUL *for* HIRE

HIDE AND SEEK

Hitmen tended to inspire fear, yet even among paid assassins, Vince Argus was a legend. People said he never missed; that he could shoot a dime out of the sky or the wings off a fly. Some say he was so tough that he chased down the Devil and forced him to give him supernatural aim.

That part of the rumors was partly true. The Devil did indeed offer Argus abilities but it was something he paid dearly for, and in the Devil's usual choice of payment. Argus had barely entered manhood when he witnessed his family gunned down in front of him. All the Devil did was offer him a chance at vengeance.

Argus took it and ended the lives of those who slaughtered his family. He could've stopped killing then but Argus didn't want to. His soul was already lost to Hell so Argus decided to put the time he had left to use by killing those who did to others what was done to his family. The Soul for Hire was very particular about what hits he would take but was more flexible about how he took his targets out of this world an into the next.

Sure, Argus loved his guns but there were some situations where guns weren't an option.

His current job fell into that category.

Even though Argus did his best to keep things quiet, sometimes word leaked out to his targets. When that happened, most of them had the good sense to try and run far away. Some were better at hiding than others.

Bobby Jablonski wasn't so good at hiding, but he figured he had a way to keep himself alive. Jablonski purposefully went to jail on a small charge – about seven hundred and fifty dollars' worth of unpaid parking tickets. The judge ordered him to pay when he said he couldn't, the judge ordered Bobby to be locked up for ninety days. Jablonski didn't fight it or even ask for bail. He figured that the cops would protect him, even bragging to his friends but that's what he paid taxes for. Though the police would probably disagree as to the reason why Jablonski actually paid if it had come up in conversation.

Because of the relatively minor infraction, Jablonski was spending time in the local jail as opposed to being shipped out to a penitentiary. He got three squares a day and the correction officers kept the hitman away.

Jablonski figured ninety days would be long enough for him to come up with the next part of his plan.

The thing with an arrest is it makes the local papers so it was an easy matter for Argus to learn Jablonski's whereabouts.

Even if Argus wasn't a professional, he would know that breaking into a jail with guns blazing to take out a target wasn't the wisest course of action. Besides being loud and messy, Argus might be forced to shoot innocent cops or corrections officers and the Soul for Hire didn't do that. No collateral damage, no innocents. Period.

Plus, cops and COs were trained for just such a scenario and might end up killing Argus before he got to his target.

At the same time, he couldn't just let Jablonski flaunt that he was smarter than Argus. It was bad for business, not to mention his reputation. The day Argus got outfoxed by a nobody like Jablonski was the day he stopped being the bogeyman to others.

On the other hand, a hitman who could kill a guy while he was in police lockup and get away with it would only increase his reputatioArgus found out that Jablonski knew he was a target because the woman who hired him confessed to the hitman that she had let it slip. Or rather had bragged about it when Jablonski came over to try and pick up some of her sister's belongings, the same sister who'd been married to him and that everyone knew he had killed. But that's the thing about law and order; if there's no evidence there's no time served.

Argus didn't blame the woman. There was a lot of anger and loss over her sister's death and she just wanted to hurt Jablonski. Since she couldn't do the deed herself, that's where Argus came in. And as always, he checked her story out. Turns out there was evidence Jablonski was guilty but it was collected an hour before a warrant was signed by a judge so another judge ruled that it was fruit of the poisonous tree and tossed it. It didn't matter that they found the murder weapon in his house, with his fingerprints. It couldn't be used in court.

Plus, the sister had sworn on a bullet engraved with her name. She knew the consequences of lying to the hitman. The bullet would be coming back at her very quickly.

Some hitmen would come up with an elaborate plan to imitate a corrections officer, cop, or some other staff member of the jail to get them access but that had far too many chances not only for failure but for being caught. What Argus needed was a legitimate excuse to be in the jail and to make sure no one knew who he was.

Argus poured some cheap whiskey on himself and did a fine imitation of a drunk stealing a dozen donuts in a shop full of cops.

His arrest was swift and un-resisted. Argus was processed but he had taken some precautions. He dyed his coal black hair bleach blonde and wore a Hawaiian shirt. His arms were covered with tribal tattoos. Like his hair color, they were only temporary, as were a Hollywood grade prosthetic nose, brow, and chin, all topped off with a Fu Manchu mustache. It wasn't much, but it would be enough to throw off facial recognition software.

Lastly, they took his fingerprints. Although technically they weren't his. Argus' real prints were already in the system. He'd been arrested but never convicted. Like Jablonski, there had never been enough evidence to go to trial.

Argus used a compound that was similar to – but much more durable than – school glue to cover his fingers and palms. Argus didn't want some innocent person to have this crime matched up with them because he stole their fingerprints, so he used a substitute. As bizarre as it sounds, Koala bears have the same type of fingerprints as humans and Argus figured nobody was going to the zoo to arrest the furry fellow he took the prints from.

There was a huge gap in his plans. He could get himself into the jail, but there was no guarantee he'd be put anyone anywhere near Jablonski. He'd be arraigned the next day and had enough cash on him to post his own bail, so his blond surfer persona would simply disappear after that.

Argus had no problem with the hair dye or makeup. The thing he hated leaving behind the most was his sunglasses. Ever since he'd avenged his family, his eyes scared people. But he knew he'd never be allowed to keep his shades and wearing a pair of regular glasses might draw attention to the idea of sunglasses to somebody with a sharp eye looking at a mug shot book. Instead, the hitman used some drops to make his eyes bloodshot which would give people a logical reason for being uncomfortable looking at his eyes.

An even larger hole in the plan was he was going in with absolutely no weapons. They even took his belt and his shoelaces. Anything to kill Jablonski with would have to be found in the jail itself and it was the type of place noted for making sure there were no weapons available.

It turns out the fates must've wanted Jablonski dead too because Argus was put in a cell diagonally across from the wife killer. Of course, the fates were never one to make something easy and Argus had a cellmate – a large biker by the name of Viper who was in for drunk and disorderly. Viper wasn't done with being either yet. The last thing Argus needed was a witness and although Viper might've been guilty of something, he might've been innocent too, so killing him was not an option.

The idea behind the disguise was for no one to suspect who Argus really was, so being a tough guy was out. Being an annoying one was still on the table.

"Yo, roomie, how're they hanging? Great hotel, huh? Any idea what time the pool and the gym are open to?"

"Ain't no hotel, you moron, although would be nice if it was," Viper said.

"Too true. Then we could head down to the bar and I could buy you a drink." Even though there was no way they could actually get alcohol, the idea that the blonde man would buy a drink was enough to make Viper smile. The biker slapped he disguised hitman on the back.

"I'd let you too."

"What would you be drinking?" the hitman asked, sounding a bit too much like any number of characters from eighties movies that used the word dude a lot in dialogue.

"Boilermakers all the way. I had six but I had to stop before I had too much. "

"I hear that. When we get out of here, I'm buying you that drink."

"Appreciated."

"So where is the food in here? You think they let us order a pizza? Cause I'm really wishing the cops had let me eat the donuts before they arrested me."

Viper tilted his head and squinted. "What you in here for?"

"I was hungry and went to a donut shop and took a dozen donuts and forgot to pay. Unfortunately, the guy who actually ordered them was a cop. They brought me here but they didn't let me have any of the donuts, even though I offered to share. Said the donuts were evidence, which is dumb. By the time the donuts get in front of a judge, they'll be stale and it's so wrong to waste a good donut."

"Bet the cops felt the same way."

Blonde Argus chuckled. "You know they did."

"I wouldn't worry about it too much. I've been here a couple times before. Food should be here in about half an hour."

"Excellent."

Over the next thirty minutes, Argus and Viper made small talk. Argus use the time to case the cell block. There was one full cell between him and Jablonski plus eight feet of corridor across. The hitman could just barely see into part of Jablonski's cell but his bunk was on the far side which was good. It meant there were possibilities.

When the food came, it was handed to each of them through a small gap in the bars. They had to rest the trays on tables in the corners that were bolted down to the floor

Viper dove right in. "The powdered mashed potatoes are runny, the steak is tougher than shoe leather, and all they give us to eat it with is a plastic spork and butter knife. At least the little piece of chocolate cake looks good."

"I'm not a fan. You want mine?" Argus said.

"Hell yeah."

Argus used his napkin to scoop up the cake then walked across the cell where he purposely stumbled and fell onto Viper's bunk, his hands going right to his throat. Argus pressed with his thumb and index finger to put enough pressure on the sensors pressure receptors in the carotid arteries to knock the big man unconscious. Argus left the napkin with the cake on his tray went back over to his own.

Using the plastic spork, he scooped up some of the mashed potatoes, held it parallel to the bars and pulled it back. The starchy gob flew through the air and landed on the lens of the only camera covering the cell block corridor. He hoped the mashed potatoes were moving fast enough that they'd have difficulty figuring out which cell they came from. Next, Argus cut up a piece of the tough steak, leaving enough fat around the edges to make it greasy and walked to the edge of his cell.

The hitman just barely had a line of sight to Jablonski's mouth. There were bars in the way and with the angle this was going to be a tough shot, even for him. It was further complicated by the fact that Jablonski would have to have his mouth open wide for this to work.

Jablonski wasn't opening his mouth much which meant he'd only get hit on the lips with a piece of meat.

Argus took Viper's spork and put it on top of his, then put the meat on the end of the spork. The hitman stood by the bars of his cell and started yawning and stretching his hands. Most people seeing someone else yawn tend to respond in kind with the exceptions of sociopaths or worse.

Jablonski may have been a wife killer but it turns out he wasn't a sociopath. His first yawn still wasn't wide enough so Argus waited a little bit then yawned again.

This time Jablonski's mouth opened wider, so Argus took aim with his doubled-up spork. The hunk of grizzle flew diagonally between the cells, narrowly missing a bar and went right into Jablonski's mouth, past his teeth, to lodge in his throat. As luck would have it have it, they'd given Jablonski a cell to himself since he was there long-term and put short-timers in the other cells. There was no one in his cell to give him the Heimlich maneuver. Jablonski stood and rushed to the bars, trying to get someone's attention but no one noticed except for Argus who stood staring. It was something he felt he owed his targets, to look them in the eyes whenever possible before they died. As Jablonski saw him, Argus nodded slightly and the man knew that his escape plan didn't work out so well after all.

A moment later the wife killer passed out from lack of oxygen and fell to the floor. The prisoners in the cell next to Argus finally noticed and started shouting for the guards. Corrections officers are not noted for running just because an inmate calls, so by the time they got to the choking man, Jablonski was beyond saving.

An investigation ruled the death to be an accidental choking. The mashed potatoes on the lens was deemed an attempt by Jablonski to get the guards' attention. The only thing that happened was that particular cut of meat was banned from the jail menu.

The next morning Argus was marched out of his cell, went to his arraignment, pleaded not guilty through a public defender. He posted his blonde persona's bail and walked out a free man.

Jester to King Arthur,
Knight of the Round Table,
Sir Dagonet was the first knight to find the Holy Grail.
Camelot is gone but Dagonet
lives on through the ages,
upholding a forgotten code of

The Infinite Jester

THE GARGLER'S GAME

I was in prison yet again. Despite my current predicament, I bore my captors no particular ill will. After all, they thought I was a murderer. They had no way of knowing the man I killed was an evil monster who had been feeding off their souls. Or some of them anyway. They just thought Achard Mauvoisin was a noble that seemed to take a particular interest in the common folk. They didn't yet realize that his motives were far from altruistic. And now that I had taken him out of the picture, they probably never would.

Don't get me wrong. I'm not one for unnecessary killing. The point at which taking a life becomes necessary is different for each man and woman. I have known good men who would kill at the drop of a hat if they thought their cause was just. Around them, one is always careful, both in word and deed. Not to mention the dropping of any particular headgear. However, in thirteenth-century France, there really was no good way to imprison a mage. Even the least powerful magic user could get out of the most impressive prison eventually so if killing an evil man saved innocent lives, so be it. If it also meant time incarcerated, my comfort would just have to suffer for the greater good.

Not that I planned to suffer for long. I was no mage but I was going to get out of this prison. I was just biding my time. Of course, I was. But all jesting aside, which is an unusual situation for me, I needed to be out very quickly. Otherwise, the locals were quite intent about seeing me put to death for my crimes. I think the only reason I was still among the living was they hadn't yet decided on the method of my execution. Having found some evidence of what they called witchcraft, they were considering burning me at the stake. Although I do enjoy warmer climates, walking unharmed among the flames is not one of my abilities. In truth, any mystic abilities I may seem to demonstrate are due to an enchanted sword that stays hidden. I had it now but preferred a non-lethal means of escape.

My captors were not entirely without heart: they left me a small, barred window through which to view the outside world. Sadly, it was too small for even someone of my stature to squeeze through. Since it looked out on to the Rouen city square, it made plans of widening it problematic, as any number of the locals would see my work. I did, however, get to watch the town folk going about their business.

There was some excitement, judging by the gossip. Several people had been found dead.

The talk worried me. I had enough experience to know that death isn't always a certainty when dealing with magic. I was proof of that. It was possible that the mage had survived and was continuing his killing games, only now if people were dying it meant he was stealing whole souls instead of just pieces. It could have been enough to save him from the reaper's grasp. Even if it wasn't him, it made no difference. I first took my vow to the Round Table centuries ago, but I had renewed it every year, ever since its fall. It was my job to protect the weak and the innocent. And sadly, the stupid and the ignorant, when they overlapped. I had not shirked that responsibility in my long life and I was not about to start. Now I had another reason to get out of my cell—to save these people. Again. Maybe they'd be so grateful they won't try to kill me this time. And maybe Arthur has returned.

The question was how to get out without hurting my captors. No answer appeared before me, but there was an unusual sight outside my tiny window on the world. A portly man I recognized as Archbishop Romain was frantically moving through the town square. He approached and spoke with all the able-bodied men and a few that were questionable in that department. After each request, the men quickly moved away from him, some even go so far as to go inside buildings and shut the doors. He came close enough that I could hear.

"But you have to help. The creature in the Seine is killing people and we need to stop it," the archbishop said.

The man shook his head. "I'm sorry your eminence, but I have a wife and children to think about. I'm no soldier."

The archbishop grabbed him by the collar of his shirt. "But you are a man, confound it. We need men to stand up and take care of this, otherwise more will die."

The man broke away from the archbishop's grip. "I'm sorry. Pray harder and maybe God will send you the soldiers you need." With that, he ran away. The archbishop bowed his head and crossed himself, remaining silent for a moment. He crossed himself again and lifted his head up.

Which was of course, when I decided to intrude into things.

"Congratulations, Father. God has answered your prayers," I said.

The archbishop glared down at my window, annoyance on his face. "I doubt that a murderer is the answer to my prayers and it is Archbishop, not Father."

I chuckled at that. "Wasn't it Jesus himself who said we should not assume importance and those at the foot of the table will be the first into the Kingdom of Heaven?"

That got me another look. Outside of the nobility and clergy, not many people read or knew enough to be able to reference scripture. "You're butchering the passage."

When I recited it correctly from memory and in Latin, the archbishop's eyes opened wider.

"Were you ever a priest?"

"Nope."

"The son of a nobleman?"

I laughed at that one. "The man from whose loins I sprang was a good many things and even more bad ones. Noble was not one of them."

"Have you ever spent time in court?"

He meant the current regime of France of course. I hadn't under the current monarchy, but had in a past one as well as other royal courts dating back to my first under the greatest king there ever was and likely ever will be. "I've spent time among royalty," I hedged.

"In what capacity, pray tell?"

"In many, as a knight." That almost got a chuckle from the archbishop. A man of my height doesn't usually make knight. I was used to the cynicism. "And as a jester." There were other positions, but those were the ones I was best at.

"What is your name?"

"Dagonet." I let off the "Sir" as it was unlikely he would believe my claim that I was once not only King Arthur's jester, but a knight of the Round Table.

"So what's got you in such a distressed state?" I asked.

"There's a gargouille in the Seine."

"A water dragon." That explained why the men of the town were avoiding the archbishop. "Nasty business." Actually, that wasn't strictly true. Dragons are much like people. There are good ones and there are bad ones. "Some gargouilles can even flood entire towns."

The archbishop raised an eyebrow. "You seem rather well informed about dragons."

As knights in King Arthur's court, we did have to deal with the occasional dragon, although not all of them as foes. It wasn't quite as common as romanticized, but I wasn't exactly a stranger to the tactics involved.

"Has anyone actually tried negotiating with it?" I asked.

"Why, pray tell, would we do that? It's been attacking people! There are six dead in the last day alone. It must be destroyed," the archbishop said.

The man was brave, I'll give him that, but he didn't strike me as any sort of a fighter, at least in the physical sense. A little too heavy and soft, but then again, he wasn't giving up, even though those around him were fleeing, so maybe he had a little fighter in him after all.

"It always amazes me on how quick people are to jump straight into fighting and death instead of a little common sense and talk," I said.

"An odd comment coming from a murderer," the archbishop said.

I shrugged, although I doubted he could see it through the small window. "I tried to negotiate with Achard, but he refused to stop hurting the people he was supposed to be protecting. I was left with no other choice."

"Ah yes, your defense that he was *sucking bits of people's souls away.* Not the most inspired thinking," the archbishop said.

"Doesn't make it any less true."

"The Lord gave each man a soul. He would not allow another to take any of that away. Even the Devil must tempt and have consent to take a soul," he said.

"I don't presume to speak for God, but it is possible and it does happen."

"I'm glad you do not presume to speak for the Lord because your talk alone already borders on heresy," he said.

"So you'll kill me for murder and then bring me back and kill me again for the heresy?" I said.

The archbishop actually chuckled. "I think the one killing would be sufficient."

"Yet the Bible and the Ten Commandments specifically state thou shall not kill. How do you justify that?" I said.

"It also says an eye for an eye and a tooth for a tooth," he said.

"Yes, but did not Jesus come and make a new covenant and invalidate that premise?"

"You argue theology well for someone who has never been part of the clergy," the archbishop said.

"After I was abandoned by my parents, I was raised by a priest," I said.

"He was a good man?"

I hesitated a moment before I answered. I would say he was good but had not always been so. And Sundry wasn't exactly a man. "Yes. And he would be most disappointed with you just tossing off these comments."

"I am the archbishop. I hardly think I need to be concerned with what a mere priest would think about my actions," he said.

"That sounds like pride, one of the seven deadly sins." I could have told him that Father Sundry was Jesus's thirteenth apostle, who before that had been one of the demons called Legion. Sundry alone among his brethren forced the pig he had been exorcised into to return to Jesus and bow before him, begging forgiveness. The Lord forgave his sins and transformed the pig's body into that of a man. Mostly anyway. Sundry had been wandering the earth ever since, guarding and watching out for the true intent of the Church, not necessarily what man had fogred it into.

"Well, we can argue all day, but I have things I have to take care of," I said.

"And what, pray tell, do you have to do?"

"A nap, for one thing."

"You're in a cell big enough for you to lie down in?" the archbishop asked.

Barely. "Plenty of room in here, thank you for asking."

"And after your nap?"

"It is Ascension Day, so I was hoping to get out to church."

"Doubtful."

"Well, there's some breathing to be done, both in and out. And there's this rat who's been visiting me, whom I would like to train to do some tricks," I said.

"Sounds engrossing."

"Oh, it is. Well, have fun fighting your dragon. All by your lonesome."

I moved away from the window, just far enough so my face was hidden in the shadows, but I could still see his. I could practically hear his brain swirling with a question he hated to ask.

"Excuse me…" He grimaced and swallowed hard. "Dagonet?"

I moved back to where my face could be seen. "Yes?"

"Would you be willing to help me fight the gargouille?"

"Would you be willing to commute my sentence and allow me to live?" I asked.

"No."

"A pity." And it was. Would have made things easier. Sadly, my oath to the Round Table didn't allow me to take the smarter route and hold out until he agreed to my demand. "But yes, I'll help you."

"You did hear me say that I would not commute your sentence?"

"Oh, yes. My hearing is quite good."

"Why should you help me and the people who have sentenced you to death if there's nothing in it for you?"

"An excellent question. I have only a simple answer. Because it's the right thing to do."

The archbishop stroked the beard on his chin. "Very well. I will allow you out, but you will remain tied to me at all times. Should you try to escape I shall put you back in your cell. Is that understood?"

"I suppose, but could I borrow a parchment and quill to leave a note in case the rat arrives? I don't want to disappoint him and I *had* told him that I would teach him some tricks," I said.

The archbishop ignored me and walked into the building where I was imprisoned. I heard some arguing, but in the end, Romain won by invoking not only his authority but by offering to take my guard in my stead if said guard did not release me into the archbishop's custody.

With the turn of a key and the clanking of the door, my cell was opened. Romain looked as if he expected me to bolt and was ready to tackle me. His face showed surprise when I held my hand up to be tied.

"Follow me, convict," the archbishop said.

"Sure, Romain," I said.

The archbishop stopped short and turned to glare at me. The veins in his forehead and neck were budging through his reddened skin. "You will refer to me as 'Archbishop.'"

"Sure, but I'll address you as Romain." I punctuated my words with a large grin.

"Then you can return to your cell."

I slipped out of the rope, did a backward cartwheel and went into my cell. "Ratty, I'm back. Ready for those tricks?"

I didn't think it possible but the archbishop's face became an even darker shade of crimson. Then he glanced out my miniature version of a window. People were running by with their possessions on their backs or carts.

A second guard ran in. "The dragon is destroying the homes along the shore. We need to go."

Romain grinned at me. "The soldiers are finally being ordered to face the beast?"

"No, we are to help with the evacuation."

The two soldiers ran out, not bothering to close my cell door. The archbishop collapsed to the floor, holding his head in his hands. "All is lost." "I was lost." I stepped out and put the rope back on my wrist. "But now am found. Let us go find a dragon." The archbishop looked up at my face, not seeming to believe what he was seeing. "Come on, Romain. We're losing daylight."

He stood and brushed the dirt of the jail cellar off his cassock. "Yes, yes we are."

We walked out into the square. People were either barricading their homes or taking what they could carry and leaving the city.

Romain begged a group of soldiers to join us. They, in turn, asked him to join them. Neither side convinced the other and we went our separate ways.

Before long, we had exited the city and were making our way along the Seine.

"Were you actually a knight or was that just talk?"

"I spoke the truth," I replied.

"How are you at battle strategies?"

"Better than many."

"So how do we go about defeating a gargouille?"

"First we try to talk, but before we do, we have a plan of attack ready." The archbishop tilted his head as if confused. "Just because we are trying to negotiate with the dragon does not mean he will be interested in doing the same. Have you ever been a soldier?"

"No."

"Then leave everything to me."

"Why should I trust a convict?"

"Because I give you my word as a knight that you can."

"I'd like more than that."

I sighed. I slipped out of the rope, rolled away from Romain and shot off the ground into a tree, a good twenty feet off the ground.

"Blessed heavens."

"Not quite," I said. My high perch was not due to divine power but an invisible, elongating sword named *Hayden*. When I hold onto the hilt and plant the tip, I can propel myself off the ground. It was a useful weapon that more than compensated for my diminutive stature and limited reach. Combined with my acrobatics, its ability to lengthen and shorten at my mental commands gave me a unique fighting style and an unseen way to both attack and keep away from my enemies.

I stepped off the branch and Romain's eyes went wide. Instead of plummeting to my death I used Hayden to lower me slowly to the ground. Not as easy as it sounds since the balancing involved without falling off took no small amount of skill.

"How did you do that?" asked Romain.

"Magic."

"So you are versed in the dark arts?"

"Hardly. Most magic is not good or evil in and of itself. It is a tool."

"Most?"

I shrugged. "There is evil and good magic. What you witnessed is controlled by me. I am not evil, so neither is the means I employ. I can leave anytime I want. You would have no chance of stopping or catching me. I am here to help."

"Such selflessness in a murderer is unheard of."

"Then perhaps you should rethink the premise that I am a murderer."

Romain looked down into my eyes and nodded. "Yes, Dagonet, perhaps I should."

A wave then splashed against our boots, unusual in that we were near a river, not an ocean. Also, because we were on land that normally would be dry, but the river had overflowed its banks and flooded the nearby countryside.

"I think we are close," Romain said. I nodded and pulled him down. Out in the river, a serpentine head loomed above the water, its mouth open and spouting water with the force of a hundred-foot-tall waterfall into someone's house. "Can all gargouilles do that?"

"Not to that extent, no," I said, wondering about the wisdom of talking first. My only advantage was surprise. By negotiating, I gave that up. "The dragon is likely a mage."

The archbishop crossed himself and raised himself up to kneeling to pray. He raised an eyebrow when I knelt to join him. As a knight of the Round Table, I had seen many instances of the power of the Lord even before the Holy Grail healed me and gave me a very long life.

When we were done, we got back down on our bellies.

"Dagonet, I think I should be the one to talk to him."

"I agree."

Romain's eyes narrowed. "I felt sure you would want to be the one."

"I do, but if I remain hidden and things do not go well, I will have surprise to aid me in an attack."

"Attack with what? You have no weapon."

"I do."

When I did not elaborate, the archbishop sighed. "Suggestions for how to open talks?"

"Try to look non-threatening."

Romain looked down at his prominent belly, then at the dragon destroying the riverside with the streams of water pouring out of his mouth. "I do not think that will be a problem."

"Then simply find out what he wants and if you are able to give it to him."

"And if I can't? Or he doesn't want to talk?"

"Be ready to run away very quickly."

His once red face was now pale. It took him a moment longer than it should have to stand, but despite his fear and shaking knees, he went to the riverside.

Archbishop Romain stood on the shore until the dragon noticed him. The stationary man in the cassock without weapons seemed to interest the beast and he swam toward him.

"Greetings, mighty gargouille. I am Archbishop Romain and I have come so we may speak together."

The dragon snorted, spraying Romain. "And what would we have to speak about, Archbishop?"

"Your actions are hurting and killing people. I would like to see what it would take for you to stop."

"You would, would you? And if I don't, how will you stop me?"

"I will trust in God to handle that."

"Very well. I will play your game if you will play mine. I would like you to provide me with a sacrifice every full moon."

"What sort of sacrifice?" Romain asked.

"Does it matter? Agree and I will stop my rampage. You will win the game you came here to play. What's more, you will be the savior of these people."

"There is only one savior and I am not Him."

"Their deliverer, then."

"I cannot agree without knowing what you want."

"Very wise. It is hard to effectively play a game when you do not know or understand the rules. What I want is a little thing. Literally. A child or infant."

Romain's anger overwhelmed his fear as he stepped toward the dragon and pointed an accusing finger. "You monster."

"Heh, why yes, I am. My game is a trifle one-sided, but it is simple. I allow you to try to appease me. Succeed and I will not harm any others outside of the appeasement. Fail and I start the harming with you. So, Archbishop, do we have a deal?"

"By all that is holy, we certainly do not."

"What would you offer me instead?"

"Cattle, sheep, oxen. Enough to keep you well fed," said Romain.

"Animals don't taste as good as humans. And their souls are barely a snack. I was hoping for maybe a virgin or two. Tradition you know."

"I will never give you a single person," Romain vowed.

The dragon moved his tail and a wave of water came up past the archbishop's ankles. "You give up too easy. Perhaps an old woman, already near death, can be brought to me."

"No."

"Perhaps criminals, those already destined for death. What harm is there in handing over one who will die anyway?" the dragon asked.

Romain actually paused to consider the offer. I began to worry. Romain could simply hand me over to seal the deal. "No. Even convicted criminals can have something in them worth redeeming. My offer of animals still stands."

"Still not interested. If you have no more counteroffers, you have lost the first game and I have you as my spoils. Now we play a new game and we shall see if you can walk on water like your Lord as you try to get away from me. If you survive the next minute, I'll even give you a head start."

The archbishop made the sign of the cross and held his ground.

As the dragon opened his maw, I leapt out of hiding and pointed Hayden down his gullet. My invisible sword elongated, slicing into the beast's upper palate. The water he was about to belch up caught in his throat and mixed with his blood. Some sprayed out onto Romain, who grimaced.

"Run, Archbishop, run," I shouted. Romain sprinted toward the tree line as the dragon turned his attention on me.

"You!?" it shouted, which startled and confused me.

"Have we met?" I asked, fairly sure I would have remembered.

"Not since you killed me," he said. "Separating my head from my neck with one fell swoop by some foul magic of your own."

Hayden was hardly foul magic, but my enemies not knowing how I did what I did gave me a certain advantage. However, even with a magic blade, I hardly had the strength to slice through the creature's barrel-sized neck with a single stroke. In fact, the only head I had recently decapitated belonged to…

"Achard."

"You recognize me." The dragon crouched low, crawling closer toward shore.

"At least you aren't as ugly as you were. Good trick, not dying," I said, backing away.

The dragon opened his mouth, not so much to smile but to make sure I got a good look at the long rows of sharp teeth. "I wasn't about to lose our game that easily."

If you call Achard chasing me down with a pack of hounds and black magic easy. I hadn't known he was also a water mage, let alone a dragon. Water mages can keep air in the blood and stop breathing for a time. I guess he was powerful enough to do it even with his head separated from his body.

"How'd you survive?" I asked, trying to buy more time for the archbishop to get away. Just in case Achard decided to attack instead of talk, I had Hayden's blade aimed at his eye.

"I should thank you. Beheading me broke the spell trapping me in human form." Hayden can sometimes cut through enchantments. My mistake. "The gravedigger was foolish enough to touch my bare skin. Draining his soul mended me." The dragon rose up from the river as if to show me his magnificence. Water splashed down from his scales forming a short-lived waterfall.

"You are restored to being a dragon. Why keep killing?" I moved again. His head was too high for me to have a good shot at his eyes. I aimed at a point on the belly where the scales were softer.

"Why?" Achard splashed back down in the river, the water soaking me, even my face. I quickly wiped my eyes, not wanting to be eaten because I couldn't see the beast lunging for me. "As you know, I like to play for life and death. My own games of course, but those are the best kind. I even allowed the occasional traveler such as yourself the privilege of playing when I was trapped as a human."

"If you call attacking unarmed and unsuspecting people a game," I said moving toward drier land. Achard had the water flow so that it matched my steps.

"I allowed them all, including you, a head start. Very sporting of me, as I could have killed any of you while you slept. Too sporting in your case."

"Like you said, hard to play when you don't know all the rules. Not exactly sporting to feed off your servants' souls," I said, my nervousness growing as the water now up to my shins and I hadn't moved. It was if an ocean high tide was suddenly coming in on the river bank.

"That was simple payment for allowing them the right to continue living. The best part of the game is to hold someone's fate in your hands or claws. I like to see how far I can push people, what I can make them do to avoid death. Any of my servants could have fought me or refused to do my bidding. True, they'd have likely died, but they had that choice. Some even chose to help me. I gave one a choice between butchering his own wife or me killing him. We had her for dinner that night. Sadly, I had given her the same dilemma first and she picked death over killing him. When I told him, he committed suicide. His despair was delicious. I had so hoped that given a choice between saving others and sacrificing someone, the archbishop would have acquiesced. That would have been such fun. Now as my fame spreads, more will come to play in an attempt to vanquish me. Much like you and the archbishop."

The dragon grinned and the water moved up to my thighs. Much more and I'd have to start treading water. I didn't want to look for Romain, but I could still hear his feet pattering in the distance. I needed to buy him a little more time.

"So little man, what will you do for me in order for me to let you live? Perhaps kill the archbishop? Or maim him and bring him to me so I can finish the job." The dragon was lazily moving toward me.

"No," I said as an undercurrent started to pull me into the river and the beast's jaws.

"Hmm. How about I allow you to bring wayward travelers to me? I kill them, you get to live."

"Not going to happen," I said, fighting to not lose my footing. "I have a counter offer. How about you give up killing and instead try to help others."

Achard was almost close enough for one of his claws to rake at me. I hoped Romain was far away because I had to put some distance between me and the scaly killer. "What would my incentive be?"

"I'll let you live."

The dragon tilted his head back and laughed. The undercurrent lessened and I used the distraction to turn and run to dry land.

"Very amusing, little man, but you need to give up those delusions. Vow to become my servant and I will still consider sparing you and only feed on you on occasion. I am a dragon and you are certainly no knight. What chance do you have against me now?"

"You'd be surprised. And you are wrong. I am every bit as much a knight as you are a dragon."

"Don't make me laugh again." Achard had one foot on dry land and his tail was posed in the air as if ready to strike me.

"I wouldn't dream of it, Achard. You are not worthy of it."

"You still address me by my human name."

"Yes, and you may address me by mine. Sir Dagonet, Knight of the Round Table."

"You jest," the dragon said, but with the slightest hint of worry. He even stopped his advance. The legends of Camelot pale in comparison to the real thing and despite Le Fey's spell to make the world think we were just legend, there were those who knew and even remembered the truth.

"I do. Superbly. However, I am deadly serious now when I say to you surrender or die."

The dragon's answer was to lunge and open his jaw. I didn't have a clear line to an eye so I shot Hayden deeper inside his throat. I felt my blade sink into the unprotected flesh and strike bone. This time it did not stop the stream of water from blasting at me, battering my body like I was caught in rapids. I held on as long as I could, but my arms eventually gave way. I retracted my blade—it was that or risk losing it—and was swept away more than a hundred feet, where a tree broke my sideways fall and a few of my ribs. Almost out of air and no longer sure which way was up or down, I made my best guess as I pointed and elongated my sword to push myself up and out of the blast stream, repeating my trick with the tree. Only this time, I was at an angle and further away from the trunk. The branch I landed on could not hold my weight and I fell. I aimed Hayden toward the tree and shortened the blade to pull me toward it. I managed to wrap my limbs around the trunk to try to get a moment's rest and my bearing. The dragon redirected the stream, blasting me further back into more branches that battered and tore at my skin.

I tumbled down, branches slowing my momentum until I landed on the forest floor. I scrambled to hide.

"Come out, little knight. I'm not done playing with you yet. You refused my chances to live, so now you must die and I shall feast upon your soul. This time I won't need my hounds to find you."

I didn't stop moving inland as I shouted, "You play a coward's game, but you can come and get me if you dare."

"You think I am afraid of you?" Achard bellowed.

"Yes. Afraid because you know you will lose to little old me and there is nothing you can do to stop me from beating you," I shouted. The dragon was angry enough that he came out of the water to give chase. Excellent. For the first time since the battle started, I had a hope of surviving and possibly winning the gargler's game.

A gargouille is at his most powerful when in water. His waterspouts were fed by his contact with the river. The dragon could only store so much water in his body and once he ran dry, he wouldn't be able to spit any more water without re-submerging.

"Where are you, little knight? I grow tired of this game."

"Too bad. I could play all day and into the night. However, I will accept your surrender and forfeit now if you are not up for it."

The dragon's head spun toward me and sent out a stream of water. He was smart and had narrowed the flow so it had more pressure and conserved his aqueous supply. The jet's force was so strong that it snapped the tree I was hiding behind clean in two. Had I been any slower rolling away, I would have been trapped beneath the fallen trunk, an easy feast for the scaly soul taker.

In the woods, I had another advantage in our deadly game of dragon and knight. I was smaller and could fit between the trees. Achard had to plow through them, which slowed and hurt him, each shattered tree bruising his hide or worse. And each injury made him angrier, which was good. I didn't want him thinking. I needed him charging ahead blindly. Gave me more opportunities.

I was doing well until I came to the bottom of a cliff. I pointed my sword down and elongated it to lift me up, but before I reached the top I was hit by another blast stream that knocked me to the side and down I went.

Nothing more was broken, but the wind was knocked out of me. That wasn't the worst of it: I had dropped Hayden.

When the dragon came to stand over me, I was only able to get to my knees. I grabbed a rock in one hand and I heard the beast laugh.

"You are going to fight me with a rock?"

I managed to get enough air in my lungs to say, "Ready to surrender now?"

The dragon's open jaws loomed as he leaned in toward me and I threw my rock. He spat it back at me. "You lose. Your soul is mine."

Which is when the miracle happened. Archbishop Romain seemed to drop from the sky and land on the dragon's neck. Somehow, he had managed to get to the top of the cliff and jump down. Even more amazing, he managed to wrap both legs and his cloth stole around the gargouille's neck. He held onto the stole like a bridle.

"His soul belongs to the Lord. I command thee in the name of

God to surrender yourself to me."

"Never!" the gargouille shouted, proceeding to buck like a wild horse in an attempt to throw Romain off, but the more he struggled, the more steadfast the archbishop's resolve was. The dragon even tried to use the last of his water to make his neck too slippery to hold, but it did no good. Romain held on through it all, although to this day I'm still not certain how.

I used the distraction to try to find where I had dropped Hayden. Finding an invisible sword is not as hard as it sounds, mainly because I could see it. At least somewhat.

Achard decided to turn back toward the river. My guess was he planned to go into the water and drown the archbishop. He never got the chance, for a cold blade was pressing in on his tail and two important parts of his malehood stopped him short.

I had found Hayden. I managed to get my sword between the scales on his tail at just the right angle to go all the way through the flesh and out the other side until the blade was cutting into that most tender of male areas. Yes, I know it was fighting dirty, but believe it or not, that wasn't against the code of the Round Table, at least when dealing with a foe of greater strength, magic, or one who was better armed. Achard qualified on all three counts.

"I wouldn't move unless you want to see how well you can reattach something other than your head," I said. "I think the game is over."

The dragon growled but stopped.

"What shall we do now, Romain? I'm sorry… Archbishop?"

He laughed with the joy of someone who has realized that he should be getting ready to be laid in the grave but has managed to snatch victory from the jaws of death anyway. Or in terms Achard would understand, the archbishop had just won a deadly game that had been stacked against him.

"After this, you can call me Romain." His face got more serious for a moment. "Just not in front of others, if you don't mind."

"No problem. We need to find a way to imprison him."

"And this creature was disguised as the man you were supposed to have murdered?"

"Yes."

"Can he turn back to a man?"

"Yes." Not all dragons are shapeshifters, but those that can don't lose the ability without a reason.

"I'll never…" The wiggle of my blade cut off his words with the threat of cutting off something else.

"Let us go back to Rouen. I have an idea," said Romain.

From my angle, I saw the dragon grin and I knew why. A new game was presenting itself. "It may not be the wisest idea to bring him around so many people." And so many souls.

"You once told me I should trust you. Will you do the same for me?" asked the archbishop.

"After saving my hide? You've earned that much."

I climbed onto the dragon's tail and gave him careful instructions to not even attempt to throw me since I could cut him with just a thought. He must have believed me because there were no incidents as he walked into the city.

We were a sight. A dragon walking into the city, Archbishop Romain riding atop his neck, and me, a convicted murderer, sitting on his tail. People began to follow us and talk about how God had given the archbishop the power to control the dragon. I was fine with him getting the credit. Besides, the only way for an overweight man of the cloth to make that jump and hold on to the neck of a fighting dragon that long was some kind of divine intervention.

Romain climbed down and ran into a blacksmith's shop, leaving me to guard the dragon. Since no one could see my sword, they all assumed that it was the archbishop's power that kept him from attacking or fleeing.

Romain eventually exited the shop, the blacksmith trailing in his wake.

"Turn back into your human form," ordered Romain.

"Go to blazes."

The archbishop crossed himself and I wiggled my sword. A moment later a naked man crouched where the dragon had stood a moment before. I retracted Hayden as the transformation began, but I quickly repositioned it so Achard didn't get any ideas. Romain had the blacksmith put a very thick and sharp-edged iron collar around Achard's neck, making sure he wore gloves so there was no skin-to-skin contact.

"It's okay, Dagonet. You can stop." I looked at Romain. "Trust me."

I retracted my blade but had it at the ready. In human form, I already knew I could separate parts of Achard. If I saw even a hint of scale, I'd butcher him.

"Achard, I blessed that collar myself. It will not allow you to transform back into a gargouille. I give you the chance to be tried for your crimes and have your confession heard."

"You are a fool. You think a piece of metal can hold me? You think you have won this game? I refuse your offer and chose the consequences. Then I shall kill you all." And Achard turned from man into dragon. The collar was large for a man, but flimsy for a dragon. It should not have held, but it did. This time I did not have to do a thing as Achard lost his own game and his head at the same time as his neck expanded but the metal collar didn't.

Romain took the blacksmith's gloves and dragged the head away from the body and ordered a pyre built around the remains. Now the soldiers leapt at his command. It wasn't until most of the corpse had burned to ash that he threw the head in.

He then doused the ashes in holy water and had them buried. I almost told him that I didn't think the holy water would make a difference but decided to hold my tongue. Romain had managed pretty well on his own so far.

Archbishop Romain then arranged for my pardon in exchange for my part in helping beat the gargouille. And from then on there was a new custom in the city of Rouen—on Ascension Day a criminal was pardoned. The tradition was kept every year from 1156 until 1780 when some idiots in the French Revolution stopped the custom. They called it the archbishop's privilege. Romain was later canonized, achieving immortality of sorts as a saint.

Even Achard achieved lasting fame as the gargouille, or in English, the gargler. The locals built waterspouts into their buildings and churches to commemorate his defeat. Every time someone in France looks at a grotesque, it is a remembrance of him, even if most people these days mistake them for gargoyles

Of course, I am barely remembered as the nameless convict who helped St. Romain. Not that it surprises me. It's not like most people even know I was a knight of the Round Table. I don't do what

I do for the glory, but it would be nice if somebody occasionally remembered me.

Sadly, it turned out the holy water was a mistake. Not so much the holy part as the water. Not that I found out until the French Revolution, but that is a story for another day.

*IT WAS FAERIE'S DARKEST HOUR WHEN THANDAU RULED
THE LAND. POWERS GREAT AND SMALL FLED,
HID, OR BOWED TO THE TYRANT.
BUT THERE WERE SOME WHO DARED TO FIGHT BACK.
THE GREATEST OF THESE WERE THE DAEMOR, FEMALE
WARRIORS, THE ELITE OF MAB'S REBEL ARMY.
THEY RISKED ALL SO THAT FAERIE
WOULD ONE DAY AGAIN BE FREE.*

THE SWORDS OF THE
DAEMOR

SAD DAYE

A tale of Daye the Deadly

Another day, another death. Hell of a way to make a living. Heh. It'd be almost funny if it weren't so sad. A few years back if someone had told me I'd end up as the hired blade for Queen Mab's Daemor, I would have told them they were insane. I was a mother and a wife. Now I'm neither thanks to Thandau's graycoats.

I'm still amazed at how deftly I took to killing. True, death is something every banshee is familiar with in ways most fey and gentry will never understand, but to call the Reaper instead of herald his arrival… it channels the hate and anger into something besides tears and sorrow. At first, I hope if I killed enough graycoats the holes in my soul would be filled. Now I know no matter how many I send to the Reaper's embrace that I'll always miss my babies' smiles and my husband's embrace, but the memories of their murderers and their fellow soldiers dying at my hands does actually help me make it through the night.

I do not kill indiscriminately. My job is to kill those who would impede the Daemor and Mab's army and our hopes of an eventual defeat of the tyrant Thandau. And since most of those I send to the Reaper could only be described as evil if you are being charitable, guilt does not stay my hand. More apt descriptions involve words I would never have said in front of my babies. In honor of them, I try not to say those type of things now. Odd I know, an assassin that won't curse, but there you have it.

I walked toward the town of Rough Woods in search of my next gift to the Reaper. Her crime was especially hateful. Daemor cannot compete with Thandau's forces in numbers, materials, or magic. What we did have were our reputations which actually helped keep us safe. People know we follow a code of honor and they know where we stand. Thandau has tried on occasion to turn this strength against us by dressing up women as Daemor and outfitting them with an imitation Daemor badge with a raven's head on a silver circle, then sending them out to do all manner of heinous and evil things to turn the people of Faerie against us. It started to become effective and endanger us, so Mab issued an edict of death against any who dare to impersonate a Daemor. After the imposters' heads were hung on strategically placed pikes, the number of impersonators dropped off, but you still get some willing to play the odds. It's my job to find them and made sure they lose that game.

Rough Woods was a Thandau stronghold mainly because he had a large enough army to hold it and strategically it's not vital enough for us to commit our very limited reassures to taking it back. That means the people here have to live under graycoat rule. It's not optimal, but in war, choices have to be made.

There was a Daemor rumored to be operating in the town. One major problem with that – Mab knows where all of our Daemor are and none of them were stationed in Rough Woods. Which of course means the assassin g has to ride in and dispatch the imposter.

The woman I used to be is disturbed that I am more troubled that I find myself occasionally speaking in the third person than I am by the prospect of killing a woman.

Sneaking into a Thandau controlled town isn't as hard as one would think. Any town has a need for laborers and most of the laborers don't get more than a cursory examination. Since the poor typically can't afford a glamour, that is the first thing the sentries at town gates look for and why I hardly ever use magic to disguise myself. I find hair dye and body makeup make a much more an effective disguise. However, the key to passing as one of the downtrodden is to lose yourself. And by that, I mean any traces of pride and confidence need to be expelled from how you walk and carry yourself. No making eye contact and no mouthing off regardless of how justified your barbed words might be. It means occasionally having to endure things you would never allow, like a blow or a wandering hand touching flesh that they had no right too. Any hint of defiance is enough to bring you to the attention of even the most dimwitted graycoats.

There were three graycoats on duty at the north gate. Unfortunately, it seemed as though there wasn't as large of an influx of laborers as I had hoped. Only three men and me.

They let the men through after examination and a small bribe from each. Fairly common practice.

It was my turn.

"What have we here?" the ranking graycoat asked.

"Begging your pardon, sir, I'm just looking for some work for my hands to do. My cousin said that her mistress had need of a seamstress and a cook and I am able to do both of those things."

The graycoat sneered as his eyes wandered up and down my body hungrily. "I see. What do you have to offer us to gain entrance to Rough Woods?"

This was the difficult part. The men had offered handmade items, things that cost nothing but the time and skill of making them. The person I was trying to be would not have much in the way of coins. She would also possibly be unaware of the need for a toll. But I had come prepared.

"I had wanted to prove my skills to my cousin's mistress, so I baked this pie." I opened the canvas sack of was carrying and pulled out a fruit pie in a wooden bowl. I had, in fact, made it myself. My mothering skills may have been rarely used these days, but they were far from gone.

"It smells delicious," said the youngest looking of the graycoats. He would not have his first beard for a season or two yet and judging by his sleeves, he was a recent recruit without rank.

"Yes, pie is all well and good but you can give that to your cousin's mistress to prove your culinary skills. I have another toll in mind," said the ranking graycoat, as he placed his hand upon my buttock and squeezed roughly, with no trace of tenderness.

"Sir, I'm a married woman," I exclaimed, feigning shock.

The ranking graycoat laughed, as did the older, fatter graycoat standing next to him. "Then it is probably best that you don't tell him about it, don't you think?"

"But sir, I don't understand," I lied. It must be pretty bad in Rough Woods for the graycoats to be allowing this to go on in the light of day. It pretty hard to keep people in line when they know you are taking advantage of or outright raping their mothers, sisters, daughters, and wives. Even the most downtrodden of people start plotting rebellion and worse when faced with that.

"I'm afraid the toll for you will just be a small service," Rank said. "It won't take very much. We can step over here to take care of this business and then you can be on your way."

I figured playing dumb was a better first tactic to take than gutting them in the streets. "But I don't understand …"

"What he is trying to tell you—" the fatass graycoat said. "—is that you are going to service our manly needs." Fatass pumped his pelvis forward a few times to let it be known in no uncertain terms what he had in mind.

"But I can't do that. I'm married," I said.

Rank shrugged. "Then like I said, I guess you had better not let your husband know about it. The pity for you is that it might just ruin you for other men for the rest of your days, but that is a chance I'm willing to take."

The third graycoat spoke up and I expected him to join the evil fun, but Beardless surprised me.

"Sir, I don't think this is right."

Rank raised his eyebrows. "Excuse me?"

"She's a married lady and she is not willing. There are plenty of women that come through that are more than happy to pay that particular toll," Beardless said.

"Are you suggesting that I take her measly little pie and allow her to come into Rough Woods?"

"Yes, sir. It would be the soldierly thing to do."

Rank and Fatass looked at each other then back at Beardless. Rank smiled then shoved his fist so far up Beardless' gut that I expected to see his hand come out the other side.

"Then who is going to wax my pole? You? Being a soldier means you take what you are strong enough to get and I do not take insubordination. Consider yourself on report and you are going to be on guard duty for two shifts straight without getting to keep any of the tolls you collect." Beardless was on the ground puking his guts out. It had been an impressive blow. "Do I make myself understood?"

"Yes, sir."

"Good. Get back on your feet and guard this gate while we take this lady for the time of her life."

I started to back away, but Rank grabbed hold of my arm and yanked me inside of the gate and pulled me towards an alley between what their garrison and what passed for the city wall.

I had already decided I was going to kill them, but it didn't pay to let that be known that ahead of time, so I acted the opposite of how a Daemor would. I screamed and pulled and begged and pleaded for mercy. There was none to be had.

Fatass tried to calm and coax me. "We are really experienced and gifted men. You will truly enjoy it. Trust me."

I trusted Fatass about as far as I could throw his decapitated head. I responded by dropping to the floor kicking and screaming. The soldiers laughed. Fatass grabbed me under the legs and Rank grabbed me under the arms and around the chest, apparently mistaking my breasts for handles. The two of them carried me into the alley and ended my unpleasant journey with a toss into a wall. Fortunately, I had anticipated their action and moved so the blow was spread out throughout my body. Rank had already undone his sword belt and had his pants dropped down to his ankles.

"You best get your dress up and off, Missus. Things will go better for you if I am not forced to beat you."

I decided now would be an excellent time to take them out, maybe see how far I could throw Fatass's decapitated head. I was again surprised. Apparently, I was not the only one planning to stop the graycoats.

"Step away from that woman," came a voice from atop the city wall. The three of us looked up to see a woman in form-fitting armor that exposed as much skin as it protected. I realized this limited the effectiveness of the armor, but the bits that shown through had been known more than once to distract a male soldier. While the Daemor looked like we dressed like that, it was a glamour that hid our armor. On this woman's chest was a circle of silver with a raven's head on it. These idiots had helped me find the fake Daemor.

"It's her. Sound the alarm," said Rank to Fatass, but before the big man could move the woman leapt off the wall, her boot connecting with his face making the back of his head strike the garrison wall. Fatass closed his eyes and sank to the pavement.

The woman already had her sword drawn and Rank's was on the ground next to his fallen pants.

"I thought you graycoats knew that the people in this town were under my protection. The protection of a Daemor."

"Shut up, whore," Rank said, spitting on the woman's face. She brought her boot up into his groin, with him hitting the ground harder and faster than when he struck Beardless. Although it was no doubt satisfying to hit the graycoat in that most sensitive of male places, it was an amateur move because it knocked him to the ground where he was able to reach out for his weapon. He pulled the sword from the sheath and thrust it towards the woman's heart. With a deft movement of her wrist, she knocked the blade away and made a thrust of her own directly into Rank's throat. The sword exited out through his spine, causing his body to twitch and then lie still. She removed the blade and there were a few gurgles as Rank's own blood started to drown him. Within moments he was dead, the loss of blood getting him before the suffocation.

The false Daemor offered me her hand. I took it. I should have ended her right then and there, only something seemed odd. All the other imitation Daemor had been working with the graycoats to make us look bad. This one seemed to have her own agenda and I wanted to find out exactly what that was and if there were any more like her.

"Are you okay?"

Making sure to maintain my character I answered, "I am, thanks to you. How can I show my appreciation?"

The woman smiled.

"No need for thanks. A Daemor's job is to help the helpless. Do you have a place to stay in the city? Or should I help you get outside of the wall before this comes down on you?" she said.

"I had the possibility of a job, otherwise I really have nowhere else to go. The graycoats conscripted all the men in my town and took the woman for worse. I managed to sneak away and I have been looking for a way to support myself since," I lied.

"An all too familiar fate these days, it is sad to say. Okay, I have a place for you to get your bearings straight. They will take care of you, feed you, and see about finding you some gainful employment." The false Daemor reached into a waist pouch and pulled out a hooded cloak and quickly put it on. She stood in such a way that the too large robe made her look masculine. She offered me her arm. It was a way for men to offer a woman their protection from others. I took it and we walked quickly out back past the garrison and down another alleyway to merge onto the main street.

"What is your name?" she asked.

"Janna," I lied. Daye is not an overly common name but it is well known as the name of the Daemor assassin and I didn't want to give her any reason to disappear on me. "What is yours?"

"Mace," she said and led me on a complicated path. We walked weaving back and forth through alleys and side streets with Mace constantly looking behind, above and around us to make sure we were not being followed. I had to admit she was very competent. As we turned to go in an alleyway I noticed her go out of her way to step on a stone and seem to stumble and hit another stone on a wall. She then changed her gait to step on several more stones. As we turned the corner the ground literally opened up.

"Stay close to me, otherwise you will be caught when it closes," Mace said, grabbing hold of my hand and leading me downstairs that had appeared below the sprung trap door. Our heads had barely cleared the ground, which became the ceiling once the opening closed. The place was pitch black. I fell out of character, readying for an attack.

Instead, Mace led me through the darkness. I heard her pushing a combination of stones on the floor again. A door opened and light filled the corridor.

"It was designed so that the two doors can't be opened at the same time. This way if it was ever used at night, the light couldn't betray where we were going to anyone that was watching from above," Mace said.

"Amazing." I was suitably impressed. That only increased as I looked around. The underground chamber was housing men, women, and children. Nearly fifty by my count.

"Who are all these people?"

Before I could get my answer, a young girl ran over, her arms flung wide, directly at Mace. The imitation Daemor scooped up the girl in a hug.

"Mace, you're back! Was there any trouble out there?" the girl said.

Mace laughed. "Nothing I couldn't handle."

"You mean nothing a Daemor couldn't handle," the girl said. "I want to be a Daemor just like you when I grow up."

"A very worthy aspiration, but it is a lot of hard work and training. Until then you have to listen to everything your mother tells you and not give her a hard time," Mace said.

"I know. Who is the lady?"

"This is Janna. Some mean graycoats were trying to hurt her," Mace said.

"But you saved her, didn't you? Just like you saved the rest of us," the girl said.

Now I was truly confused. Why would Thandau's imitation Daemor be helping his victims?

"Mace helped all of you?"

"Oh yes. She helps others too but many of them had places to go to. All of us didn't have anywhere else to go. We couldn't go home after they killed my father," the girl said. "The soldiers tried to take mommy and me away, but Mace stopped the slave transport and rescued all of us."

"You stopped an entire slave caravan by yourself?" I said incredulously. That was a feat worthy of a true Daemor.

Mace smiled modestly and shrugged. "It was weeks in the planning and I had to lay out many traps. But yes, I did."

"Before Mace got here everyone was afraid of the graycoats. The Daemor didn't bother much with us because we were kind of in the middle of nowhere. That all changed when Mace got here because now the graycoats are afraid of her."

"I wouldn't say they were afraid of me. I'd say I'm more of a huge pain in their bottoms. Now Janna, can we get you something to eat?"

I hesitated a minute sizing up Mace. She was behaving like a real Daemor would. In fact, by housing these people, she was going above and beyond what most Daemor had to do. Mab ran havens for refugees, so usually all a Daemor had to do was drop off anyone in need of hiding or a home and then head back out to the field. It seemed Mace was truly a freedom fighter, dedicated to the same cause as Mab's forces. It was just unfortunate that she chose to claim to be a Daemor. There were no exceptions in Mab's edict allowing for mercy just because the impersonator meant well. For the first time in a very long time, I felt sorry for one of my targets.

"Thank you, but I'm not very hungry right now," I said truthfully. I felt sick to my stomach over the thought of losing her to the Reaper.

"Nonsense, you have to keep up your strength," said Mace.

"I have a pie, although I'm happy to share." I handed it to the girl.

"Excellent. We shall have dessert tonight, but what good is a snack without a meal? Have some soup and maybe some bread. Janna bring her some."

The little girl did and I ate it. It wasn't bad, no worse than the army food I was used to. My slender piece of my pie was much better. Everyone who wanted some was given a small slice. It was good enough that many of the eaters liked me immediately. Good food has that effect. Maybe even why the false Daemor fed these people.

I made my way around the underground hideaway and talked with the other people. Mace seemed to be genuinely helping these people. One of them was even her cousin. Apparently, her parents were well off and were able to pay bribes to the graycoats to leave their family alone, but Mace couldn't look the other way when helpless people were being hurt. She dyed and cut her hair as a disguise so her family didn't get any retribution for her actions. According to her cousin, she disappeared for a couple months and came back as a Daemor. I kept silent on the truth that it took much longer for a woman to become one of Mab's elite forces.

After what was likely nightfall, Mace left to go out again. I snuck out after her, following her like a shadow. Again, no magic, just stealth training. She didn't notice me as I followed her onto the streets.

She took to the rooftops, which made sense. Most people tend not to look up and the buildings in Rough Woods were close enough to allow people to leap from one to the other. It was a way to patrol and minimize the chance of being caught. As the night went on, I watched her stop thieves who were attacking a single man, then steal food many times over from the richer neighborhoods only to drop it at the poorer ones.

My reservations about introducing her to the Reaper were increasing. If nothing else, we should recruit her for the army and she could make her way up to Daemor.

I was trying to think up a way to convince Mab to recruit rather than kill when I heard a woman scream. I ran back the way I came along the rooftops until I came upon an alley where Fatass from earlier had cornered a girl all of twelve, bolstered by a half-dozen other soldiers looking for an especially evil way to spend their downtime. Fatass already had his pants down around his ankles and was pointing a sword in the girl child's direction. The other soldiers were lining up behind him in wait for their own turns. I leapt down, feet hitting against the far wall and pushed off again towards the wall of the building I started on to land on the ground between Fatass and the girl.

"You have one chance to live. Walk away now," I said.

Fatass laughed in my face. "I am not afraid of you, woman. I have no reason to be."

"You should. I'm a Daemor."

That stopped Fatass from laughing, but he didn't look like he believed me. I was still in character both in posture and manner. It was enough for his companions to draw their swords and one of them to pull a bow.

Now there are plenty of stories about Daemor – how we're are stronger than giants and faster than flying arrows but most of them we allow to be spread to give us a psychological advantage over our enemies in battle. Yes, an arrow can be caught by most Daemor – we are trained to do it– but at this close a range there isn't time to prepare properly so I wasn't exactly confident at my odds.

"Shoot her just in case she's speaking the truth," Fatass ordered.

The bowman let the shaft loose. I reached out in hopes of catching it, but it never reached me. Instead, Mace jumped from the rooftop straight down, taking the arrow meant for me right in her chest.

"Mace," I said. I wanted to ask if she was okay, but I knew she wasn't. They had gotten her heart. The native magic of Faerie extends life, but it has its limits. She had moments.

I cradled her in my arms and she grabbed my chest. "I have a confession …" she said. As she reached for my shawl, her hand touched a round disc underneath it. Mace pulled the cloth off and saw my Daemor badge. Her eyes went wide in amazement and awe.

"No need for confessions. You are one of us," I said. Loud enough for both her and the graycoats to hear.

"I knew you would come. Did you mean that I really was one of you?"

"In almost every way that counts," I whispered.

"Somebody has to take care of Rough Woods," she whispered.

"Rough Woods will be taken care of. I promise."

"The word of a Daemor, so I know it's true," she said with a smile. I sang my song of death and the light went out of her eyes. I reached in her scabbard and drew her sword, then gently laid her body on the ground before I stood up to face the murdering, raping bastards that killed her. Fatass took a step back, now able to see my Daemor badge.

"Maybe we will give you a chance, Daemor. There are seven of us and one of you. Walk away and we will let this go," Fatass said.

"You don't understand. You just killed a Daemor."

Yes, I was supposed to kill her and, in a way, I guess I did. Mace put herself in harm's way to save my life. I wasn't so far gone that the irony and guilt didn't eat me up inside, which only fueled my anger. I pushed it down inside. Anger in battle makes a warrior sloppy.

Mace had behaved with the honor of a Daemor. Everyone believed

Mace to be a Daemor. I came here to enforce one of Mab edicts and I was damn well going to do it. I was just choosing a different one.

"Anyone that harms a Daemor pays the ultimate price."

"We still outnumber you," Fatass said.

"Think so? Then perhaps I should tell you my name. I am Daye." I saw the color drain out of Fatass's face. "It's nice to see my reputation precedes me."

"Shoot her again," he ordered.

The bowman tried, but now I wasn't barehanded. With the sword I swatted the arrow aside, making sure it didn't hit the girl who was the greatcoat's original target. I lunged forward and my blade was through his throat and out the back of his neck before he could blink. Without breaking stride, I grabbed two arrows from the archer's quiver and rammed them through the eyes of two more of the graycoats. I used my bare hands to snap the neck of a fourth and a pair of poison-tipped hairpins on the fifth and the sixth. That just left Fatass. I turned toward him and he started to run away. I was on him before he got out of the alley. Fatass wasn't getting off that easy – his introduction to the Reaper was going to be something extra special.

"Go on get out of here and get home," I said to the girl. "Tell everyone to stay indoors. The graycoats killed a Daemor. By morning, there will not be a single graycoat left alive in Rough Woods." The girl nodded and ran off. It was good because I didn't want to scar her by having her watch what I was about to do to Fatass. I had barely begun before he started screaming and as much as I hate to admit it, it was music to my ears. And it turns out that I got quite some distance when I tossed his head.

I was good, but to take out an entire garrison of soldiers – that took more than one Daemor. I needed reinforcements. Of course, that didn't mean I couldn't soften things up a bit. I made a few preparations to the garrison for my return and left Rough Woods by going over the wall. Of course, to do so I had to send two guards to the arms of the Boneman. That just meant they were going to get a head start on their fellow graycoats.

Daemor have an asset that Thandau doesn't and it is one of the few things that's allowed us to stay alive and fight Thandau's superior numbers and resources. Her name is Tralla and she is a pathmaker. There are lots of mages that are pathfinders, but Tralla can make and change fairy paths. On a path, time and space warp so you can make journeys that would take weeks or months on foot in a matter of seconds. Of course, go down one the wrong way and come back at a slightly different angle and everyone you ever knew could be ancient.

As part of Daemor training, we have to memorize the paths so we know how to get from one part of Fairy to another. I ran for almost an hour to get to the nearest path but it took me less than four minutes on the paths to get to Mab's castle. It was the middle of the night when I got there, but Mab was woken up to hear my report. I waited for her in the throne room. It didn't take her long to arrive dressed in full armor. You would never know that moments before she had been asleep.

"Any particular reason this couldn't wait until morning?" said Mab. "I assume the imposter is dead?"

"Yes, but therein lies our problem. It seems that the imposter was not working to discredit us. In fact, if anything she was bolstering our reputation."

Mab turned her head and narrowed her eyes. "Explain."

I did, telling how Mace had worked to protect the innocent, feed the hungry, and house the homeless. "And she was killed by the soldiers because they thought she was a Daemor."

"I see." Mab became silent. I could see the muscles in her jaw tighten. "So you feel since people thought she was a Daemor, that we should avenge her?"

I nodded. "I do, my queen."

"We could simply disavow her."

"Mab, she died saving me and a child. She embodied everything the Daemor stand for. I owe her a debt that I can never repay directly to her. I respectfully request that she posthumously be declared a Daemor for service above and beyond. Therefore, she would be deserving of vengeance upon those who killed her."

"Strategically speaking, there is nothing to be gained by taking the town."

"While that may be true, from a perception standpoint there is much to be achieved. People will see that you don't hurt a Daemor and come away from it unscathed. They will be shown that the Daemor care enough to free a town that is not strategically important. It will help us win the hearts and the minds of some. And maybe it will give others hope against the tyrant and that might even lead to new recruits for our army."

"Excellent points all, but it is not worth the deployment of manpower. I will have to turn down your request."

"Then I tell you that I will have to resign my position," I said.

Mab's head snapped as she stared at me. "You will no longer be a Daemor?"

"No, once a Daemor always a Daemor. However, I will not be able to serve as your assassin. You know it is a job that I find distasteful, but necessary. However, my debt to Mace will force me to take her place in Rough Woods. As a Daemor, of course. I will not have the time to function as your blade."

"I could order you to remain," said Mab.

"Yes, you could, but that would be in direct contradiction to our agreement. When I became your assassin, you told me I could quit anytime and name my new position. I am evoking that part of our agreement. Should you order me to do otherwise, I will of course obey, but we both know you will not break your word."

Mab took a deep breath in. "Very well, here is my compromise. You can accept it or not. You may take any Daemor who are in residence with you so long as they are willing to volunteer for this mission. Should you get enough takers to join you in this… foolishness, I will grant your request that Mace be made an *honorary* Daemor."

"Thank you, Mab." She nodded again and my audience was over. I left quickly and headed to the dormitory tower. I woke several Daemor from their slumber and got my volunteers. Kande, a human from Earth who joined our cause and fights with sword and one of the few guns that actually works in Faerie. Terrorbelle, half ogre, half pixie, all warrior. Bristlebrite, a pixie with the heart of a giant. Saraid the roane, a shape-changing seal woman who, like many of us, lost much to Thandau including one of her human eyes. Elon, an intelligent horse who worked her way up from a mount to a full-fledged warrior. And last, but certainly not least, the mighty Smaze, who was the offspring of a fire and a water dragon. Seven women against two hundred soldiers. My head knows that the odds are in the soldiers' favor, but my heart knows that they don't stand a chance.

Once we left the path, it took us a third of an hour to return to Rough Woods. Terrorbelle and Bristlebrite flew under their own power while Smaze carried Saraid and me. Kande rode on Elon. The pair had been friends since they accompanied Mab on her return from a brief exile on Earth, back before the mare gained intelligence.

A full-frontal assault would be suicide if the graycoats had found the bodies and heard what I had told the girl about us coming back.

We needed cover. Because of her parentage, Smaze's body was constantly at war with itself. While she could neither breathe fire nor water, she was able to put out various mixtures of the two. The dragon opened her mouth and exhaled a heavy fog that covered the main gate and the surrounding town. Bristlebrite went in first to recon the garrison.

Before I left, I had weakened the support beams of the soldiers' barracks. The pixie emerged from a window to hover above the fog and gave the all clear sign. Terrorbelle flew over the wall, as did Smaze who carried Elon in her talons and Kande on her back. Each took a separate wall, except for Kande who took a rope I had prepared and tied it to the mare. The wall closest to the graycoats on sentry duty was left empty so as not to attract undue attention too early. Bristlebrite flew from wall to wall to make sure everyone was set and gave the signal by changing the sound of her wings buzzing. The dragon, the horse, and Terrorbelle pulled, then pulled again. Smaze's wall was the first to fall. Next went Terrorbelle's and finally Elon's, until the roof collapsed, crushing the sleeping graycoats within.

Next Saraid and I slipped over the wall of the main gate, hoping the distraction of the falling building would cover our entry. It did. I dispatched the graycoat nearest to me, Saraid did the same. She got to the third before I did, her blade pulled back for the killing stroke.

The last graycoat was Beardless.

"Stop!" I whispered and Saraid stopped her blade a finger's width from Beardless' throat. "He tried to stop the others. He'll be our messenger." We needed one alive to tell the tale.

I took some rope and tied Beardless, tearing his own sleeve to gag him. "You live only because you tried to do the right thing. Try to escape or sound an alarm and you will suffer the same fate as your fellows. Clear?"

Beardless nodded and Saraid cocked him on the back of the head with the hilt of her sword. We weren't about to simply trust the boy, should he happen to wake up before we were done he will hopefully think better of doing something foolish. We blindfolded him as the less he could relay to the graycoats, the better.

What happened next was not pretty. According to Bristlebrite's estimation, almost one hundred and fifty enemy soldiers had been inside the garrison when we brought it tumbling down. Smaze covered the rubble with scalding steam she spat out, boiling any flesh inside, making sure the Reaper claimed any of those who might have survived beneath the fallen mortar and timbers.

We hit the three other gates next. Terrorbelle and Bristlebrite rained death from the skies at the east and west gates respectively, each taking out a trio of sentries. Kande and Elon took out the three at the south gate. Saraid and I each went down the main street, looking for graycoats while Smaze watched from the air, able to see through her fog better than the rest of us. The roane and I came up empty until we hit the first tavern we found. Everyone but Smaze joined us as we entered. The dragon kept watch outside. Inside we found twenty drunken graycoats.

"We Daemor claim vengeance for our fallen sister," I announced after I had already started killing. Three of Thandau's soldiers hit the wooden floor before I finished the sentence.

Bristlebrite's armor was a weapon, her helmet and gauntlets functioned as blades. The pixie dove down, slicing one soldier's jugular with an arm and literally going in one side and out the other of a second soldier's throat using her helmet. Elon bucked, her hooves crushing rib cages. Kande shot again and again, each time hitting a graycoat. Saraid's blades seemed to swim through the air with a deadly grace, finding target after target. Terrorbelle grabbed two soldiers by their heads and smashed their skulls together, reducing them to a bony mush.

I simply sang, reducing most of the remaining soldiers to trembling cowards who quickly tried to run away. The song of the banshee is not for the weak hearted.

Not a one made it past me.

It was much the same in the next several bars and a whorehouse. By dawn's first light, Beardless was the only remaining graycoat left alive in Rough Woods. And although we received our share of wounds, no Daemor fell.

I dragged the boy soldier out the city gate he had guarded, untying his legs and removing his gag, but leaving his hands tied behind his back and his blindfold on.

I shoved him to his knees so he faced the city wall before removing his blindfold. Beardless opened his eyes, looked up at me and screamed.

He had good reason to. I allowed some of my banshee aspect to show through. When the Reaper is coming to call and for a while after, banshee are able to take on some of Death's many aspects. Right now, my face looked more skull than flesh. Even more terrifying than my visage was the dozens of his fellow graycoats looking down upon him, their lifeless heads placed upon pikes atop the wall.

Beardless crawled away from me, his legs pushing so hard that he slid on his back in the dirt.

"Tell your masters this is the price of hurting a Daemor. This city is ours now. Any graycoats who dare return will suffer the same fate."

Beardless rolled over and managed to get to his feet, running away as fast as his legs could carry him, still screaming all the while.

I stood and watched until he was out of sight. Only then did my fellow Daemor allow themselves to come out of hiding. Again, the less the greatcoats knew about who had taken the city, the better it would go for us. We knew they would return to attack in force. We had time to fortify Rough Woods and train the citizens to defend themselves against the coming attack. In our favor now was Rough Woods was of no more strategic value to Thandau than it was to us. If a full attack failed, the tyrant might leave it alone for a time.

And with luck, by the time he was inclined to try again, we'll have his head upon a pike. Unlikely, but the thought of it warms the cold parts of my heart and gives me a reason to go on.

*It was another time, another era. One woman strides through
mean streets, cloaking herself in pink and darkness
and uses the forces of science to ensure that truth and justice
triumphed over the forces of evil.
Kaye Chandler is*

THE PINK REAPER

EVERY DEATH YOU TAKE

As the woman in pink stood over the corpse in the alley, all color drained from her skin.

"It can't be," she thought. "I ended the King of Killers."

The Pink Reaper had put an end to the murderous killing spree of Rex Hill, the man the press dubbed "The King of Killers," named for the lion's head scar that he burned onto the face of each of his victims. She knew that, but evidence to the contrary was right before her eyes. The dead man's left cheek bore the all-too-familiar lion's head scar branded into the cold skin.

When she didn't wear the mask, the Pink Reaper was Kaye Chandler. Depression-era New York was tough on a lot of people, especially the poor. Kaye had inherited more than wonderful gadgets and notebooks filled with inventions when her uncle was murdered. She also received money and several real estate holdings in Hell's Kitchen and had turned one of the buildings into a soup kitchen. The kitchen had many regulars, people who showed up like clockwork. Earlier this evening, Herbert Mendez had missed dinner for the first time that anyone could remember. He had lost everything in the crash and had been reduced to selling apples on the street corner. He never missed a hot meal.

Kaye asked about him, but no one had seen Herbert, so she donned her mask and pink work clothes then went out looking for the missing man.

The Pink Reaper found him but was too late to be of any help.

A search of the alley for any other clues was unsuccessful, so she pulled the alarm box at the nearest corner, leaving a note instructing the police to check the alley.

Then she went to see Rex Hill.

Hill had claimed twenty-three victims before the Pink Reaper cornered him on a Manhattan rooftop. The two fought. Hill had assumed his size, strength, and cunning would win him the battle, right up until he plummeted to the street below. In a just world, he would have died. Then again, in a just world, there would be no need for a woman in pink to hunt in the night to protect the innocent.

Hill had merely snapped his spine, although *he* might argue that his injury was tragic. And to add to the unjustness, doctors found him moments after his fall. Not surprising since the building the pair had been fighting on the top of was a hospital. His spinal cord was injured at C4, paralyzing all movement below the neck. The doctors managed to keep Hill breathing long enough to place him in an iron lung they had on hand to treat polio victims.

The machine was a large metal cylinder with a pair of vacuum pumps and an electric motor. Hill's entire body below the neck fit inside. The pumps created positive and negative pressure, causing his diaphragm and rib cage to expand and contract, simulating breathing. Without the machine, the man would die.

A paralyzed man does not a good killer make.

Hill had never been charged with his crimes. His family's wealth and power had squelched both the charges and the truth.

The Pink Reaper didn't press matters because Hill ended up in a worse prison than the courts could ever send him to; his own crippled body, tortured by the constant drone of the iron lung as it kept him breathing and alive. The Reaper imaged it as akin to an incessant Chinese water torture and smiled.

Iron lungs didn't come cheap. Hill's was $1500, the average price a family might pay for a house. Add to that the care he needed and the upkeep on the machine and it cost a small fortune to run. It was no surprise that the hospital didn't raise any objections when Hill insisted he be moved home with round-the-clock nursing care, even splurging for a gas-fired thermo-electric generator for power back up. A small fortune was nothing to a man with a large one.

After landing her black sky rider – a brilliantly constructed glider with two silent electric motors – on the roof of Hill's Manhattan home, the Pink Reaper lowered herself down the side of the building. While technically breaking and entering, the task required no actually breaking as the third story window with no fire escape was left open. It was a simple matter for the Reaper to let herself in. Slowly, she crept down the stairs. The upper floors were empty of people, the expensive furniture covered with sheets and layers of dust. The rooms echoed eerily with the beat of the machine downstairs as it breathed for a man who couldn't.

Having round-the-clock nursing care was far different than having round-the-clock security. A nurse in white uniform and hat sat at a table reading through a newspaper, practically asleep.

The Pink Reaper made sure there was no "practically". Pointing her large pink gun, she twisted the dial so a pellet shot out, striking the floor by the woman's feet. It burst on impact, releasing a measured amount of sleeping gas. Any more was dangerous to the person gassed. The Pink Reaper caught the woman's head in time to gently lower it to the desk in front of her and realized she recognized the woman. Her name was Cassandra Nolon. She had been Hill's mistress. The Reaper wondered how much he was paying her to stay on and hoped for her sake it was a lot. Nursing a paralyzed man was much harder than sleeping with a rich one.

The outside of the Reaper's cape and hood were black to better to blend into the darkness which she made sure was present by turning off the lights.

Silently she stepped to a spot behind Hill where he couldn't see her. The Reaper's outfit and mask were pink, down to the inside lining of her hood and cape. There were reasons for the pink, just as there was a reason for the skin the outfit revealed.

The Reaper began to laugh, then switched on a flashlight she wore on the wrist of her glove. Using her uncle's designs, the tiny bulb generated as much luminescence as a spotlight, with a battery that would last years. Despite the light, Hill's pupils stayed wide, but it did reveal his face had become even paler. The Pink Reaper stepped forward to stand over the dethroned King of Killers.

The Reaper imagined that from his perspective, she appeared to be upside down and saw no reason to help him focus by changing position, although she bent forward to make sure Hill could see her face in the light.

"Rex Hill, the Pink Reaper has come for you."

At the sight of the pink mask, the former King of Killers tried to scream, but no sound came out until the iron lung reversed itself to allow air to be pushed out through his throat and mouth.

The Pink Reaper smiled. The effects of her fear gas still lingered in his system even after all these months. For some reason, exposure to the gas altered the brain to have a fear response at the sight of the color pink. Since she and her outfit were what Hill saw at the time of his exposure, the sight of her pink mask triggered a flashback. The more pink he saw, the more afraid he'd become, so she started off with a small amount, covering everything but her mask with her cape.

"You've been a very bad boy, pretending to still be hurt when you're well enough to go out and kill the innocent."

"Don't know…" Hill had to pause while the machine switched to inhale for him. "What you're talking about. Still paralyzed from you, bi…" Again, his speech was cut off from the iron lungs switched the direction of the air flow. "…itch."

"We'll see about that," she said, her gun pointed at Hill as she flipped the power switch for the breathing chamber. The generator sat useless without someone to turn it on.

The Pink Reaper expected Hill to initially behave like he couldn't breathe, but then his autonomic nervous system would kick in. After all, no one can hold their breath forever.

Hill's expression became even more terrified. His mouth opened as the veins in his skin began to throb. He looked as if he was trying to scream, but without air, the sound couldn't come out. The Pink Reaper waited a minute, impressed by Hill's control. By the two-minute mark, his lips were turning blue and he still hadn't drawn in a breath.

Realizing she'd made a mistake, the woman in pink flipped the switch back on, but not without some hesitation. Keeping the switch off would ensure Hill could never hurt someone else if he somehow got better, but the Pink Reaper couldn't do it. The Reaper could kill when she needed to, but never in cold blood. And certainly not a helpless victim. That would make her no better than the scum she fought against.

The iron lung clanked back on and Hill color improved with the next few breaths.

"You crazy…" Those words were cut short with a pink-gloved index finger placed over his lips.

"You don't get to speak unless I say so. Maybe you didn't do this new killing, but that doesn't mean you aren't behind it somehow. I would like to know exactly how you arranged it."

"I'm not…" Another pause. "…telling you anything."

The Pink Reaper opened her cape, exposing her pink outfit and lining. Much skin was showing, from her cleavage down to her navel. There was a reason for that too. Under the effects of the gas, the male mind typically is unable to focus on more than one thing at a time. That meant men's eyes were drawn to her body, which made it hard for them to try to attack her. For the weak-willed, it also made it harder for them to lie. Sadly, Hill didn't fall into that category. The sight of more pink made his face twitch while his eyes practically popped out of their sockets to stare at the beautiful and dangerous Reaper.

The woman in pink considered using a fresh dose of the fear gas but decided against it. In his condition, it the increased terror might trigger a heart attack. Instead, she leaned forward in over to give him a better view in hopes of distracting him to the point where he wouldn't even realize what he was saying to her.

"Tell me how you did it. Explain to me how you had that man killed."

Hill's eyes were twitching now, but now it was his turn to laugh. "There's nothing you can do to me that's…" Inhale. "…scarier than being more machine than man…" Pause. "I will do nothing to help you."

"We'll see," the Reaper said, turning off the light and leaving the way she came, but not before leaving a little something behind.

The knock out gas wore off Cassandra about thirty minutes later. The poor woman woke to Hill screaming at her – at the machine's indulgence – to call somebody. Hill had actually been screaming for the entire half-hour, when the iron lung allowed, but it hadn't been enough to wake his former mistress. Still, she fussed and fretted over Hill like she was still love-struck, even going so far as to curse the Pink Reaper for what she did to Hill. It took her a few minutes, but she eventually made the call.

The woman in pink heard it all through the listening device she had placed under the tray that supported Hill's head.

To the Pink Reaper's disappointment, Hill didn't make a phone call to an accomplice, but rather an old crony, stating he needed a bodyguard. The Reaper waited until almost dawn and learned nothing. She set up an antenna on the roof to boost the listening device's signal. The Reaper needed to make it back to Hell's Kitchen before the sunrise. In the night, no one would be likely to notice her sky rider, but daylight would steal away that anonymity. The last thing she needed was the entire city of New York knowing that she had a device that let her soar through the sky.

The Reaper landed on the roof of her brownstone, part of which lowered to become a ramp into a room on the top floor that had no door into the house proper. The only way out besides the ramp was a hidden stairway that led down to the subbasement that housed most of her late uncle's inventions. Not to mention some of her own, including a listening station with a two-reel magnetic tape recorder that was triggered by any noise over the receiver. She set it to ignore the beating of the iron lung so she'd be able to listen to any of Hill's conversations at her leisure.

Taking off her costume, Kaye Chandler put on a bed gown and crawled into bed. Her schedule was blessedly empty so she slept until the crack of noon.

The first thing she did on waking was flip a switch on the wall behind her nightstand which activated the autochef which her uncle had designed to cook gourmet meals, then went into the shower. By the time she went down to her kitchen, the table had a fresh cup of coffee next to Eggs Benedict, buttered toast and two links of sausage. She took a sip of the coffee, got the morning paper and read while she ate.

The story on page three covered Herbert Mendez's death. The reporter drew the same conclusion Kaye had – that the King of

Killers had returned. Of course, he had no way of knowing that the King was in a unique prison of his own. The police had refused comment.

Kaye flipped to the classifieds out of habit. Another masked avenger known as the Stringer worked for the *Gotham Sentinel*. Sometimes she would leave messages in the personal section. There were none today.

When breakfast was finished, Kaye went into the subbasement, changed the tape on the recorder and played the recording back at a higher speed, slowing it down when she had trouble making out the high-pitched voices. Hill's bodyguard had arrived. His mistress turned nurse seemed to whisper a lot of sweet nothings in his ear, with him answering yes and no a lot. Cassandra turned him, gave him medicine, changed his diaper and fed Hill through a tube. Kaye grinned that another of life's pleasures was taken from Hill. Part of her reveled in it and another part of her was ashamed by the reveling.

Hill had used a very unique ring to do the branding on his victims. It had an intricately carved lion's head, which was then covered by a gold top made to look like an ordinary piece of jewelry. The top held kerosene jelly. Hill would wear it over an asbestos glove, then set the jelly on fire. It had been a terrifying sight for his victims to see a man with a flaming hand coming to kill them.

With Hill inside the breathing chamber, Kaye had not been able to tell if he was wearing the ring, but she thought it was likely passed along to his new protégé. If she found the ring, she'd find the new Prince of Killers. It would be as easy as finding a needle in a metal hayfield.

The question was how did he find someone to follow in his murderous footsteps? It's not as if he could advertise in the *Sentinel's* classifieds. It had to someone he had a previous connection with, perhaps someone who looked up to him. Someone Hill had known since their childhood maybe.

Kaye Chandler made her way down to the police precinct in the late afternoon and went directly to the detective's room. No one stopped her. In fact, a few officers greeted her by name. She had become a fixture during the investigation into her uncle's murder. She placed an apple pie on the desk of Detective Ray Cervantes.

Cervantes looked up, first at the pie, then at the beautiful blonde woman would put it there. He smiled and stood up in greeting.

"Why Ms. Chandler, what an absolute pleasure it is to see you again," he said, extending his hand.

Kaye was tempted to turn her wrist in such a way that would imply that he should kiss it, something that Ray would not have been comfortable with. Instead, she took his hand in her own. "Likewise, Detective Cervantes."

"To what do I owe the pleasure?" Cervantes said, pulling out the chair next to his desk for her to sit in.

"What, can't a girl bring an apple pie to one of the two detectives who helped catch her uncle's killer?" Kaye said.

Cervantes leaned in close and kept his voice low. "We both know that you had as much, if not more to do with that than either Eastman or I did. And I don't know how many times I have to tell you what a bad idea it is for you to wear pink in your civilian life."

"Why? I look fabulous in pink," Kaye said, smiling.

"It's too easy to draw an association between you and the Reaper."

"It's only a blouse. Besides you're wearing a blue suit. Aren't you worried that people will draw conclusions about you and Detective Mydnight?" she whispered.

"Blue's a much more common color," Cervantes said, leaning forward to smell the pie. The cop licked his lips. "Did you make this yourself?"

"Technically it's homemade."

"That's not what I asked you."

"It was made in my home and I prepared the ingredients that went into it. It's better than homemade. It's scientifically crafted."

"That contraption of your uncle's in the kitchen?" Cervantes sniffed the air hungrily. "So why are you here? Lion hunting?"

"Mind if we talk somewhere more private?"

Cervantes got up and lead her to a private room the detectives used. It even had a couch the detectives slept on when they couldn't go home. It was vacant and he led Kaye inside to catcalls from his fellow officers. He noticed one circling his desk and went back to get the pie and took it with him, then closed the door.

"Ray, did you catch the King of Killers case?"

"As a matter fact, I did. Been investigating all day. One dead end after another. Problem is, we both know the real King is paralyzed and stuck in an iron breathing machine and didn't do it. Unless he suddenly regained the ability to get up and walk," Cervantes said.

"My first thought too. He hasn't. I checked," Kaye said.

Cervantes raised an eyebrow and smiled. "The other problem is we rank-and-file police simply don't know that Hill was involved, so I can't even question him without six kinds of hell raining down on me from City Hall."

"I already guessed as much. My best guess is he's got a protégé. I was hoping you might have some insights as to whom that might be."

"Great minds. I was looking into leads along those lines as well. I don't run in the same social circles as the Hills, so all I was able to find so far are the names of family members. Almost all are idle rich. No way to determine which might be so bored with their place in society that they'd be willing to throw it all away for some thrill killing. And Rex wasn't exactly well-liked by most of his family. He was the object of ridicule by many, particularly his father. Not exactly an authority figure among his own. I think your best bet is to look outside the Hill clan for someone whose life he had touched in a very powerful way."

"Still going to check the family out though?" Kaye said.

Cervantes smiled. "We detectives live to hit our heads against walls, follow up dead-end leads and be generally looked down upon by society snobs who think they pay our salary because they pay taxes. I'd think you'd have more luck with that aspect, being part of said high society."

"Normally I might, but there was bad blood between the Hill patriarch and Uncle Dash. Apparently, Hill's mother rather fancied my uncle. As his heir, I'd be told less than nothing."

"Of course, we both know what's coming next."

Kaye sighed and nodded. "Hill always killed twice in the same location, or at least the same vicinity to thumb his nose at the powers that be."

"With one rather notable exception," Cervantes said.

Kaye smiled. "True."

"Although I'm certain it was being thrown off a roof that put him off his game."

"I like to think so."

Cervantes smirked. "Going out on patrol tonight?"

Kaye rolled her eyes. "No way around it I suppose. Thanks."

"You're welcome. Thanks for the pie."

The reason for Kaye's reaction was simple. Unlike cops, the majority of the night avengers did not go on patrol. Their advantage lay in surprise. In mystery. Any sort of pattern would eventually lead to them getting caught by the bad guys or the cops. This Prince of Killers had chosen her adopted neighborhood of Hell's Kitchen and she wasn't going to let him succeed in killing someone else.

A quick review of the day's tapes revealed nothing except the bodyguard was a snorer and his nurse had left, promising to run some errands. She even said she would miss him and apparently kissed him. The things some people will do to keep a job.

Watching from a rooftop gave one a good view of certain blocks or alleys, but the Reaper had an entire neighborhood to watch over so she took to the skies. Dashiell Chandler, the uncle she had become the Pink Reaper to avenge, had been quite probably the most brilliant scientific mind of the last century, probably longer. Dash didn't believe in patents as it gave away the details of what he worked on. He figured if somebody wanted something that he created, they could try and do it themselves. That's not to say he didn't have any use for patents. He had sold more than a few and had become extremely wealthy. One of his hidden advances was in silent electrical engines like the pair that powered the Reaper's sky rider. It took the designs of Chinese gliders in the sixth century, those of gliders of the 19th century, and the aircraft of the early 20th century and spit out something new. With its pair of silent electric engines, each powering a pair of pivotable propellers, it could even fly over a small area in very small circles. The Pink Reaper used it sparingly as its greatest advantage lay in the fact that almost no one even suspected something like it existed.

Flying patrol over Hell's Kitchen for hours on end, even under the cover of night, presented a high risk of discovery. The prospect of saving a life was more important. The woman in pink had a single goggle over one eye. It acted like a telescope, allowing her to see details in the Street below.

Hill's later victims were targets of convenience, but the first of each pair of his earliest kills were chosen for personal reasons. The second kill was someone chosen randomly just for being in the area. Made it harder for the police to connect him to the killings or figure out a motive.

Hill always struck at night. His fiery ring would not have been as effective during the day. The victims were almost always alone. The Pink Reaper worked under the assumption that the Prince of Killers would do the same.

Her first night of aerial patrol was a bust. The only thing she caught was a cold. Dressed in a warmer, yet still pink, outfit, she returned for a second night. It seemed as though it was to be as uneventful as the first until a few minutes after a clock had struck three. A man stumbled drunkenly down 39th Street. The fellow was barely able to stand, let alone walk. He lurched from building to building, using his arms to remain upright.

Out of a darkened doorway stepped someone in a long, dark coat and a hat that covered their face in shadow. Their paths crossed at the mouth of the same alley in which Herbert had been slain. The drunk looked up in time to see an arm shove him into the darkened alley. He stumbled toward the back as the shadowy figure removed a cover from a ring. A lighter flashed and flames danced a jig on the end of a hand. Shadows joined the murderous dance, the flickering flames making the figure in the long coat seem like a vision from hell. The other hand sported a rig with three blades jutting out like claws. Hill had used a knife. It looks like the Prince had changed things up a bit.

The Pink Reaper landed on a roof above the alley and fastened one end of something that looked curiously like a compact fishing pole and repelled down the side of the building.

Before she reached the ground, the woman in pink had her large pink metal gun out to spray her pink fear gas at the Prince of Killers.

Hill had trained his heir well, because this killer was prepared for her interference and wore a gas mask. Fortunately, her gun fired more than gas. She turned a dial, aimed and pulled the trigger again. This time a shock dart took the Prince in the chest. The electric charge was purposefully low. The Reaper had questions for this killer and it wouldn't do for him to pass out before she got answers.

The Prince of Killers stumbled back into the alley wall, knocking off the hat. The drunk ran past them both. The Pink Reaper pulled off the gas mask, surprised that she recognized the killer. It eliminated the need for all questions save one.

"Why Cassandra?"

"Because Rex Hill is the greatest man who's ever lived. He was doing wonderful work before you crippled him. Somebody needed to carry on his legacy. After everything he'd done for me, I was honored to be chosen," the Princess of Killers said, swinging the steel claw at the Reaper.

The arm length pink gloves the Pink Reaper wore were made from material that was bullet and knife proof. The gel padding underneath cushioned the force of any blow. She blocked the claw, then twisted the killer's arm and tore the slicing device off the killer's wrist. The Reaper again pointed her gun at Cassandra's now unprotected face and gave her another dose of the fear gas. The crying and screaming began almost immediately.

By the time the Pink Reaper was done, the Princess of Killers was more than happy to confess all to Detective Cervantes, from Hill plucking her off the streets as a child to him making her his mistress and how she became his nurse after his spine shattered. It turns out she had plied the world's oldest profession at too young an age and Hector had been her first client, back when he had money and had been none too gentle. Cassandra Nolon held a grudge. She used the same pattern as her mentor of having her first kill being for revenge and the second simply to cover up a motive. But even in her fear and terror, her loyalty to Hill was unshakable and she would say nothing to implicate him in the new killings.

That was okay. The Pink Reaper had other plans for Rex Hill.

The Pink Reaper waited until the next night. The news of the capture of the Princess of Killers had been released and broadcast over the radio and in the papers. The woman in pink took some small pleasure in listening to Hill struggle to rant as the machine breathed for him. He was promising to bring the full weight of his fortune to bear to have his protégé freed and found innocent of all charges.

It was a simple matter to knock out Hill's single bodyguard. He was more alert than the Princess had been, so instead of sneaking in she simply knocked on the front door, her body and gun hidden under her cloak. The cape parted to let her fire a shock dart into his neck when he opened the door. This one had enough of an electric charge to send the bodyguard to dreamland.

The Pink Reaper strolled in the main entrance, with a middle-aged woman by her side. She slammed the door closed behind them and went into Hill's room.

"You…" Clang. "Did this. I will…" Hiss. "Make you pay."

"Your days of being able to threaten anyone are over now, Rex Hill. How did you twist Cassandra Nolan's mind so that she would kill strangers just to make you happy?" the Reaper said.

"Everyone. You. I. Them. Are…" Hiss. "Twisted. It's simply a matter…" Pause. "Of letting it out. And with Cassandra, it helped starting her early." Clang. "Pity you seem morally unable to kill me so there's nothing you can do to stop…" Inhale. "…me without breaking some misguided code of honor."

"I think you misunderstand. I would not have lost a moment's sleep because of misplaced guilt had your fall killed you. I have killed and will likely again, but never in cold blood. I don't have that right. If you had killed someone close to me, then that would give me that right."

"Give me…" Smile. "…time."

"No need. This is Mrs. Greta Heinrich. I don't know if you remember her son Erik. I promised her I would do everything in my power to bring his killer to justice. Erik was your fourth victim and her only child."

"I would say I am sorry for…" Clang. "…your loss, but why lie? You have rather made…" Hiss. "…my day by showing me that my work lives on."

Greta Heinrich walked up to the man in a machine who looked little more than a metal tube with a head sticking out and slapped

Hill's face. "You bastard. I hate you for killing my son. He had two babies of his own that no longer have a father because of you."

Hill's smile simply widened.

Greta turned to the Pink Reaper. "Are those the wires down there?"

The smile suddenly vanished from Hill's face as he realized that *this* woman had the right the Reaper spoke of.

"Yes, they are," the Pink Reaper said, her eyes and face seemingly set in stone.

The older woman bent down on her knees and ripped the wires from the machine, with a dark smile of her own. The room was filled with a sudden silence. Hill tried to scream, his mouth and lips moving, but without the machine breathing for him, there was no air to bring sound to his silent screams.

Greta Heinrich stood and watched as Rex Hill's face first became pink, then blue. Veins on his face throbbed and his eyes bulged. The Pink Reaper put her hand on the old woman's shoulder and nodded. Greta spit on Hill's face. The two women turned and walked away.

The King of Killers was finally dead. The Pink Reaper hoped that no one else would come vying for the throne.

Faerie is destroyed in a mushroom cloud and the survivors flee to Earth. Darkness and the things that once had to hide in shadow now cover the land. It is a horrible future that a group of tricksters managed to prevent, but the stories of those that suffered through it live on in the tales of

THE MYSTICAUST

IRON BARS

featuring Terrorbelle

<u>**Author's Note:**</u> *This story takes place in the dark alternate future that was stopped from happening in Fools' Day and is not part of Terrorbelle's current continuity.*

I'd like to say the world went to hell after the US nuked Faerie, but it was more like Hell came to us after the Mysticaust. I'd never seen radiation burns close up, but I've seen people that had been fried by magic. The mystic fallout that leaked through the rifts that linked the two worlds did a lot worse. The first wave of nuclear magic was akin to an explosion, leaving empty craters all over the world around the rifts that were left open.

Many thousands in this world died, but that was only a fraction of the dead in Faerie. Combined, the numbers were barely a drop in the bucket compared to those that were either transformed or brought back from oblivion by the influx of power.

Most humans had assumed they were alone. Those of us who could have proved them wrong tended to keep a low profile or out and out hide. After the refugees started pouring through the rifts from Faerie, a lot of the more magic-based folks started to come out of the closet. There was no longer any point to keeping a low profile, or so we thought.

That's before racial tensions elevated and the news services reported on baseless stories claiming that what happened was a terrorist attack from Faerie, completely ignoring the fact that our entire world was destroyed and most of Faerie's population was slaughtered by US missiles. Not that there wasn't cause for alarm. My old boss, Queen Mab, had stolen a nuke from an Air Force base in Arkansas. From what I've been able to piece together from survivors, she was planning to use it to intimidate the rulers of a rival kingdom. From all accounts, Mab is dead, but I almost wish she wasn't. For one thing, I owe her my life. For another, I had served as an elite soldier in her all-female Daemor during the Thandau War. She was our greatest hero, the woman who freed Faerie from tyranny. Now she'll go down in history as the woman who destroyed Faerie. I would love five minutes just to ask her why.

That and four fifty will get me a cup of coffee.

When the monsters started appearing, bloodshed followed in their wake and regular Faerie folk got the blame. We were no more responsible for the deaths than someone who had gone to the same high school as a serial killer would be for the murderer's killing spree. That didn't stop the press, politicians, and plenty of others from saddling us with culpability.

The president signed an executive order starting the camps, being careful that the word *concentration* was never used in the same sentence. Might make regular folks draw a connection to Hilter's camps and no politician wants to be labeled a Nazi, not even one who's acting like one.

I'd been living in Manhattan for years when it all went down. While I never hid, I didn't broadcast either. I'm not the most attractive woman, but with a Mama who was an ogre that's to be expected, I guess. A friend of mine, a bartender named Murphy, has helped me get past that, as much as a girl who is beauty challenged can expect. To be honest, Murphy's okay to look at but I've got the hugest crush on him. He's funny, in an annoying, yet endearing kind of way, and he's got a good heart. He's a little thing, at least compared to me, yet he stood up to Hercules and Hermes for me and they're gods. Hercules could have thrown him into orbit and Hermes could have done worse, but they *backed down* from him, a powerless human. He made them apologize for calling me ugly. Actually, what they said was much worse, but I'd rather not repeat it. Sadly though, I'll probably hear it again. Despite being a war veteran, I'm only about twenty and change in human years. My mama was slaughtered in front of my eyes and I was taken prisoner. I was nothing more than a slave until one of Mab's Daemor freed me. I survived by acting tougher than I really am and overcompensating in most areas. Murphy saw through my tough veneer to the frightened little girl beneath and he tried to protect me. That's when I fell for him. I'm still working on the part where he falls for me.

Murph had offered to help me with this, but I turned him down. It might take me months and he's needed at Bulfinche's Pub. His boss, Paddy Moran, is one of the few men, actually leprechauns, willing to stand up to the feds by housing refugees and refusing to turn them over to the camps. Paddy has a lot of muscle, money, and clout. So far, he's been left alone. I worry that the day is coming when that won't be enough and the feds will decide to come for him.

I was searching the camps one by one, looking for friends and my only remaining family, my Papa. Ever since Earth's magic levels were increased, I've been able to use my large dragonfly wings to actually fly. Before that, the best I could do was hover briefly or slow a fall. I get my wings from Papa's side. He's a pixie. No child likes to think about their parents having sex but considering the size deferential it makes my conception an especially impressive accomplishment on Papa's part. I'm enormous for a pixie, but small for an ogre. Even though I can fly short distances, it takes a lot out of me. However, my wings are hardly fragile little things. They are razor sharp and Mab taught me to use them like the deadly weapons they are. Better than a pair of swords or battleaxes.

Of course, on Earth PM (Pre-Mysticaust) they kind of made me stand out, so I got in the habit of hiding them under a specially padded trench coat. It was safer too. It would be very unfortunate if I yawned in a crowded subway car and accidentally sliced off another passenger's arm while stretching my wings.

I had made it to the Pine Barrens in New Jersey. It was the fourth camp I'd checked and I was hoping to have better luck.

I slowly pulled up to the guard booth on my motorcycle. I'd learned it doesn't pay to spook armed soldiers.

The soldier on point took one look at me and radioed for back up. Five soldiers armed with automatic weapons, undoubtedly loaded with bullets with at least a partial load of iron, surrounded me.

"All this for little old me?" I said. "I'm flattered, boys, but I'm not into group stuff. I'm not that kind of girl."

"You ain't a human girl, that's for sure," said the Soldier-boy on point.

"Why? You looking for a little variety in your love life, soldier? I'm afraid you'd have to buy me dinner before I'd even consider anything like that." And a barrelful of whiskey at least.

"I'd shoot myself in the foot first," he said.

"Oh, you're into S&M stuff. Not my scene, but thanks for the offer. Now before you boys go getting yourself in a tizzy, you better look at my papers," I said slowly lifting my fingers off the handlebar. Thinking ahead, I knew it would be very bad to reach inside my coat pocket as these yahoos were looking for an excuse to perforate my voluptuous body. My face may not be pretty, but very few centerfolds can match my cleavage in either size or firmness. Ogre skin is tough, pixie bodies perky. In that trade, I got the best of both worlds.

Soldier-boy took the envelope out of my hand.

"Says here you have clearance to access the camp and remove certain individuals if you find them," he said.

"Wow, thanks for reading that to me. I thought I was dropping off a pizza order," I said. "I guess I shouldn't have skipped breakfast."

"Listen, fitch..." New slang combining fairy and... well you can guess the second word. "You should be in this camp, not given free reign of it."

"And yet here we are, sweetcheeks. Now give me back my papers and open the gate," I said.

"I don't know about that. Maybe we say you were trying to escape and we kill you and leave your fitch ass lying dead in a ditch."

"Hmm, let me think about that. Nope, that's a bad idea in so many ways. First off, I won't be the one dying. There's just five of you and you only have guns." Humans have discovered painfully that there are things much worse than guns. Now guns can kill me, but these bozos had no idea what I could and couldn't do. Most humans were amazingly ignorant of our abilities. I've learned to make that work in my favor. I can bluff with the best of them and truth be told, if it came to it, I probably could take all five with only a little luck.

Two of them still had their safeties on. "Second, my credentials are authorized by the DMA." PM the Department of Mystic Affairs was thought to deal exclusively with cranks and conspiracy nuts, even though they told everyone different. This year, their budget is more than the FBI and CIA combined.

"How'd a fitch like you get DMA authorization?" growled Soldier-boy.

"I've done some work for them. And they know I'm here," I said, both of which were true enough. They've hired my boss Nemesis on a freelance basis often enough and I've helped out. Plus, Uncle Sam, the Director of the DMA, owed both Nemesis and Murphy a favor, which they both called in on my behalf. The fact that I work for one of the most dangerous people on the planet is what's kept me out of the camps. Sadly, other than the few people on my list, there was nothing in my power that I could do to help the rest. It broke my heart each time I left a camp.

"Listen, fitch..."

It was one insult too many. I grabbed Soldier-boy by the throat and pulled him toward me with one hand and bent the barrel on his weapon with the other, all without getting up from my bike. The other four soldiers all trained their weapons on me, but I ignored them like they didn't matter. Besides, they couldn't hit me without risking Soldier-boy's life.

"No, you listen. You use the F-word again and I'm going to ram every one of your teeth down your throat. I'm an American citizen." Which was true. The US has always had provisions for non-human citizenship and I applied when I was nineteen. It didn't hurt that Nemesis insisted on it as part of her payment for a case. "And I'm not going to tolerate this disrespect." I turned to the number two soldier. "You, open the gate. Direct me to your C.O. I'm going to drop your friend off with my personal reprimand."

Soldier number two just glared at me.

"Don't make me repeat myself."

The gate lifted open and number two pointed at a building. I started the bike. I held on to Soldier-boy, forcing him to run alongside me or be dragged on the pavement. He chose to run.

I arrived at the building and dismounted before dragging Soldier-boy behind me. The MP at the door seemed confused. I smiled and winked at him and breezed by him before he could stop me.

I went up to the receptionist, who looked up at me terrified.

I tried smiling at her. While I don't think I have a pretty face, I've always thought I had a nice smile. The woman behind the desk didn't seem to agree.

"Hello," I said.

The woman stammered for a moment before she managed to say, "Hi. Can I help you?"

"Yes. Ms. Terrorbelle to see Colonel Redmond," I said.

"Do you have an appointment?"

"As a matter of fact, I do."

"He's in a meeting." People in charge always are, especially when they're not. They seem to think it helps we peons realize our place in the grand scheme of things.

"That's fine. I'll wait," I said, sitting in a chair that was barely big enough for my curvaceous bottom. I still had Soldier-boy in tow. I switched my grip to the back of his neck and planted him in the chair next to me. He was fuming, but powerless to do anything about it. Soldier-boy was still holding his gun, but the bent barrel insured using it would hurt him a lot more than it would me.

The MP from outside had come in and was staring at me. The fact that I had said I had an appointment and sat down to wait made it seem reasonable for me to be there. However, holding a soldier by the scruff of his neck did not.

"We're fine. I have him under control. I'm bringing him to the Colonel to be put on report," I said.

"And you are?" he asked.

"With the DMA," I said, stretching the truth, although I did have a consultant's badge ID. "If you feel uneasy and would prefer to keep your weapon trained on me while I wait, that's fine. It won't bother me none, but you might as well pull up a chair. You know how these officer types are. We could be waiting for hours. Of course, I'm bulletproof," Big lie there. My coat is, but bullets still hurt like hell. The bruises last for weeks. "So if you decide to fire, please make sure your ricochets don't hit you or the other people in the room. I'd hate for you to accidentally kill someone."

The receptionist blanched at that and picked up the phone. A moment later the colonel stepped out of his office.

"What's going on out here?" Colonel Redmond demanded.

"Good morning, Colonel Redmond. I'm Terrorbelle. I called ahead."

"Right, right. DMA said you could examine our residents and take some of them into your custody. I'm assuming you are looking for criminals, although if you had sent pictures, we could have saved you the trip."

"Unfortunately, no know pictures exist of these individuals, but I would recognize them," I said, deciding it was best not to explain my true purpose.

"That's fine, but why the hell are you dragging around one of my soldiers like he's some God-damned rag doll?" yelled Redmond.

"Behavior unbecoming a soldier. Violations of the military code of conduct. Racial insensitivity and violation of my civil rights," I said.

"What did you do soldier?" demanded Redmond.

Soldier-boy looked sheepish. "Called her a fitch, sir."

"You assaulted one of my soldiers because he called you a name?" Redmond said, rolling his eyes.

"That and the fact that he and four other soldiers threatened to kill me and leave me in a ditch rather than do their duty and let me inside," I said.

The Colonel fell silent at that. "MP, take this man into custody as well as the other men involved until we can investigate this matter further." I finally let go of him as the MP removed his bent gun and let Soldier-boy outside. "I apologize for their behavior, Ms. Terrorbelle."

"Apology accepted," I said.

"Very well. Ms. Terrorbelle, please allow me to show you around the Alamo."

"Alamo? I thought that was in Texas," I said.

"The original was, but the men and women stationed here named our camp that because this is where we are making our last stand against the darkness poisoning our world." What a load of hooey. I guess my face must have betrayed my thoughts, because Redmond added, "No offense meant to present company' of course. For you to be working for the DMA means you were here before the attack."

"I was," I admitted, although I'd be willing to be my entire savings account that each of us had a different opinion of what the attack in question was.

Redmond nodded as if he had made some great point. I wasn't keeping track of points today, so I let it go.

"Ms. Terrorbelle, if you'd be so kind as to wait outside, I'll join you in a moment."

"Sure," I said, but if I had known then what would happen much later, I would have unfurled my wings and decapitated the bastard then and there.

The military had taken to enlisting and even drafting mages. They all went in as officers and, in addition to wearing the traditional uniform, wore a hood that covered their eyes in shadow, based on the concept that looking into a mage's eyes was dangerous. The color of the hood matched the uniform. Redmond was Air Force blue, but many of the people under him wore army green.

The mage that walked out of Redmond's office had a khaki hood.

"What do you think about the halfbreed?" Redmond asked.

"I sense that she is here for what she says, but I'm not sure. Call Washington and verify her credentials," she said.

"Thank you, captain. Dismissed," said Redmond, as he came out to join me. "Ready, Ms. Terrorbelle?"

"Yes," I said. The Colonel started walking and I followed. We walked the better part of a mile across the camp until we came to an area enclosed by razor wire fences twenty feet high, including across the top. Can't risk some Faerie flying off, now could they? The iron in the steel was supposed to discourage ideas of escape. In case it wasn't enough, at the four corners and at two spots on the long edges and one on the short there were guard towers, each with a pair of snipers with laser sights. If this was anything like the other camps, the snipers were rotated every four hours to keep them sharp.

"Must be rough for you to see this," probed Redmond.

It was, but I wasn't going to give him the satisfaction of an answer. I just nodded.

"Must make you question your patriotism and loyalty," he probed.

"Let me ask you, Redmond," I said, dispensing with his title. "You agree with every war and police action you've been ordered to fight in?"

Redmond smiled. "Yes."

That made him either a liar or a fanatic. Either was dangerous. "Would you have fought even if you disagreed?"

"Of course."

"I do what I can. I donate to lobbying groups. I write my congresswoman, senator, and even the president to change things."

"Good for you," said Redmond, the condescending twit. "Here we are. The holding area. How long will you need to look for your prisoners?"

"An hour should do it," I said. This was one of the newer camps and it wasn't full yet. There were reported to be at least four hundred prisoners.

"Very good," said Redmond. "I'll be back to meet you then."

He instructed the guard to open the gate and into the valley of death I went.

The camps were put in isolated areas for a reason. It was much easier to control what people saw that way. Although I had not seen any abuse personally, I saw people who looked beaten and battered. When I mentioned it, I was always told that the prisoners fought among themselves. The guards were outnumbered and couldn't be expected to risk their lives to break up every little fight. The usual crap. Unfortunately, I couldn't prove they were lying and even if I could, what would I be able to do?

As soon as I entered, I was the center of attention. There were those that looked at me, walking freely in, that viewed me as a traitor, which is interesting since before the disaster Faerie had been nothing but factions and kingdoms since the Dagda disappeared lifetimes ago. There was always infighting. The hatred united the Faerie folk as much as it did the humans. Other stared, wondering if I was a new prisoner. The worst were those who viewed me with hope, that I might be here to take them away.

Honestly, it made me want to kill something, but that wouldn't help anyone.

I was greeted by a *wernun*. No, it wasn't someone who turned into a nun when the moon was full. It was a word from the old language which literally meant one who steps on others for scraps. It was what we called the collaborators who Thandau let govern for him. In the camps, it was someone who sided with the soldiers against the prisoners. They had nominal power, appropriately colored gray uniforms instead of the orange ones the rest wore. They even had a room to themselves. The rest slept in barracks or tents lined up in the yard. Not much protection against the elements. Despite common misinformation, we get cold, hot, wet, and uncomfortable too.

"Welcome, welcome," the wernun said, gesturing as if he was welcoming me to a resort.

I ignored him and brushed by. Unable to get the hint, he followed me. "How can I be of assistance, gentle sister?"

"You can't. Buzz off."

"You appear to be a guest of the soldiers. I would hate to offend them by not offering you the correct hospitality."

"So you offend me instead," I said.

"How have I offended you?" he asked.

"Just the gray togs were enough to do it," I said.

He became indignant. "Someone was going to do it. It might as well be me. I do whatever I can to protect everyone in here."

I hated people who justified their actions with excuses. I would have a tiny bit of respect for him if he admitted he did it because he was weak, that it was easier than growing a backbone. "Whatever gets you through the night."

"How dare you judge me. You have no idea what it's like in here."

I stopped and stared at him. "I was a prisoner in one of Thandau's slave camps. This place is horrible but not as horrible as that."

"So they beat the dark one and you were freed. It's not like you did anything."

"Wrong. I joined the resistance. I *helped* beat him. I didn't become a lapdog to his lackeys' lackeys." I wanted to flash my Daemor emblem, a black crow's head on a silver circle. When we won the war, we were heroes. Wearing that emblem would get me free booze, food, and lodging. That was then. Now, thanks to what Mab wrought the Daemor are considered below scum, so it doesn't pay to broadcast. There are too many memories for me to just throw it away, so I still wear it on my belt, but these days I hide it in a flip top buckle. Just the thought of things was making me angry. "Just point me to the pixies."

Even in the camps, like congregate with like. Pixies with pixies, gentry – leprechauns, banshees, and such – with gentry, fey with fey, ogre with ogre, and so on.

The wernun pointed to the far end where they had set up birdcages like you might find in a pet store. Inside were dozens of pixies, lying still. It was a sad sight. Pixies by nature flutter like hyper-hummingbirds. This lot was too depressed to care.

"Greetings *wingrethren*," I said in flawless pixie. Most faerie folk could easily communicate with a simple spell that allows them to be understood. As long as the person on the other end did the same, the conversation could ensue. On Earth, most humans don't know the spell, so conversations tend to be one-sided. The fact that I bypassed the spell and used the native speak got their attention. I had to. Pixies have a tendency to not bother with the spell so they didn't have to bother with small talk with other races. I learned as a child that in order to speak with my smaller relations and have them talk back, I had to talk the talk.

"Salutations, *barerethren*," one replied, using their word for one without wings, considered a handicap among the pixies.

"Incorrect," I said, lifting my coat and top so only those in the cages could see the bottoms of my wings. "I am *wingrethren*."

That got me a smile and a flutter of wings. "So you are. Why do we speak?"

Like I said, they're not into small talk. "I come seeking blood of my blood, Thunderrod." At this point, I should point out that what you think the rod part of Papa's name refers to is probably correct. My paternal grandmother had issues. Named all of her kids after their most prominent body parts. My father was a legend, even as an infant apparently. I always felt especially sorry for my Uncle Treenose and Auntie Mountainbutt.

"Which blood is that?" he asked.

"Father." Normally, a pixie told that someone my size is seeking her pixie dad would laugh hysterically.

This pixie appeared to have at least heard of Papa, so he just nodded knowingly. "Your name?"

"Terrorbelle."

"I am Tigglehym. Your father has spoken of you with much pride."

I smiled. It was good to hear. I've always been Daddy's little girl, even though I was bigger than him on the day I was born.

"My blood is here?" I said, excited that I might have actually finally found him.

"Your blood is cavorting," Tigglehym said, pointing to a corner of the steel mesh that had been bent up and put back.

"Bending the cage must have given much pain," I said, trying not to jump up and down with joy.

"You know Thunderrod. There is a banshee that attracted his eye. He goes to make her give the scream of life instead of death," said Tigglehym, pointing to one of the barracks.

"My gratitude," I said.

I went into the barracks but stopped short at the screaming. The wail of a banshee is enough to give one reason to pause for obvious reasons, but this wasn't that kind of screaming. And it wasn't just one voice. Cautiously, I opened the door a crack. It was Papa and he was pleasuring not one, but two banshees.

I shut the door quickly. "Yuck."

Rather than interrupt, I decided to wait until he was done. It was the polite thing to do and he wouldn't notice me until then anyway.

It wasn't long, at least by Papa's standards, maybe forty minutes. When I heard the lull in the festivities, I walked in quickly, unwilling to risk Papa getting his second wind.

"Only two ladies? You're slipping," I said, strolling up to the bunk the trio were occupying.

"Terrie!" Only family calls me that. Papa flew up to me and kissed me on the cheek, wrapping his arms as far around my neck as they would reach. I hugged back. I was so happy, I started to cry and tears fell down my face and onto Papa's head.

"Careful there, little girl. You don't want to drown me."

I kissed him on the top of his head, then I noticed the banshees getting huffy.

"Who is this whore?" one asked.

"We are not going to share, so you can just tell this slut to get out," said the other.

"Both of you, stop being so rude to my daughter or I'll leave and not come back," said Papa.

"Daughter?" said one.

"Sorry, Thunderrod. Please don't leave," the other said.

"It's not me you need to be apologizing to," Papa said.

"Sorry, Thunderrod's daughter," said the one.

"Very," said the other.

"I'll let it go," I said. Papa brought out that in women. It had happened before. It would happen again.

"Ayn, Potrice, allow me to present my daughter Terrorbelle, the Daemor," said Papa.

"Daemor?" growled Ayn.

"Oh, stop it. *She* personally helped beat the Dark One. She retired long before the Blasts," Papa said.

The banshees seemed to accept that.

"I'd like to steal my father, if you don't mind," I said.

Reluctantly, the banshees nodded and left the barracks.

"You're not a prisoner? I assumed your Nemesis would keep you free," said Papa, worry creeping over his face.

"She has." Nemesis had a hand in Thandau's fall as well. It's how we met. "I'm actually here to get you out."

"Out?" Papa did an airborne jig. "Just me or all of us?"

I frowned. "Only you and maybe a few others, if they're here." I told Papa the names of my friends.

"No, none of them are here," he said.

I was disappointed, although I had no guarantees any of them had been caught. They could still be free and hiding out. I heard Saraid and Bristlebirte were down south working for the Louisiana National Guard.

Still, I searched the rest of the camp with no luck. Papa said his goodbyes and there was a large group of disappointed women to see us off.

When we got to the gate, Redmond was waiting and he wasn't alone. His mage captain was behind him. I stood and waited, but the gate stayed closed.

"Colonel, please open the gate. My business here is done," I said.

"Ms. Belle, please tell me what crime the pixie you are taking into custody committed," asked Redmond.

"I never said he committed a crime. I'm here to secure his release," I said.

Redmond shook his head. "Sorry, that won't be possible."

"What are you talking about? I have authorization signed by the Director of the DMA and the Head of Homeland security." Uncle Sam had held both offices for months since the President put the DMA over the other law enforcement agencies. .

"Correction, you had authorization," said Redmond.

I pulled the papers out of my pocket. "I still have."

"No, you have papers signed by the former director, who resigned last night. I just spoke with acting Director Zachs who has rescinded your authorization."

"We'll see about that," I said, hitting my speed dial for Nemesis, but my cell phone had no service.

"The Pine Barrens are very remote and we have jamming devices," Redmond said. "The acting Director has also rescinded the former Director's order of protection on you."

"He can't do that!" I said louder than I meant to. Zachs was a scumbag, but he should still be afraid of Nemesis.

"I assure you he can and did. What's more, he instructed me to take you into custody and intern you here at the Alamo."

I'd heard enough. I retracted one hand in the sleeve of my coat and rammed it through the razor wire, making a hole big enough for my arm to fit through. The coat had stopped any serious damage as I wrapped my hand around Redmond's throat. With my other, I pulled my gun and pointed it between his eyes.

"That ain't happening, Redmond," I said.

The bastard smiled. I squeezed tighter. "Or you'll what? Shoot me?"

"If I have to, but it doesn't have to come to that," I said. "Just let us go."

"I can't do that." Redmond nodded to the tower snipers and twenty laser sights were trained on me. Most were on my coat, but three were on my head. Papa, bless his heart, fluttered up and got between two of the snipers and my skull.

"They shoot me and I'll still have time to pull the trigger, Redmond."

"You're not afraid of dying?"

"There are worse things," I answered.

"A hero complex. Who would have figured a fitch to have that strength of character? Target the prisoners," said Redmond. "If she fires, slaughter them all. Start with the pixie."

Damn. He had me and he knew it. I let go of his throat.

"Your gun, please," ordered Redmond.

"I can't do that," I said, hitting a hidden stud on the handle. The weapons Nemesis supplied her trio of agents with were powerful and magic based. I had strict orders to never allow one to fall into enemy hands. The stud activated a teleportation function to get rid of the gun. Sadly, we hadn't been able to get one that would take the gun's wielder along.

On the plus side, it went straight to Nemesis' vault, which meant in about five seconds she'd know I was in trouble. She'd get Rudy and Gani then the Calvary would be on its way.

Redmond saw the gun vanish. "Stop it!"

His mage closed her eyes, tilted her head back and reached out her arms. An instant later, my gun was in her hands.

Double damn. His mage was a conveyor. They had the power to teleport and obviously, she was able to retrieve the gun by overriding the escape function.

"Things are as they should be now. Your ass is mine," said Redmond, a dark glint in his eyes. "Open the gate."

The guard obeyed. Redmond, his mage, and the five soldiers I had met at the gate walked in.

"Strip down, fitch," Redmond ordered.

"Not if you had a fist full of hundreds and I was two months late on the rent," I said.

"Shoot the pixie," Redmond ordered.

"Don't," I ordered back. "If he dies, your only hold over me is gone and I'll cut through your troops like they were paper soldiers and I swear it will end me with holding your severed head in my hands."

"Not in your power," Redmond said.

"Try me. I work for Nemesis. Ask your pet mage about her. I'm one of her three agents. Ask the conveyor what that means. And what will happen to you if I'm hurt."

Redmond looked to the mage.

"*Gods* fear Nemesis. She is the Enforcer for the Council of Thrones. If she comes for you, not even I could hide you. If this one is a member of her triumvirate, there must be more to her than meets the eye," she said.

"Should I kill her?" asked Redmond.

"If suicide works for you," I said.

"Nemesis probably has a link of some sort. She might be able to not only sense the death, but when, where, and who caused it," said the mage. "There would be retaliation. We would all die."

"For her, but not the pixie?" asked Redmond.

"Probably not," answered the mage.

"Fine. Strip down, fitch, or I order the pixie shot. If she retaliates, aim to wound," Redmond said.

"Terrie, don't worry about me. Save yourself," Papa said.

"I can't do that. Not after how long it's taken me to finally find you again," I said, shrugging my coat to the ground. I'm not the type to run around naked on Earth or even back on Faerie, but I've had to do it on occasion. I wasn't going to let them see that their request bothered me. I was wearing a t-shirt underneath, so I flexed my wings. The razor-sharp edges tore through the thin fabric, shredding it to pieces, which all fell to the ground.

I smiled as I watched Redmond and the rest take a step back. I stepped out of my jeans, thankful I had decided against wearing a thong.

Soldier-boy stepped up to me, a new gun in hand. "The Colonel said naked. Ditch the bra and panties."

He put his hand on my right breast and tried to pull my pink bra off. I plucked his hand off and squeezed hard, breaking his fingers. It was instinct. I was a victim of sexual assault as a child by soldiers. I was just a kid then and I wasn't able to stop it then but I'd die before I let it happen again.

"You god-damned, fitch," screamed Soldier-boy.

"I warned you what would happen if you called me that again," I said punching him in the mouth. While I didn't succeed at knocking out all his teeth, I got most of them. Then I stepped back and put my hands on my head.

"And what did I said would happen if you resisted?" said Redmond.

"You'd lose your head," I said. "Not all the guns here or your mage will be able to save you. So, the ball's in your court. How's this going to end?"

"You will stand down?" he asked.

"As long as none of your boys try to get handsy or stupid," I said.

He grabbed an orange jumpsuit from a nearby private and tossed it at my feet. He motioned for the same private to pick up my clothes. Pointing to Soldier-boy, Redmond said, "Get that man to the infirmary." Then he walked away.

I put on the jumpsuit, but it was several sizes too small. I had to tear the sleeves and legs to get it on and I couldn't close it all the way in front, but things had turned out better than they might have.

I slept near the pixie cages that night. At dawn, ten armed soldiers came to collect me.

"The Colonel wants to see you."

"Let me check my appointment book," I said standing up, pantomiming flipping pages. "I can fit him in now. Isn't that convenient?"

There was no response, so I followed them. We ended up in the Colonel's office where I was instructed to sit in a lone chair. Two of the soldiers came in with me and stood behind me, with their guns trained at the back of my head.

Redmond was sitting behind the desk and his mage stood off to the side on my right.

"Good morning. I trust you slept well," Redmond said sarcastically.

"Four-star accommodations, Colonel. Even got a wakeup call, although room service never did show up with my breakfast," I said.

"You are a funny one. You know what I find funny?" he asked.

"Pulling the wings off flies?" I said.

"No, but pixies are another matter," he countered. Pulling out my belt buckle, he hit the flip release, revealing my Daemor medallion. "Imagine my surprise to find out you were a Daemor terrorist."

I said nothing.

"Did you know, I was in command of the Air Force base that Mab stole her nuclear missile from?" I didn't but kept quiet. "My career should have been over, but they had to keep the details very hush hush because of national security. Still, a missile was taken on my watch, so I had to be punished. They put me in charge of this God-forsaken camp, where I've been taking my revenge on your kind for what they did to me and my world."

"They could have tried to negotiate for the return of the missile or sent troops in. The President is the one who decided to nuke an entire world. The Mysticaust is his doing more than it is Mab's," I said.

"That's what your kind want people to think, but it's lies. But slowly I've been getting even."

I'd heard some stories of the tortures Redmond had been inflicting on the prisoners during the night. It wasn't pretty. Beatings, rapes, torture.

"I've never been able to get my hands on a real Daemor, until now."

"I had left Mab's service years before the Mysticaust happened," I said.

"That's what you'd like us to believe when in reality you were a sleeper agent, a mole feeding her information to help her with her plans," said Redmond.

"That's not true," I said.

"Don't lie to me," said Redmond, sliding a piece of paper over the desk. "This is a confession you are going to sign."

"Like hell," I said.

Redmond nodded at one of the soldiers behind me, who opened the door. The wernun walked in. "I'd wondered why you're interested in the pixie. The guards tell me he has a way with the fitches, so at first, I assumed you were an old lover. Luckily, I checked with Stanelus." Apparently the wernun's name. "He tells me the little winged rodent is really your father. It's simple. I'm going to wrap him in iron and torture the little bastard until you sign or he dies. You so much as lift a finger to do anything but sign and those men put iron bullets in your head. I'll deal with this Nemesis if it comes to that. What do you say?"

What could I say? "Mab's dead. My father's still alive. I'll sign."

"Excellent," Redmond said, pushing a pen toward me. It was one of those fancy metal jobs. "I'll have proof that what happened wasn't truly my fault. Maybe I'll even get my old command back."

I picked up the pen and scratched it across the paper. "Pen's out of ink. Do you have another?"

Everyone had relaxed at this point, so as soon as Redmond bend over to look in his desk, I made my move. I tossed the pen with all my might at the mage and punctured her right eye. The pain and blood destroyed any hope of focusing enough to use her powers. Simultaneously, I flexed my wings and sliced off the hands of the soldiers behind me, before I leapt across the room to slug the mage. She had a glass jaw and fell to the floor unconscious. Without missing a beat, I rushed behind the desk and removed the Colonel's sidearm and put it under his chin.

By the time the eight other armed soldiers came into the office to see why their comrades were screaming, I was behind Redmond.

"Hello again, gentlemen. Please come in and shut the door behind you." They listened. "Now put the safeties on and put your guns on the desk slowly and one at a time." This time they hesitated. "Colonel, perhaps you'd like to help here."

"Do as she says," Redmond ordered.

"Don't fogret the guns on the floor," I said. The men did as they were told. I indicated the soldiers I had wounded. "Now tie tourniquets around their wrists so they don't bleed to death." They had already passed out from the shock. "And apply something to her eye too."

Once everyone was patched, I bent the metal arms of Redmond's chair to pin his wrists. "Now if everyone would be so kind as to line up in front of the desk here."

They obliged. I tried to sucker punch the entire line. Five fell down, a sixth was stunned and the seven and eight were untouched, at least until my next three punches send them to dreamland.

Next, I motioned to the wernun, who ran toward the door. "I can knock you out or shoot you in the back. You're a wernun, so which way doesn't matter to me."

Twitching the entire way, Stanelus walked to the desk and I

slugged him hard enough for my fist to hurt.

"You'll never get away with this," Redmond said.

"I'm doing pretty good so far," I said, opening his desk drawers. I found my gun, coat, and pants and got dressed. I decided to stick with just a bra instead of ripping apart the ill-fitting jumpsuit any further. Many of the Daemor used to run around fighting in what looked like armored bikini tops. It was a glamour. The cleavage distracted male enemies. I took the crow's head on silver medallion out of the belt and fastened it on the strap connecting my bra cups, the way it was meant to be worn. I activated the glamour and it suddenly looked like I was in my old armor. I tied up the mage and shot her once in the head. Nemesis's special guns have multiple types of bullets, including the one she gave me. The boss had Vulcan design them years ago after watching some cartoon around a rabbit sheriff whose guns shot bullets that did something different each time. The slug I put in her head was of the non-lethal variety but would keep her unconscious for days and a headache that would keep her from focusing enough to use her magic for the rest of her days.

It would have been safer to kill her, but I was supposed to be one of the good guys. Killing in the heat of battle is one thing, slaughtering a helpless enemy is another.

"Now we just have to figure out a way to free all the prisoners in this camp. Any suggestions?"

"Go to hell."

"That's not very helpful and I'm short on time," I said, digging my thumb into a nerve cluster behind his ear. My opinion of Redmond didn't give him much credit for strength of character. If my gut was right, a lot of very bad pain would be enough to break him. "Tell me all about your camp here. Let's start with how many troops."

Redmond broke, although I was surprised he held out as long as he did. I had him get all the non-sniper soldiers into their briefing room for an urgent meeting. Once they were inside, I locked the doors and shot in a concussive bullet, another non-lethal special from Vulcan. It combined a small shockwave, gas, and some sort of electric wave that shut off the reticular activation formation, the part of the brain that keeps us awake. In less than a minute, they were all unconscious and would be for at least twelve hours.

That left the snipers. I did some sniping of my own from nearby. Using the automatic fire mode, I was able to knock out fifteen of the guards before anyone noticed. The other five strained to find me, but I got them before they got me. I commandeered a jeep and crashed through the gate.

"Okay, people, listen up. The soldiers are temporarily unconscious, so we have to move quickly. We're all getting out of here. I'll take anyone who wants to go to Paddy Moran for sanctuary. Anyone who doesn't want to come with me, get as far from here as quickly as you can."

There was some commotion, but everyone moved. They didn't have any possessions to get, so they were out quickly. Only about one hundred and fifty took me up on my offer, Papa and all his lady friends among them. The rest preferred to go out on their own. The Pine Barrens were big enough that most could probably hide out without getting caught for a long time. I wished them luck.

We stole every military vehicle we could, loaded them up, and headed for the open road. I had called Nemesis from Redmond's office on a landline. She, Rudy, and Gani were on their way to meet us, ride shotgun, and run interference.

They'd make sure we made it to Bulfinche's Pub. Then I was going to figure a way to put a stop to all these camps, once and for all.

The

DMA
Casefiles

*Once a demon-possessed serial killer,
Agent Karver strives to make amends for his victims
as an agent for The Department of Mystic Affairs.*

PINING AWAY

The stockings were hung by the chimney with care alongside five members of the Sutton family.

It was a brutal crime, easily as horrendous as any I was responsible for back when the seriál demon possessed me. Someone had taken an ax to Mom and Pop Sutton, then their young children Jamie, Will, and Kristin. Then the killer or killers had stuck a broomstick where the sun don't shine and kept on pushing. They strung them up to the walls by hammering in Christmas lights and covered the late Sutton family with tinsel and ornaments. To top off the twisted crime, the killer took stars and rammed them through the top of their skulls, except for Jamie. She was the young and for her, they used an angel.

"Thank you for calling us in, Sheriff Weeks," said my partner Mandi Cobb, doing her best to look only at the Sheriff's face. My partner's an empath and a propath, which means she can feel and project emotions. Normally she has ironclad control and she was a pro when she was examining the bodies but I could tell it spooked her.

Not that there were any outward physical signs or change in body language. Her emotions were leaking out, a mixture of fury and disgust. That's one of the drawbacks of the job. Sure, you get to try to bring in the bad guys but you see so many things that made you doubt humanity should be allowed to exist. Fortunately, one look at my partner was enough to convince me otherwise.

Sheriff Weeks was puffing on a stogie, same as our last shared crime scene. An old trick to block the smell of a dead body. These weren't dead long enough to have rotted but much of the insides had been put on the outside and that still stank pretty bad. I still stuck to the nastiest methylated cough drops you can buy. Of course, I was blocking the smells for a different reason. When the seriál demon had possessed me, it enhanced and rewired my body. It left behind some twisted changes. While my mind was disgusted, my body still loved the smells of death and carnage.

"Why did you call us?" I said.

"Frankly, Agent Karver, you and your partner impressed me last time with the Harrison case. My medical examiner and crime scene techs haven't moved the bodies because you wanted you to see them but they did inspect the scene. The techs say those broomsticks were rammed through the floorboards and grew roots out the bottom to reinforce the, eh, staying upright. The floorboards grew branches up to the broomsticks.

"My ME says his exam revealed sticks were shoved all the way up into their throats and it was done with a single thrust each because there were no signs of them being pulled out to reshove or twisting at the entry wound. All of that screams supernatural to me. Which is why I called in my friends at the Department of Mystic Affairs. And to bask in the glow of your wonderful personality again, Agent Karver," Weeks said with a good-natured chuckle. We hadn't exactly become besties last time around but Mandi and I have found that nothing endears you to a good cop than helping them to catch the bad guy and saving lives.

"We always appreciate being called," Mandi said.

"Mandi gets called so much that she burns out the ringer on her phone every month," I said.

"And Karver usually has to blow dust away from his whenever he has to answer it."

Weeks took another puff of his cigar and made a face. It only helped so much. "Any ideas what could have done this? Some sort of anti-Christmas demon?"

Mandi looked to me.

I shook my head. "It wasn't a demon." Unlike my partner. I don't have any powers per se. Among the other residual effects of my demonic passion, it altered my body so I was at the pinnacle of human strength, speed, and endurance. As nice as that is, I trade it in a minute to bring back any one of my sixty-three dead. The only thing I have resembling a supernatural ability is on able to sense when demons or Hell magic is involved in something. I wasn't sure what this was yet but it didn't come from the Pit.

"How do you know?" Sheriff Weeks asked.

"Karver's had a lot of experience with demonic crimes. It's a specialty so if he says it wasn't a demon, you can rest assured it wasn't." Mandi had a gift of politely not giving out details of my past while making it seem like just an area of study. She also leaves out it was with the most horrific teacher imaginable.

"Any ideas what did this then?"

"That's yet to be determined but this was a crime of passion. It was very personal to the killer or killers. It a serious hate-on for the Suttons and/or for Christmas. Did they do anything unusual around the holidays?" Mandi said.

"We're looking into that but so far, nothing out of the ordinary."

I looked around. Considering how the killer showcased their kills, something important was missing. "Where's their Christmas tree?"

"We haven't been able to find it but judging by the pine-covered tree stand we found, they had a natural rather than of an artificial one."

"I think they threw it out," I said.

Sheriff Weeks nodded. "It seems likely. We found tinsel at the curb by the full garbage cans."

"But if the garbage is still in the cans, why would the garbage collectors take the tree but leave the garbage?" I said.

"Yesterday was New Year's Eve so there was no regular pickup because of the holiday."

"Maybe this was about the tree. Could they have gone to a neighbor's property and cut down a tree they weren't supposed to, maybe making a neighbor very angry?" Mandi said.

"Over cutting down a tree?" I said.

"We get a lot of calls from people complaining about their neighbors trimming branches that grow over the fence line. We've seen more than one fistfight, so it's not beyond the realm of possibility. If said neighbor was some sort of supernatural creature disguised as a human, maybe this could be the retaliation," Sheriff Weeks said.

"Nice work, Sheriff. You've come a long way."

"Thanks, Karver. To misquote Sherlock Holmes when you eliminate the impossible whatever explanation that's leftover, no matter how improbable is likely the answer. Problem is after the Harrison case, I have no idea where impossible lies anymore"

"You started canvassing the neighborhood?"

"Yep. So far, none of the neighbors hurt or saw anything, but it was New Year's Eve and a lot of people got to celebrate. And after celebrating they tend to be unreliable witnesses."

Mandi nodded agreement. If she lost focus in a bar, she could actually start acting drunk without having touched a drop. "Have your people keep an eye out for any sort of stumps that could be about the size of a Christmas tree."

"My biggest concern is how and what I tell Daphne about what happened to the rest of her family."

"Who's Daphne?" Mandi said.

"The Sutton's oldest daughter. She's sixteen and spent the night at a combination sleepover and New Year's Eve party. I'm heading there when we're done to break the news."

"Then we may not have to find the killer," I said.

Weeks seemed so surprised he almost dropped his cigar. "Why? You think the daughter did it?"

"No, but I'll bet you a year's supply of donuts that she's our killer's next target."

Not to gripe or complain but solving magic based crimes is a lot more difficult than the human base variety. You have all the joys of a human murder investigation except the list of possible suspects is a lot longer. To add to the fun there are always new instances of creatures and folks that had not been encountered before. Same with new uses of magical powers.

We did some digging but didn't come up with anything that would reveal family history with anything that would have such murderous intent. Course that doesn't mean anything. There is not always a record of a chance encounter that had in the woods a century or more ago with someone of something that swore vengeance on that person and their entire bloodline.

The mystic offender can then toddle off to someplace like Faerie. If they don't cross over just right, they can return a hundred years later here, but only a day or so has passed for them. Which of course they still have the anger and the need for vengeance but the person they swore to get is long dead so they go after innocent family members.

Mandi, Weeks, and I went through different Christmas and holiday-related motives but we kept coming back to why the fixation on the tree? What would make the tree so important to someone?

Was it someone that was dramatizing Christmas in the set things are just collateral damage? Or was it someone who had a special attachment to that tree?

The last theory was the one that made the most sense, especially with broomsticks growing roots and wood floor sprouting branches.

"I think we could be dealing with a dryad," I said.

"What's a dryad?" Weeks asked.

"Nature spirits. Some of them are set up as guardians to protect a place or a tree," my partner explained.

"Aren't fairies cute with little wings?" Sheriff Weeks said.

"The wings are optional. Most don't have them. There's some cute and cuddly but a lot more are very deadly," I said. "If the dryad was supposed to protect the tree and the Suttons cut it down, it would cause such anger."

"Then why kill the family now? They had to have cut down the tree weeks ago," said Sheriff Weeks.

"The dryad might've been touched by the family putting up the tree in a place of honor in their house, after decorating and seeming to worship it. An evergreen tree still had a chance to be saved and brought back to life, especially by a dryad. Maybe she thought they were going to take care of the tree," Mandi said.

"She?"

Mandi nodded. "Whether sexist or otherwise, all dryads seem to be female."

The Sheriff nodded. "Agent Karver, you still think it'll go after the surviving daughter next?"

I nodded. "Anger like this doesn't just disappear. This dryad won't be able to stop until the entire family is dead."

Weeks frowned. "So how do we stop this murdering dryad before she kills the kid?"

"We don't." We have one agent who might be able to track her. Unfortunately, he's on an assignment where, for his own safety, he couldn't be contacted. Which was very bad for us because I was fairly confident Hunter would be able to find this dryad. And I don't have many friends these days but Hunter and I went to the DMA Academy together. He's always treated me straight so it would be nice to see a friendly face who knows what I am and likes me anyway. "We need to guard this girl twenty-four/seven and hope that we can stop her before she succeeds."

Week shifted his weight to the side, then back "You're talking about using a teenage girl as bait for a supernatural killer?"

"We are. It's going to be after her either way. At least this way, we will hopefully get the killer first," I said.

"Don't you guys have someone who can impersonate her to get her out of the line of fire?"

We tried to get Gus. The changeling would be able to take Daphne's place and the dryad would be none the wiser.

"We already put in a call to get him but he is deep undercover right now and if pulled could risk the deaths of hundred. The home office is not about the many for one, so we're on her own," Mandi said.

"We stop this thing? Silver bullets?"

Mandi shook her head. "Iron, not silver. We can use our badges to cloak ourselves from the dryad. She'd have to physically see us to know we were there."

"How can my people help?"

"This won't work if it knows anyone is there. We have training and experience in dealing with this kind of thing. Let us do our job," Mandi said.

Weeks sighed. "If we didn't have history, I'd tell you both where to go. You two did right by me and my town, so we'll do what you suggest. Don't fail my trust and don't you let this girl die."

"You have my word that I would die before letting something hurt her," I said.

"Thanks, Karver. I guess my first impression of you being an ass was wrong."

"No, he is an ass. But he'd take a bullet to save a life. Somedays it's worth it to put up with him to have him around when stuff hits the fan," Mandi said.

"Stop, you're making me blush," I said. "Something, judging by your social life, you are unable to do."

"Is there anything else you need?" Weeks asked.

"Actually, can we head to a hardware store?" Mandi said.

Two hours later we had everything set up in the Sutton home. The sheriff let us use it despite the fact it was still an active crime scene.

Daphne was a mess.

"I don't know if I can do this." She blew her nose and the latest in a never-ending flow of tears from her eyes.

"I understand but if we don't stop this creature, it's going to get you too," I said.

Her sobbing intensified. Which got me a glare from Mandi.

"What my ever tactful and often clueless partner is trying to tell you is this killer is going to coming after you, regardless. With us playing bodyguards, the thing that killed your family will be stopped."

Instead of being comforted, Daphne curled up in a ball on the floor.

Mandi sighed and used her powers on the girl. She projected confidence and bravery then did her best to dampen the pain, loss, and terror that was gripping the girl's heart. Even with all that, it took Daphne a couple of minutes to stop crying but then she sat up. She looked surprised by what she was feeling and assumed that somehow it was coming from within instead of without. Mandi wouldn't correct that thinking.

"I'm sorry. I think I can do it now," she said

"Good girl," I said.

Mandi gave Daphne a hand up and we went into the living room where her family had been killed. The crime scene techs had done their best to erase traces of the horrific murders. Sheriff weeks hadn't told her exactly where they happened yet. There would be time for that later if she survived.

"So, all I have to do is sit there and watch TV?"

Mandi nodded and handed her the remote. Daphne sat down.

"That's it. That and as soon as anything odd starts to happen we'll tell you everything. Can you handle that?" Mandi said.

"Yes. Just make sure you get their killer."

Mandi smiled. I knew my partner well enough it was because that last flash of bravery was all Daphne.

Mandi drew her gun and hid behind a reclining chair from which position she had a perfect view of Daphne and plenty of room to jump out.

We had shifted our DMA badges to stealth mode. We both had our earpieces. I took the outside of the house in hopes of getting the dryad before she got inside.

I searched for a good hiding spot and talked into my earpiece. "Sorry we couldn't set the trap somewhere else in the house. I know you'd get a kick out of being in a strange new bedroom and getting to see more than the ceiling."

"At least I get invited into people's bedrooms. Not sure you'd even know what to do in one except sleep," Mandi shot back with a chuckle.

We coped with uncomfortable situations by picking on each other. Mandi's as far from a loose woman as you can get. And I'm not exactly emotionally equipped to be romantically involved with anyone at this point in my life. The demon did too many horrible things to others using my body. It takes the magic out of a romantic evening when you're flashing back to the dying screams of so many people.

"I'm outside the front window. I can see the front and one side of the house. Initiating radio silence."

"Be safe, Karver."

"You too, Mandi."

I stood as quietly as I could. One of the few beneficial effects of my possession was my body was almost always at its peak. While I didn't have any supernatural ability to see in the dark, my eyes adjusted quickly.

Sometimes things go bump in the night and sometimes they don't. Dryads can move silently in the woods but we were in suburbia. I was hoping that would decrease any stealth abilities this murderer had.

It didn't. It was pure dumb luck that I spotted our perp. The dryad clocked in at maybe a foot and a half tall. No wings, but various appendages that had natural camouflage that looked like evergreen needles hanging off of them. She crept silently up to the house until she could see in the living room window.

The killer wasn't expecting to be expected because I stood less than three feet from her and she didn't notice me or even bother to look. She had eyes only for Daphne Sutton.

Unlike my partner, I hadn't drawn my gun. Instead, I held my knives. The seriál demon had liked to slice our victims and left me with an almost supernatural ability with blades. The DMA had gotten me a very special set that contained a mix of silver, iron, and several other alloys and topped the whole thing off by engraving runes on the blades. For me, they were the perfect weapon to take on supernatural bad guys because they were designed to hurt most things mystical.

I reached out and pressed the tip of one of my blades against the back of the dryad's neck and whispered, "Don't move. You're under arrest. DMA agent."

As a federal agent, I was obligated to follow procedure and say exactly what I said. Not that I was above skipping that part if there was a clear and present danger.

The problem is an awful lot of supernatural criminals don't really understand the idea of an ethical more enforcement system so the dryad burst forward toward the glass window. I pushed my blade to cut her, slicing off what looked like several needles and a bit of skin but it wasn't enough to stop her.

"Incoming!" I said through my earpiece, using my blades to smash the rest of the windowpane. I know a lot of action heroes will jump through a glass window, but that's a good way to cut an artery and die. I went right after her but Mandi had already taken a couple shots at the dryad, but the murderous guardian spirit was too fast and dodged the bullets. The shots slowed the killer long enough for Daphne to dive out of her chair into a specially modified dog cage and shut the door behind her. Instead of having mesh, it was covered in stainless steel with the highest percentage of iron that we could find. Steel didn't hurt those from Faerie as much as iron did but touching it wasn't exactly pleasant.

Daphne was safe. At least for the moment.

"Surrender and we won't hurt you," Mandi said, training her gun at the small dryad.

"Nettles already hurts. Been protecting that line of trees for centuries. Suttons kill the last in the line. Not only they kill tree, they doomed Nettle. They all must die before I do."

"That's not happening. If you don't surrender, you will die," Mandi said, pouring on the emotion to try and convince the dryad to relax and give up.

It wasn't working. Her anger and hate were too strong.

"There's another option. One where neither of you has to die," I said.

"Liar!"

Nettles lunged at the steel encased dog cage and grabbed hold an edge of the sheet metal. The dryad pulled with a deceiving for her size and tore the side of the cage free, leaving only the metal mesh of the cage between the murderous dryad and Daphne.

"I don't have a shot," Mandi said.

Well, she did but it might also take out the girl we were trying to protect. That left it to me.

As a rule, I don't like throwing my knives. There are really closer in length to short swords but once one is out of my hands it could just as easily be used on me or Mandi, but this dryad was ignoring the pain and the burning on her hands and had the steel layer peeled away and was starting on the mesh bars of the dog cage.

Daphne's screams rang out from inside.

Needles was so focused on killing the girl that she never saw my blade coming. It caught her in the side and swept her away from the cage and pinned her to the sheetrock wall like a butterfly in a collector's shadowbox.

"Nettles is done and so is the tree line she swore to defend. Nettles has failed her oath and dies in shame."

Mandi moved to stand between the cage and the dryad. One of the first things you learn in the DMA is just because something is wounded doesn't mean it isn't dangerous. I knelt in front of Nettles so I could look her in the eyes but I still kept my other blade in front of me.

"No. In your anger, you forgot there was another option." I reached into my suit jacket pocket and pulled out a tiny pinecone one of the crime scene techs had found under the couch. "You could've taken this to save the line. You can still take it and save yourself."

Dryads were typically asked to watch after trees that had some magic properties, even if they looked ordinary. There was enough life left in the pinecone for the dryad to take and heal herself. She'd still be going to jail but at least she'd be alive. I'd caused enough death in my time. These days I wanted to swing the scales in the other direction. I wanted a win. I wanted Nettles to live.

Despite being sliced nearly in half, Nettles smiled with genuine joy when she saw the pinecone and she held out her arms in front of her. I took out a tiny pair of handcuffs and put them around her wrists. DMA charms would keep her abilities contained. She might drain the magic and make her getaway or try to kill Daphne again. The cuffs would stop that.

I handed the dryad the pinecone and she cradled it to her chest like a mother might a baby.

She reached down to her stomach wound where my blade still pinned her and filled her palm with blood, then wiped it on the pinecone, gently kissed it, and held it back out to me.

"You didn't take its energy."

"Nettles failed. In choice between my life and the tree line living on, honor demands the tree live."

"But you will die," I said.

Murderous dryad smiled and nodded. "I shall."

"But it's only a pinecone."

"But if someone plants it, one day it will be a tree. You are human and the bond between guardian and guarded is something you can never understand. You ended Nettles. Will you also end my failure and redeem my honor by making sure seedling is planted so the line lives on?"

Our eyes meet and for a moment, the hate in hers was replaced with hope.

"I will. You have my word."

"Thank you, human. Perhaps now the great woods will allow my spirit to dwell there."

And with that, Nettles died. I didn't need to check. I'd seen far too much of dying to know when the Reaper called.

I left my one blade in the wall and put my other one in the back sheath under my suit jacket. Mandi had to bend the sheet metal back on the dog cage before she could get Daphne out of the cage.

The angry teen crawled out and onto her fee then charged the dryad's corpse. I stepped between her and the dead killer before she made contact.

"Get out of my way! That thing killed my family! I want to tear it to shreds and stomp on it."

"But you will not," I said. "What she did was terrible but, in her mind, she was avenging *her* family. This is done. The only thing that comes out of an eye for an eye is that the people who make eye patches get rich.

"You're not really going to plant that thing, are you?"

"I gave my word."

"But she was a killer. She doesn't deserve anything."

"Even a killer deserves a chance at redemption."

Daphne slapped me across the face. She telegraphed the blow so I could have moved out of the way but I didn't. Hitting me would be therapeutic for her in the short term. The long-term would last the rest of her life.

"Yes, he does," Mandi whispered in her earpiece so only I heard her, then she stepped up and wrapped her arms around the girl. Daphne collapsed crying.

I called the DMA cleanup team and then Sheriff Weeks. I put the pinecone in an evidence bag and put that in my pocket. That was one piece of evidence that the locals wouldn't be getting back.

The BAMBI MYSTERIES

*The original bad girl succubus
has changed her ways
and now works for Hell PD*

XPLOITATION

Some days I can't believe how far I fell. Or maybe I'm finally going in the other direction.

It wasn't that long ago that I had men – of the demon and damned variety – tripping over themselves, groveling, and offering to do *anything* I wanted just for the hint that they might have their hell rocked by the hottest succubus this side of Paradise.

I've never had any issue with modesty. Nor much need.

My current situation started when I lost my virginity. That might seem like an odd statement coming from a succubus but right after the Fall, I saw what was coming for the Fallen. And worse, what my lot in the afterlife would be. I mystically removed my virginity – much like a mage seeking immortality would his heart – and hid it in a safe place. I know full well that any man who took it would have power over me for eternity. I've certainly never been the type to believe that any man was my equal, let alone my superior. That attitude probably contributed to my choosing the wrong side of the war in Heaven.

Still, I wasn't about to let that happen so I hid the physical manifestation of my maidenhood away in a dark corner of the Pit and then someone found it. I needed it back and I thought I could manipulate Negral, the Chief of Hell's police, into getting it back for me. I mean he was just a man.

He turned out to be a little bit more. Negral is a Sumerian god of the sun, fire, plague, and a few other nasty things. He ruled over their afterlife for centuries until a split with his ex-wife didn't go well.

His power works differently than the demons down here. The Chief can control flames including hellfire, which runs everywhere throughout the Pit. Gives him a lot of ammo. Add to that his ability to generate sunlight, which hurts demons, and it makes him a force to be reckoned with. He was even man enough – and foolish enough – to fill HPD's badges with the bright stuff, which gives us a weapon against the keepers of the damned.

In hindsight, it's funny. I had never had any trouble manipulating any man to do exactly what I wanted. Turns out Hell's Detective was a little bit more complicated and didn't like me setting him up to be killed. Since I broke our agreement, he claimed my virginity and got complete control over me.

Sometime later, through an unusual turn of events with a rebel monk who came to Hell to save the damned, I got my virginity back. Where I was originally forced to work for Hell's Detective, I'm now a willing member of Hell PD and help keep order in the Pit.

Then the worst thing that can happen to a succubus happened to me. To quote Negral's vernacular, I fell in love with the mook.

Now I'm the Assistant Chief of Hell PD. I don't lord over my own domain anymore. I've even released all my thralls to go have afterlives of their own. I have a lot less power – I was in line to become one of the Lords of Hell – but oddly enough I don't even miss it. I'm actually happy now.

Don't tell anyone. Here that's a crime punishable by eternal torture.

Negral wanted to see me in his office.

"Good morning, Chief." That's a sign of respect. When I was on the job, at least in the 666th precinct, that's what I called him. In private was another matter entirely. "You wanted to see me?"

"I got a case for you. It's going to involve you going Earthside. You up for?"

"Won't be the first time I've gone Earthside." Succubi do some of our best work among mortals.

"But it will be your first sanctioned mission there as a member of HPD which means the rules are different," Negral said.

Men have a habit of thinking they are saying what they want to say while missing the mark by a mile. What Negral meant was could I handle the restrictions he put on his cops. His cops could do we wanted to demons or damned but living innocents were another matter.

The Chief acknowledges collateral damage but he doesn't like it. Involve a kid or an innocent and that "doesn't like" gets upgraded to hate. Negral wasn't born here in the Pit nor did he make the transition like those of us veterans who survived the war.

It gives him some pretty messed up ideas about right and wrong, starting with he thinks they exist. When I came to him to find my missing virginity, I thought he was a fool. A powerful fool, but a fool nevertheless. Oddly enough, spending time with him changed my mind about that and a lot of other things.

Do you want to know the real reason I fell in love with the mook? I double-crossed him more than once when he was looking for my virginity. So, he did what any man would do and popped the red jewel that represented my virginity. He had near total control over me. Anybody else in Hell would have just made me their sex slave or worse.

What did Negral do? Told me not to do anything to hurt him and gave me a job as a cop. We didn't become intimate until after my virginity was restored to the jewel and given back to me.

I've never encountered a man who wouldn't just take me – with or against my will – in a situation where there were no consequences. For the powerful in Hell, there rarely are. Then there's Negral, a man who had a set of rules that went beyond taking care of his libido.

Damn sexiest thing I have ever seen. Add to that the fact that I've seen him willing to die to protect innocents, his cops, and even me and one thing I can tell you for sure is Negral is too good for Hell by far.

Basically, he's a forgotten god on Earth so he can't survive without manna. Since he doesn't have any religion worshiping him in the mortal world, he had to make a deal with Nick – what we call the Devil so he doesn't know we're talking about him – or fade away to oblivion.

A while back the Chief had a chance to get out of Hell with enough mana to survive for centuries. Negral threw it away to save the cops of Hell PD and me, which ensures something that I had never given any other man before – my loyalty.

That meant I would follow his rules, however foolish.

"I can handle it. What's the case?

Once I got the skinny, I used a hellhole – a mystic portal – to travel to a small town outside of Bogotá, Columbia. The case was simple. The demon Darfin had permission to manifest on Earth and do the usual mischief, death, and destruction that came with it.

Turns out this demon was a jonz – basically they specialize in increasing mortal addiction be it sex, drugs, booze, hoarding, or even shopping. The goal is to increase the addiction to the point where it controls the mortal's life. That in turns makes many mortals more willing to do evil to support said addiction.

Darfin's sub-specialty was drugs and he took over a drug lord's cartel in the usual way; by killing him. Although the way he killed him was unusual as he removed the drug lord's limbs and head, then ate them in front of his new troops. Gory but brutal enough to ensure an ascension to power. Then Darfin came up with the evilly brilliant idea of cutting the product in brimstone scraped off the slopes of Hell itself. This laced it with hell magic which made coming off the drug a waking nightmare of terror and horrors.

Demons on Earth are supposed to abide by the Host-Horde Accord which puts strict limits on the number of deaths a demon is allowed to cause. Darfin's direct kills were well under that number but by Negral's figuring, all the people who died from the brimstone-laced cocaine got tallied into his body count and that put him way over.

Darfin had already been issued an order to return to the Pit through traditional channels. Not surprisingly, he ignored it. Thus, it felt to Hell PD to bring the jonz back to the Pit.

Because Darfin had manifested physically on the mortal plane that made him a little bit tougher to take in but I've always enjoyed a challenge. Before I could take him back to Hell, I had to find him.

The hellhole manifested on the outskirts of a small, isolated town. A lot of people have the impression that demons don't do recon. Some don't and things usually don't go as well for them as it could.

While it's true I could walk into wherever Darfin was hanging his horns and try to take him into custody, odds are he wouldn't be alone. While the Chief might not give me much grief over hurting or killing a bunch of drug dealers there'd be Hell's Detective to pay if I hurt one innocent child, so I went to get the lay of the land. Although there was a time I might've held that title myself.

The first thing I noticed were emancipated and unhappy looking humans working in a field of coca leaves. I wasn't a great detective yet but I was pretty sure they were there against their will, at least if the armed guards with machine guns were any indication.

I was careful not to be seen and went into a warehouse which was the only decently constructed building I could see in the entire town. Inside were more unhappy and underfed humans, this time cooking leaves they then made into a paste and cutting it with brimstone among other things. Again, more human guards with machine guns

There was no sign of Darfin anywhere. However, up on a hill outside of the town, I spotted a mansion with a ten-foot-high fence and a patrol of guards with even more machine guns and dogs.

If I were a demon – and I am – with limited time on Earth, would I be wasting my time doing the actual labor or enjoying the fruits of said labors?

Which meant my next stop was the mansion.

Sneaking around in a field or a large warehouse doesn't require any special skills beyond stealth. Getting into this mansion fortress wasn't going to be as easy.

Now I could wait for nightfall and trying sneaking inside but I've always been a more flamboyant sort, which I know is not all that difficult to believe.

Instead of wasting hours coming up with a way to break-in I went to the front gate.

I like the color red. It's the color of my skin, hair, and the majority of my wardrobe. However, for this case, I'd chosen a black catsuit with a zipper in the front. I lowered the zipper down to my navel and strutted to the gate.

Here's the funny thing about succubus magic – you can get men and even women to do a lot for you. The amount that they are willing to do depends on a combination of their inner fortitude and personal value system. Yes, it even works on gay men. However, it doesn't work on those who have known true love. In the short term, those who are in love with someone have a limited immunity. There were two guards at the gate, each held a machine gun and a leash for a dog. The one on the right was ripe for the picking but the one on the left had a wife and kids that he loved.

As hard as it might be for some to imagine, even scumbags can care about other people. It would take too big an expenditure of power to turn him. The two dogs were another matter. I can generate uncontrollable lust. If I don't work to control the focus, the desire automatically turns toward me. I aimed my power at the two dogs so that the object of their lust was the guard on the left.

The two trained guard dogs took him down to the ground so they could have their way with his legs, arms, and anything else they could hump.

His companion thought it was hilarious allowing me to get within a few feet of him before he noticed me.

I held off using my power on him. I like to do that every so often. Sometimes a woman wants to know that she still has it.

He was intrigued but not enough to be stupid and he pointed the machine gun at me. "My, you are sunburned."

"Centuries of hellfire can give a gal quite the tan," I said.

"What are you doing here?"

"I'm here to see your boss."

"I thought Darfin had already gotten his evening whores."

Many women – human and demon – get insulted when a man calls them a whore. I don't because that's exactly what I was. Whores have sex for gain and I did that for millennia. I was good at. At one time, I liked to think I was the best. Who am I fooling? I *was* the best.

It's the *was* that gets to me. It's funny how even a fallen angel can change.

"Thank you for noticing the physical aspect of my skill sets. However, I'm retired and on a different career path. I'm not here to see to Darfin's sexual needs, which I'm sure are large and twisted. I'm here to bring him back to Hell so if you kindly bring me to your boss, I would appreciate it."

"Hands up."

The guard looks like he might actually shoot me so I hit him with a jolt of the lust juice. His gun went down and something else went up. Now he was all smiles.

"I'm sorry, my angel."

Talk about tacky, calling me that. "There's no need to get insulting. Take the gun away from your friend so he doesn't hurt the dogs."

The guard did as instructed.

"Roberto, please help me," said the guard who loved his wife and kids. The dogs were acting with such ferocity that whenever he tried to get up, they'd bite into his clothes and drag him back down. Another benefit for males is my power can make them go as long as I want before they finish up. In fact, there were times back in the day where I wouldn't grant that release. It wasn't a Tantric thing. I was just a bitch. And a demon.

"Take me to Darfin."

"Of course, my sweet. Perhaps along the way, we can find a secluded spot…"

"Excuse me? I asked you for something and you're not going to give it to me right away? Are you trying to make me unhappy?"

Roberto dropped to his knees and groveled. "No, no, my sweet love. I will do anything that your heart desires."

"Then get off your knees and bring me where I want to go."

The mansion was equal parts tacky and opulent. I'd been in demon Lord's palaces that weren't as impressive.

It took us several minutes to arrive at what Roberto said was the master bedroom. The hallway outside of it as larger than any two of the villagers' homes. There were two dozen guards stationed in the hallway alone and they were all surprised to see Roberto and me.

"Roberto, what are you doing here with her? I thought the boss's whores for the evening were already here."

I smiled. "Thank you for noticing."

"She's here for him," Roberto said.

The guard at the door frisked then grouped me. Don't get me wrong – I like a good grope as much as the next succubus but there's this little thing I like more – the groper asking nicely first.

If this was Hell, I would've ripped his arms off then beat him over the head with them. But it wasn't, so I didn't. In the Pit, wounds heal and death is not a possibility. I didn't know if there were enough bullets here to kill me but there were a sufficient number to rip me to shreds so I kept my yap shut. There would be time enough to settle up before I left.

Gropie opened the twelve-foot-high double doors and led me into Darfin's bedroom of horrors. My bedroom was an impressive exercise in opulence and decadence and had room for a hundred. I had parties where there were so many suitors, most had to wait outside. This place was designed for fear and intimidation and no one's pleasure other than Darfin's.

There were five women – one was unconscious and three were having a bad trip from the brimstone laced cocaine. Darfin was busy pleasuring himself with the fifth but I doubted she was getting very much out of it. Corpses rarely do.

"So, she decided sex with you was a fate worse than death."

Not bothering to stop pumping the girl, Darfin spun around to look at me.

"If it isn't the whore who thinks she's a cop. Mind standing right there where I can watch you until I'm done?"

I stepped forward. "You're coming with me, Darfin."

"So that's how it's going to be? Fine. Carlos, get my insurance policy and bring it here," he said to Gropie. The rest of you surround the whore from Hell."

Darfin got off the girl and stood up to his full eight-and-a-half-foot height. The jonz demon was a bright shade of yellow with short horns and a tail that would do a lizard proud. He reached down to the girl whose corpse he been desecrating and ripped her arm from her shoulder then proceeded to eat it as if it was a chicken leg.

"To what do I owe the pleasure? You shouldn't be here. I'm well under my kill ratio."

"You're not. All the deaths from the brimstone-laced cocaine are being tallied against you. It's time to go back," I said.

"I'm a little insulted that Negral didn't come for me himself. And he sent you? I'm beyond insulted. Why don't you just strut your way back to the Pit and tell your boss to be a man and come for me his own self."

"Not going to happen. We can do this the easy way or the hard way."

"I was heard you were easy and liked it the hard way, so how about I give you little toss on the mattress and you fogret you found me?"

I laughed. "I doubt you've ever managed to pleasure a woman or even heard one real orgasm, let alone know how to make it happen."

He angrily took a bite of the bicep and swallowed, then pointed his snack at the dead girl. "I made her come. I couldn't even stop her from screaming."

"It's probably because you were killing her. Those were screams of pain, not pleasure."

The yellow demon shrugged his shoulders and devoured the tricep. "It looked close enough and worked really good for me."

I had been trying to avoid using my using my power on Darfin. The connection was a two-way street. I can deal with what's in a human's mind. The evil there is usually pretty tame but, in a demon, it's not pleasant. I've been trying to fight my baser urges so I didn't need to expose myself to something that might bring back things I'm trying to bury.

I may take the form of a slender woman but I'm still one of the Fallen. I can call on a lot of physical power when I wanted to.

I took a step towards Darfin.

He shook his finger side to side and said, "No, no, no. Since you're working for the Chief, I figure his issues are now yours."

The demon motioned with his hand to the door behind me where Carlos the groper brought in twenty women and children, all with guns pointed at them.

"One of the drawbacks in coming to Earth is that eventually I knew I'd have to go back to the Pit so I kept an insurance policy ever since I arrived. Figured if the Chief came after me, I could use them as hostages. So, surprise – that's what they are. If someone with some balls came for me, I figured I could offer them a snack to distract them long enough for me to get away. Now not only are you going to let me get away but before you go you're going to show me why so many of the Lords of Hell made idiots of themselves over you."

This situation brought home the difference between the old me and the new me I was still becoming. It also limited my options.

Despite his appearance of greater size and strength, Darfin was born in the Pit. I could outmuscle him. As to who had the better martial skills, that was yet to be seen.

Adding hostages meant I couldn't just take him on with tail and claw. It looked like I was going to have to get my mind dirty. Or dirtier.

I hit the yellow demon with a fistful of power and did my best to block out his mind. It was much easier than I thought. Now all I had to do is open a hellhole and Darfin should follow me home like a horny little puppy.

"You had enough fun and games. Let's go back to the Pit." I motioned for him with my index finger to follow me then turned my back. It was an incredibly stupid thing to do because Darfin smacked me across the very large bedroom with his tail, throwing me through the wall. When I got up and looked, I confess I was expecting a rather more shapely hole.

I've met more than a few lovers in my time who liked the rough stuff, so I was able to recover quickly but my mind was still reeling. Why was my power not working on him?

Darfin laughed then stuck the rest of the corpse's severed arm in his mouth and stripped off the remaining meat with his teeth.

"You're trying to figure out why am not your little lost thrall, aren't you?" He didn't bother to wait for me to answer. "I couldn't be sure the Chief was coming for me. I'd heard about your demotion to Hell PD so I figured out a way to negate your lust magic. All of these men here have not only sworn their loyalty to me but they sealed the deal by selling me their souls." Twenty souls give a demon a lot of extra power, but nowhere near enough to resist me. "I used that bond to grant each man a portion of my power and link them to me."

"What do you get by giving power away?" It was a very undemonlike act.

"Simple. I can spread out any magic used against me among all of them so it doesn't affect me."

That was actually a pretty intelligent plan for one of the rank-and-file to have come up with. With a mind like that, Darfin had serious potential to move up in Hell's hierarchy.

However, there is a difference between a good plan and a well thought out plan.

And let's be honest – when a woman looks like I do most people be they demon or human – underestimate me. Anyone with my face and body has to be stupid because the Creator wouldn't be so unfair as to give the same woman both beauty and brains.

Well, guess what? The Creator isn't fair or I would get to go back to Heaven and wouldn't have needed to be a succubus to survive in the Pit these past millennia.

It took me maybe thirty seconds to figure out a way around Darfin's plan. Admittedly if I hadn't done the move with the dogs it would have taken me much longer.

Then, because he was a lower rank than me, I committed the same sin and underestimated the jonz.

Turns out Darfin wasn't a one plan wonder. The yellow demon nodded and Gropie lobbed a very thin glass canister that hit me square in the chest on my exposed skin.

It burned and melted my flesh. It wasn't the glass that did it but what was inside.

Holy water.

It didn't matter that I was now one of the good guys, at least relative to the rest of Hell. Things aren't that easy with the Creator.

She holds a grudge.

There are certain things that will harm any demon, save the Devil himself. Among the least fun of them is holy water.

Under the onslaught of the blessed liquid, I fell to the ground screaming and crawled away to curl into the fetal position. This of course was an invitation for the human lackeys to kick me and smash in my head, stomach, and ribs with the butts of their guns. Which apparently, Darfin he had had some priest or holy person bless so they could hurt me.

In a situation like this, it didn't matter how much power I had. Well maybe it did, but if I went into full rage mode I'd kill anything mortal near me which included the human hostages.

Also, if I went to full demon mode I would be stronger but the holy water would be able to hurt me more. The trappings of humanity in my physical shape actually shielded me from some of the water's effects.

I put my arms over my head which of course left them free to hit where my burns were. I got enough focus back that I could've let my claws pop out to hamstring then kill the ones nearest to me but that would ruin my plan.

Instead, I reached out and poured power enough into Darfin to make even a demon Lord quiver with unquenchable lust.

And just like he claimed, the yellow demon distributed the effects of the lust magic along among his twenty lackys.

That was a mistake.

This wasn't a fistful of power. It was a truckload.

All the men froze and stopped their attacks on me. I wasn't the target of this lusting. Darfin was.

I rolled away and stood near Gropie. He'd come back from getting the hostages wearing a bandolier filled with glass vials of holy water. I grabbed two handfuls of vials and threw them at Darfin who was in his full demon form. The burning made him drop to his knees screaming.

I twisted the lusting so the human lackeys found him even more attractive in his mutilated state.

The twenty killers forgot about everybody else in the room. Since most of them associated sex with violence, they all were already moving towards the demon. I grabbed hold of Gropie's shoulder.

"He's still very powerful and he's not going to let you guys have your way with him easily. How much more holy water do you have?"

"A roomful."

"Then I suggest you make sure all of you have some if you hope to have any success."

Gropie got a dark grin on his face and ordered five underlings to go get the water. None of them wanted to leave the side of the object of their affections but once Gropie explained what they needed it for, the quintet ran to comply.

"You might want this too," I said, handing him shackles that would contain his power and weaken him. I was planning to use them myself but this would be better.

I've spent most of my existence in the Pit. I've seen a lot of sick and twisted acts but what followed next was brutal even by Hell's standards.

The guards had military training and used that precision to keep Darfin strategically covered with a stream of holy water and beatings with the blessed weapons. Gropie and two friends took my shackles and bound Darfin's wrists, ankles, and tail. And then they held him down and did fairly nasty things to him over and over because I made sure I blocked their ability to complete their tasks.

I used the distraction to get the hostages out of there.

Like any good drug lord, Darfin kept a lot of cash around the place. I put my lust puppet Roberto in charge of distributing the money to the hostages and the townspeople with the promise that I would come back to check on him and give him a reward if he had done right by the locals. It was hardly my fault if he misconstrued what kind of reward I was speaking of.

Next, I freed the workers in the field and the warehouse. The armed thugs were all hit with a burst of power that would leave them with a crippling depression the moment they couldn't see me anymore. I stepped away and felt them curl up into balls.

Don't feel too bad for them. My power linked us and each of them had been a party to multiple murders of the townspeople.

Seems the townspeople remembered too and took a little vengeance of their own. Looks like some of the guards would get to Hell before I did.

Double checking to make sure nobody was in the fields or the warehouse, I destroyed the crops and the product. I think Negral would appreciate that I burned the place down.

When I returned to the mansion's bedroom, Darfin was weeping uncontrollably. I had nothing against torture used on those who deserved it, but it does reach a spot where the point is made.

I reached out and allowed his twenty personal guards to finish. They'd be happier, more relaxed and easier to control that way. I took out my transportation amulet and open up a hellhole.

"March."

Darfin didn't have a spot anywhere on him that wasn't bruised or burned but he still managed to smile which was a little disconcerting since the holy water had burned off his lips.

"You've got me but these men will stay behind and make sure nothing changes here."

"Wrong. I've already taken care of your drugs, fields, and operation. Also, since they sold you their souls, they're coming with us. And since you resisted arrest and got the souls while in violation of the Host-Horde Accord, we are confiscating their ownership." Negral doesn't care to own souls with the exception of his damned cops. Turns out *he* owns them, not Hell. Hell owns the souls in Hell but lets some demons have possession of them. It's a way to build power. Negral owns his cops free and clear. That way if he ever has to get out of the Pit in a hurry, he won't have to leave anyone behind.

The Hellhole opened up to a holding area in the 666th Precinct that wasn't soundproofed and you could hear the souls outside of the precinct house being tortured for their sins. The screams of the damned flowed out into the bedroom and terrified the twenty men who had been so brave when they held machine guns.

Actually, they still held them and, in their fear, pointed their weapons at me. I was amused since most of their ammo now resided in Darfin thanks to their attempts to keep him in place for their lust fest. Judging by the small wounds, he'd only blessed the guns, not the bullets.

They had good reason to be afraid. From the looks, they weren't going go in the hellhole willingly. Not that I was expecting them to.

I grabbed hold of the shackles and dragged Darfin to the opening and threw him through the fiery portal after hitting him with a small lusting.

The bonding he forced with the humans wasn't something he could just turn off. He needed the men's consent which they hadn't been about to give. The mystic jolt recharged all the evil bastards physically and their libidos so they ran into the hellhole after him like lemmings jumping off a cliff.

I decided to leave the house without burning it. A lot of the locals could live there a lot more comfortably than in those shacks.

Not bad for my first sanctioned case on Earth. I had a lot of pent-up lust myself. Using a lusting affected my libido too, just not as much as those I use it on. So as soon as I processed these bums, I was going to celebrate with the Chief.

A LITTLE GIVE AND TAKE

A tale of the Phoenixian

The Scranton Slasher wasn't a stone-cold killer. He enjoyed his profession too much. There were times he even whistled while he worked. To hide his true feelings behind an expressionless face—he simply wasn't capable of it. How could he not show the joy his victims brought him in their last moments?

It would be wrong to even try.

Slasher Steve, as he thought of himself, had seven notches on his trophy knife and was out looking for number eight. Fortune must have been smiling on him because "Octane" wasn't hard to find. The killer liked to give his victims nicknames of their own. Felt it gave him more of a bond with those he took life from. The latest candidate was a young, small woman with dark hair. Octane was carrying two handfuls of packages and wasn't looking around as she headed right toward the Slashermobile. It was actually an old van he had fixed up, but he liked thinking of it as the Slashermobile better. It had a much cooler ring to it and self-image was everything to someone who couldn't talk about his greatest and darkest accomplishments.

The poorly lit strip-mall parking lot he had chosen was deserted and old enough not to have had security cameras installed.

Another fifteen feet and Octane would be close enough to put the chloroform-soaked rag over her mouth and nose. Seconds later, she'd be loaded in the back end of the Slashermobile and whisked off to his funhouse in the woods for a weekend of death, torture, and screams, although not necessarily in that order. It would be grand.

Slasher Steve's skin was prickled high with gooseflesh in gleeful anticipation. Just ten feet away and poor Octane had no idea what was in store for her. The anticipation made him absolutely giddy.

Then it all went bad. Out of nowhere, a man leapt directly into the woman's path.

"Booga Booga!" the Phoenixian shouted, opening and closing his hands at face level in an attempt to be scary. It failed to frighten but passed the weirdo test with flying colors.

The woman jumped back. The Phoenixian wouldn't move from her intended path, so she went around, avoiding Slasher Steve's grasp, all the while cursing the man who had just saved her life.

Joy was incinerated, but from its ashes fury rose in the heart of the killer. Slasher Steve wished he had a knife with him, but he never carried concealed. A rag can be dropped and won't give up fingerprints. A man lurking with a large knife who is unlucky enough to be caught by the police will not be able to talk his way home.

He could grab a blade from the Slashermobile, but it was best to just walk away. The idiot probably didn't realize what he was doing. Then the idiot turned with a goofy grin on his face and waved.

"Pleasure to meet you. Which way to your vehicle?" the Phoenixian asked.

Slasher Steve was too stunned to speak or even point.

The man winked. "Probably this one. The van, right? It's almost always a van." The Phoenixian opened the side door and jumped in. "Are you coming or are you just going to stand there all day? You've got a job to do. I can't abide slackers. Slashers, even those from Scranton, sure, but not slackers."

"Excuse me, but would you please get out of my van?" the serial killer said, straining to be polite, pretending to be just another shopper having to deal with a crazy man.

"Why? I chased the girl away and I know your type hates to go home empty-handed. And I'm more than enough to fill up both your palms." Another wink.

Slasher Steve twitched and took a step back. "Are you gay?" He had gotten over any moral compunction about murder and torture, but still had a ways to go to conquer his homophobia.

"No, not really, but I'm up for anything for a good time. Listen, I sought you out because of the thorough work that you do. You're not going to disappoint me, are you?"

"I have no idea what you're talking about. I don't usually pick up strangers," the killer said.

"Right, and the pope don't poop in the woods. Or is that a bear ain't Catholic? Either way, you may not pick up strangers, but you do drug them and drag them off. You probably have a scrapbook

with all sorts of articles on what you've done, Mr. Scranton Slasher."
The serial killer did, but he wasn't about to admit it. "Why are you
waiting out there? Something the matter with you? Only go after the
girlies? Too afraid to take on a man? How very sad and more than
a little pathetic. Is your big knife just a way to compensate for being
too small where it counts?" The man was making an exaggerated sad
face and pointing at Steve's groin.

"You can't talk to me like that!" the killer yelled before he realized
his shouting was bringing him unwanted attention from others in
the parking lot. The last thing he wanted to be was memorable.

"I can and did. What are you going to do about it?" the Phoenixian
said, putting his hands behind his head and leaning back against the
far wall of the van. When the serial killer didn't reply, he added,
"Pathetic."

The serial killer slammed the side door. He had rigged it so it
couldn't open from the inside, so the man was trapped. He ran
around to the driver's side and got in, pulling a large blade from
under his seat.

"I'll show you what I'm going to do," the killer said, brandishing
the knife and climbing in the back. The blade was placed harshly
against the man's throat. "Get behind the wheel and drive. You just
made the biggest mistake of your life."

The serial killer knew he had delivered his threat in a significantly
frightening fashion. Steve had done it more than a half dozen times
before. Each time, his prey was terrified. Sometimes they trembled,
others they cried or begged for mercy. One even wet herself. Slasher
Steve just couldn't understand why his latest kidnapping victim
giggled and hopped into the front seat clapping his hands like a little
kid going to a party.

"Nice place. How you keep house says a lot about you," said the
Phoenixian, glancing around at the ramshackle property as he pulled
the van into the driveway. The landscaping looked like someone had
loaded up a trailer at an auto scrap yard and dropped the contents
randomly around the place. He pulled the Slashermobile between
the shells of a Dodge Dart and a Pinto. "Probably easier to not have
to worry about the outside of a place. Lawn care is highly overrated.

This deep in the woods, who's going to know? Besides the high grass attracts snakes and their bites are incredibly painful. I'm a big fan of them, to be honest."

"Why don't you just shut up?" the serial killer said, more annoyed than he could remember being in a long time.

The Phoenixian winked at him and put the van in park. "Why don't you just make me, you big, strong killer you?" He tried to open the driver's door, but it would remain closed unless a hidden switch was hit. The Phoenixian wasn't about to wait so he lifted up a tire iron and swung with such force that the serial killer cringed backward, thinking the blow was meant for him. Instead, it smashed only the window. The Phoenixian reached out and opened the door using the outside handle.

The Phoenixian was off and not quite running. The serial killer scrambled after him thinking it was an escape attempt.

"Don't you run away. It won't do any good," Steve yelled as he leapt out the open door. It took a moment to realize that the man wasn't trying to get away—he was merrily rushing toward the house in a manner no self-respecting victim should ever use. "And stop skipping!"

Slasher Steve ran after him. The killer didn't like others wandering around his funhouse—it made him uneasy. The thought that someone might touch or move his things made him cringe. It normally wasn't an issue as the only people he brought around were unconscious, at least until he got them shackled to the wall in the stone basement.

The killer followed the scampering Phoenixian into the house. For the first time since he began the taking of human life as a hobby, Steve felt that he was not the one in charge and it disturbed him. He tried to remember when he lost control of the situation but couldn't remember actually having it.

Once inside, Slasher Steve became frantic. His prey was nowhere to be seen. Had he run out the back door into the woods?

A toilet flushed and Steve rushed toward the only bathroom in the place and slammed into the door, but it was locked. The killer pounded his fists on the cheap wood and was answered with the sound of running water.

Stepping back, Steve lifted up his leg and smashed his foot against the chintzy lock, separating it from the door. The Phoenixian was drying off his freshly washed hands on some toilet paper.

"You didn't have a hand towel," he offered by way of explanation. "And this soap is kind of grungy."

Slasher Steve grabbed the man and smashed him into the shower where his prey ended up flat on his butt.

"If you had to go that badly, you could have just said so," the Phoenixian said. "I would have waited."

The serial killer's face turned a dark red. "What the hell are you doing?"

"I had to go potty and frankly, even though I realize we'll be getting intimate later, I tend to like a little privacy when I answer nature's call. If I had known you'd be this upset, I'd have considered letting you watch me tinkle."

"I didn't want to watch. I told you, I'm not gay," Slasher Steve said, realizing he was only a few decibels away from shouting.

"I believe you," the Phoenixian said, standing up. The killer held his blade up. The man put his finger up and ran it along the edge, drawing his own blood. "Drat. Too sharp. You wouldn't happen to have a dull and rusty one, would you? Maybe a hacksaw? Or a really jagged butter knife?"

Before the Slasher could answer, the Phoenixian walked by him, displaying absolutely no fear of being stabbed.

"So where does the magic happen? You a traditionalist?" The Phoenixian gave him the once-over, his glance moving from head to foot. "Yeah, definitely not the artistic type—no offense. I figure it's in the basement, right?"

The prey rushed to and fro, searching the house in the woods until he found a door with three locks and a chain.

"Ah-ha. Here's the way into your happy place." The Phoenixian started unfastening locks. Watching a victim touching his locks pushed Slasher Steve over the edge. They were *his*. Victims were supposed to be afraid. Victims were supposed to try to figure out a way out from the inside, not the other way around. Victims were supposed to listen and wait to be told what to do. The Phoenixian was doing nothing that he was supposed to and everything he wasn't.

Slasher Steve's hand shot out and spun his odd prey around so they were face to face and he smiled as he plunged his blade through the Phoenixian's hand, pinning it to the door. That should get him acting like prey should, thought Steve.

It didn't.

Instead of fear, the Phoenixian's eyes lit up with excitement. Rather than terror and pleading, he sighed, smiled, then whispered, "Thank you."

"What the Hell is wrong with you?" the serial killer said.

"Nothing you won't be able to fix," the immortal practically purred.

Slasher Steve ripped the knife out. The Phoenixian screamed in laughter.

"Oh, come on. You pulled it out way too fast. Take your time," the bleeding prey whined. "Do it again." The killer grabbed a dirty dishtowel from his kitchen and pressed it into the bloody palm. "What are you doing? Fixing me up? What kind of a screwed up serial killer are you?"

"You're bleeding on my floor," the Slasher scolded.

The Phoenixian glanced down and saw the blood pooling at his feet. "Oops." He held his hand up and looked at the makeshift bandage. "At least it's dirty. Maybe it'll get infected. Do you have any salt you could rub in it?" Slasher Steve stood silent and dumbfounded, unable to believe what was happening. "It could be worse. You could be a drinker. I hate those. Are you an eater? I love eaters."

"Drinkers? Eaters? What are you blabbing about?"

"Drinkers like to down the bodily fluids of their victims, blood being the most common. Not much pain, which means very boring. Eaters are cannibals. If they eat me while I'm still alive the agony is exquisite. Unless, of course, I die during their meal. Then it gets messy for them. Not a pretty sight," the Phoenixian said.

"You must be an escaped mental patient." Slasher Steve "People don't die and come back!"

"Phoenix's do." The wounded man wiggled his eyebrows.

"You ain't a phoenix."

"I am by adoption, which is why I'm called the Phoenixian. It seems obvious to me, but you seem a little slow on the uptake today,

Steve. I assume I can call you Steve?"

Ignoring the question, the serial killer undid his own locks and pushed his prey down the stairs. The Phoenixian tumbled, flipping over twice before landing in a twisted mess on the basement floor.

"Not bad, but you can do better. At least I hope you can, Steve," the Phoenixian said, sitting up and holding his dislocated shoulder. "Otherwise, you're just wasting my time."

Slasher Steve walked down a couple of steps and shut the door behind him. The basement had no windows and was plunged into darkness. The serial killer flicked on a long tube lighter, the kind that was used in fireplaces and furnaces. The flicking light from the tiny flame bathed him in an eerie light, at least as far as the pictures in his mind were concerned.

In his other hand, he had his favorite blade. He had named it Beth and occasionally slept with it cuddled to his side. On lonely nights, he had been known to rub its smooth side all along his bare skin and imagine things that would give other people nightmares, but he found terribly exciting and erotic.

"I'm not going to waste your time. I'm going to waste you, Phoenix," the Slasher said, brandishing the knife, snaking it back and forth in the flame light.

"I told you I'm called… aw, what the hell. Phoenix is fine."

The killer waited for the Phoenixian to scurry backward, but he couldn't even do that right. Instead, his prey stood up, brushed himself off, and tripped the killer so the knife plunged into the Phoenixian's abdomen.

"It's been a while for me. I was getting a little anxious," the Phoenixian said. "This is better. Sorry if I made you stab prematurely. We can take our time next time if you want."

Slasher Steve had had enough. Normally he enjoyed the torture and mind games, but only when he was the one playing them. This nonsense wasn't fun at all. Time to change that.

Beth the Blade raised and dove again into the man's flesh, with a grace Steve knew no human woman could ever match. Together he and Beth started with the extremities and he helped her work her way in toward the torso and organs, thrusting in and out like a bad lover who couldn't find his way in the dark. There were screams, loud and long, but the Scranton Slasher found them disturbing, interspersed as they were with orgasmic laughter and frantic shouts of "More! More!" and "Don't Stop!" whenever he slowed down.

Finally, the light faded from the prey's eyes and his body went limp. The killer had a ritual of standing over his kills, just to drink in what he had done with his eyes. There were times it took him hours as he replayed memories of the murder, the screams, and the terror. His eyes would gaze longingly into the dead eyes of his victims, lording it over the slain. Sometimes he'd even dress them up real nice and pretty if they had given him a lot of pleasure as his way of saying thanks. As much as he tried, this time Slasher Steve just couldn't do any of it. The smile on the dead man's face took away all the fun.

The killer left him where he lay. There would be time to dispose of the remains later. Steve just wanted to get away and de-stress. He climbed the steps, locking the door behind him. After cleaning up and changing, he collapsed on the couch. Using the remote, he turned on the TV and searched for something mindless.

Sometime later he fell asleep and was awakened by pounding from the inside of his basement door. Startled he leapt up and looked around thinking it was a raid. He waited but no doors were kicked in, no bubble lights brightened the night. Yet, the pounding continued.

Cautiously, he unlocked and opened the door. The Phoenixian was standing upright, unhurt and undead on the top step. Worse, he was stark naked and apparently very happy about something.

"Not bad for a first time. Let's go once more," the Phoenixian said. "Only this time with feeling."

The serial killer freaked out more than a bit, thinking his latest victim had returned from a grave he hadn't even had time to put him in. In his mind, there was only one reason for the dead to come back—to take revenge. They didn't come back and ask you to kill them again. The Phoenixian stepped up onto the ground floor. Slasher Steve mistakenly took the action for an attack and shoved frantically. Again, the Phoenixian tumbled down the cellar steps. The killer raced down after him. Once he caught up to the Phoenixian, he started kicking the fallen man, with each blow getting out more of his frustration at being afraid. Finally exhausted, the serial killer stopped and screamed, "Why aren't you dead?"

"It doesn't take," the Phoenixian said, spitting out a tooth loosened during the beating.

The Slasher examined the floor. There wasn't a single drop of blood anywhere, but the cement and stone were singed like it had been burned. The Phoenixian had fresh bruises and cuts from the kicks, but his naked body didn't have a single stab wound. His blood-soaked clothes were also missing, which was impossible. Steve had bricked over any way out of the basement years ago. The only exit was the stairs and there was nothing to hide clothes behind or under.

"What the hell happened to your clothes? And all that blood?"

"I'm not sure I want to tell you, Steve. I don't like the way you're acting," the Phoenixian said, his face twisted up into a pout.

Slasher Steve started kicking again, this time focusing on the head and groin. Again, the killer's foot pummeled his victim until he was too exhausted to go on.

Seconds later, the Phoenixian was crawling across the stone floor. "Better, Steve, but still too tame." He pulled himself to where the knife that had previously killed him was lying. The Phoenixian lifted it up as an offering to his attacker. "Here, use this. You really don't have the lower body strength to make the kicking work. Maybe if you took up jogging or biking it would help. Some weight training wouldn't hurt. Try low weights and high reps."

"Don't touch Beth!" And with a primal scream, the killer fell upon his prey and stabbed him again and again until he was sure the Phoenixian was dead.

The serial killer kept a shower in the basement, which made it easier to clean up after his fun. His clothes were covered in blood. It wasn't the first time, but this time it made him feel dirty. He stripped out of his clothes and moved under the shower in the corner. There was no curtain or door, just a nozzle, a drain, a bar of soap, and a bottle of bleach. He used three of the four to get himself clean.

The serial killer was washing his face and had his eyes closed when the corpse and the blood on his clothes caught fire. Everything was consumed in the flames. In the heart of the fire, an image of a fetus could be made out. It grew quickly until it was a baby, then a toddler, then a boy, and finally, a man who was free of any wounds or damage.

The Phoenixian stood and stretched, stopping to crack his neck. Looking around, he saw Slasher Steve scrubbing himself clean. The formerly dead man snuck up behind his latest killer.

"Want me to scrub your back?"

The serial killer's scream was reminiscent of a little girl's. He ran to the other side of the basement, his wet feet making him slide and crash into the wall, where he cowered and covered himself. "Get away from me, you freak!"

"You're starting to hurt my feelings, Steve," the Phoenixian said. "I've been nothing but nice to you."

"You came back from the dead. People don't do that. Only Jesus can do that," said Slasher Steve. "Oh my God! Are you Jesus?"

"Yes, I'm Jesus, come here to have you kill me and then shower with you," said the Phoenixian. "Pass the soap."

"Really?" Slasher Steve said.

The Phoenixian rolled his eyes. "No, not really, but let me get this straight – you believe in Jesus?"

"Sure. I was raised by a religious family. I'm born again," the killer said.

"Boy, do I know how that feels," the Phoenixian said. "How do you think your savior feels about your hobby?"

"Never really thought about it. It doesn't matter. I accepted Jesus into my heart, so I'm saved no matter what I do," Slasher Steve said.

"Boy, are you in for a surprise," the Phoenixian said.

"Why? Do you know Jesus?"

"No," said the man who would not stay dead.

"Before your time, I guess," Steve said.

"Actually, no. I was around, just not in the same part of the world. I did manage to get crucified a few dozen times. It was amazing, but other opinions might vary. Of course, I was younger then and less discriminating. But enough about me. I have a proposition for you, a way for both of us to get our jollies with no one having to get hurt. Besides me of course."

Slasher Steve became very aware of his wet, naked body. "I keep telling you I'm not..."

"Yes, yes. You're not gay. I've picked up on that. I do listen when you talk. Steve, I'm not talking about sex. I'm talking about death, specifically the giving and receiving of it. It's a perfect symbiotic relationship. You get to kill and I get to die," the Phoenixian said.

"Why do you want to die? And why don't you stay that way?"

"I once did a good deed for a magic creature, saved its child. I was given a reward. Whenever I die I am reborn in fire, but my nervous system was rewired in the process. Pain brings me pleasure, the worse the agony is, the greater the rush. Death is the ultimate high. I want you to give it to me," the Phoenixian said.

"What do I get out of the deal?" Slasher Steve said.

"I should think it would be obvious. You can kill and torture me to your heart's content. You can push the limits of your knowledge on what the human body can take. Improve your technique. And since I can't stay dead, no one else needs to get hurt."

"But that's part of the fun," Slasher Steve said.

"This way there is less of a risk of getting caught. Let's be honest – how long do you think you'll last in prison? With your homophobia I don't think you'd enjoy being someone's wife, do you? Assuming you don't get the death penalty. Think of this as your chance for rehabilitation," the Phoenixian said.

The serial killer mulled the offer over and looked down at himself. "I assume I can wear clothes."

"Of course."

"I prefer to take my time. I also like to shackle my victims to the wall. And I like screaming. Frightened, not happy."

"I can work on that. Just treat me like any other victim," the Phoenixian said, holding out his hand.

"All right. Let's give it a try," agreed the serial killer, shaking the hand of the eternal willing victim.

Things went well for a couple of weeks with both Slasher Steve and the Phoenixian getting what they wanted. But as so often happens in new relationships, even symbiotic ones, what flares so brightly at first burns out in time.

On their fourth Tuesday together, Slasher Steve was upstairs playing a video game, *Divine Reckoning II*. It was long past time for him to have come downstairs and perform his relationship duties, but he hadn't.

There was banging on the basement door. He tried to ignore it, but it kept getting louder. Finally, Steve got up and unlocked the door. Without looking or speaking he returned to the couch and picked up the game controller.

"Steve, were you planning on coming down anytime soon?"

"For someone who's been around for thousands of years, you sure are bitchy. I'll come when I'm done with my game. I see you got out of the shackles," Slasher Steve said, not even looking up from his flat screen.

"Dislocated and broke my wrists, used a little blood for lubrication," the Phoenixian said.

"See, Phoenix, you didn't need me. You started by yourself. I bet it hurts like hell. My extra knife's over there. Why don't you go amuse yourself with it?" Slasher Steve suggested.

"It doesn't work if I do it myself or else I wouldn't exactly need you, would I?"

The serial killer turned so his back was to his victim and crossed his arms over his chest. "It's not like you appreciate what I do."

The Phoenixian stepped closer and began to rub Slasher Steve's back. "Of course, I do."

"Really? Then how come you're always telling me what to do and how to do it? *Steve, slash higher to get the artery. Steve, puncture my eyeball. Smash in my testicle with that hammer. Stick your knife in deeper and swirl it around.*"

"It's just feedback to help you get better at what you do. Constructive criticism," the Phoenixian said.

"It's not constructive, Phoenix. Nothing I do seems to be enough for you. I can't even cut off your ear right."

The Phoenixian shrugged. "It did take you two tries to get the entire thing and it is one of the easier body parts to slice off."

"That's exactly what I'm talking about. No matter how hard I try, I just can't seem to satisfy you. Well, it's not me. It's you. I never had any complaints from any of the others," the serial killer said.

"Do you think that might be because you killed them?"

Slasher Steve spun and went back to the couch. "I'm done talking, Phoenix."

The Phoenixian spoke again, trying to be comforting, but was ignored. The immortal sat down on the other end of the couch and picked up the second controller, hitting start to join in the tournament play.

Still, Slasher Steve remained silent.

"I know the guy who made this game." Still nothing. "His name's Lucas Wilson." Dead air. "I helped out a friend of his whose whole family got kidnapped."

"What'd you do? Get them back?" asked Slasher Steve, his interest overwhelming his pout.

"Not exactly. I let the friend kill me. A bunch of times," the Phoenixian said.

"How did that help exactly?"

"Trust me, Steve, it was crucial."

"Right. It seems all you can do is get killed. Would it hurt you to pick up after yourself? Maybe wash the dishes you use? Or chip in some money for food? I usually take money from my victims to make ends meet, so this little arrangement has left me a bit on the cash-poor side." The killer started slamming controller buttons, taking out his aggression on the virtual avatar the Phoenixian was playing.

"That's the kind of passion I'm talking about."

"Shut up and die!" Slasher Steve said.

"Sure. Up here or in the basement?" the Phoenixian cooed.

"I meant in the game."

Promptly, player two's character died.

"You just gave up," griped the serial killer.

"You said die. I obliged so we could have some us time in the real world."

"That's not going to happen tonight."

The Phoenixian's brows moved together and he frowned. "Now, Steve…"

"Unless you manage to beat me in the game."

"Fine, if that's the way you want it."

The killer scowled. "It is."

The Phoenixian smiled "Bring it."

The rest of the game was fast and furious – Slasher Steve was killed fast which made him furious. "How'd you do that? I've never seen those moves before."

"Secret attack combos. I told you I knew the guy who made it. We were stuck together in a house for a long time. He taught me a few tricks," the Phoenixian said.

"You cheated," whined the serial killer.

"No, I just played better. You never asked if I knew how to play. You assumed you could beat me because you thought you had played the game more. You were wrong. Take it like a man," the Phoenixian said.

The serial killer stood up, threw his controller against the wall and stormed toward the door.

"Where are you going?" the Phoenixian said.

"Out," said Slasher Steve.

"But you said you'd kill me if I beat you."

"I lied," said Slasher Steve. The door slammed behind him and the van's tires peeled rubber as it left.

It was five hours before Steve returned. The Phoenixian had spent the time trying to clean up the house. He had even ordered food on a credit card that he had memorized the number for, as they tended to melt when he was resurrected, and even paid extra for it to be delivered to the woods.

The dishes had been washed, the floor mopped, and the windows cleaned. He had even scrubbed the toilet.

The Phoenixian hoped Slasher Steve would accept the peace offering. The problem was the killer hadn't come home alone. A girl, blond and unconscious, dangled in Steve's arms as he came in the door.

"What the hell is this?"

Seeing the Phoenixian's angry reaction, Slasher Steve grinned. "What's it look like?"

"We had an agreement. An arrangement. Of the exclusive variety," the Phoenixian said.

Slasher Steve's grin got even wider. "Yeah, about that. It's not really working for me. I think I should start killing other people."

The girl woke up just in time to hear the bit about killing and began screaming. Her struggles against the man carrying her were rendered ineffective by the duct tape that bound her hands together. Steve did put her down so she stood next to him, his arm wrapped around her neck in a traditional headlock.

"I think you should leave so I can stab this girl in peace," Slasher Steve said. The poor young lady screamed even louder.

"I can't allow you to do that," the Phoenixian said.

"What do you care?"

"I may be the biggest bastard on Earth, but that girl only gets one life. You are not going to take it from her," the Phoenixian said.

"How are you going to stop me? Get in the way of my knife as I stab her?"

The Phoenixian answered with a swift kick to the groin. As the serial killer bent over, the man who could not stay dead pulled the girl out of the killer's grasp and whispered, "Stay in the corner."

She obeyed with only some mild whimpering.

Slasher Steve straightened up and pulled a knife out from under his jacket. "You'll pay for that."

"Sorry, but we're going Dutch now. Besides you're not much of a killer."

The Phoenixian grabbed the killer's wrists, pinning them to his side. The serial killer was surprised at the man's strength, then realized that the Phoenixian had never fought back before. The Phoenixian head-butted the serial killer in the nose, breaking it. The pain made Slasher Steve attack back in the only way he could—he bit off the Phoenixian's nose and kept biting, swallowing bits of flesh and blood in the process. The maiming made the Phoenixian laugh, but the sound had a different edge to it. He let go of the killer's wrists, who promptly brought the knife up into his heart.

"Congratulations. Now you are an eater and a drinker. About time you broadened your horizons." The Phoenixian wrapped his arms around the killer, not letting go. Slasher Steve struggled but was knocked to the ground as the Phoenixian died. The killer was partially pinned by the corpse. The girl who had finally stopped screaming, started again when she saw the man who had said he would kill her push the naked dead man aside and stand up.

"You're next, girl. Don't make me chase you or it'll be worse for you when I catch you," the serial killer said, a real smile back on his face for the first time in weeks.

The girl decided to take her chances and ran anyway. The killer methodically followed after her, not wanting to risk letting her get away.

The chase of predator and prey went through the living room, bedroom, and back into the kitchen where Steve finally caught her. Before Steve could hurt her for having the tenacity to run from him, smoke billowed out of his mouth.

Slasher Steve screamed, then doubled over holding his stomach. He turned to glare at the corpse and saw it burst into flame. The killer's insides felt as if they were on fire and for good reason. They were.

Once the dead body was consumed into ashes, the flames moved on, lifting the serial killer up off the ground until he too was on fire. Now it was his turn to scream, but they weren't happy sounds. The wailing and cursing went on until the air was too hot for him to breath. Several convulsions followed and the Scranton Slasher became still, but the flames weren't yet done with him. The fire licked and ate away at the serial killer until nothing remained of his body but several piles of ashes.

The girl watched in horror and wonder as the flames coalesced into a man.

Her savior looked down at the ashes and shook his head. "What a waste." Walking over to the girl, he removed the tape from her wrists. "Are you okay?"

"I am thanks to you."

"What's your name?"

"Sadie."

"I'm the Phoenixian."

"How can I ever repay you?" she asked, hugging and kissing the naked man who had rescued her. She couldn't help but notice his toned and muscled body and that he was well endowed. Almost being killed and then being saved had left her feeling excited and grateful, with an incredible urge to do all sorts of appreciative things to her fiery knight who was without his armor. With her body language, she made it clear enough that a blind man could tell how she wanted to thank him. The Phoenixian didn't seem to notice.

"Sadie, you don't happen to have any latent homicidal tendencies, do you?" he said.

"No, I'm straight," she said.

The Phoenixian rolled his eyes back in his head. "No, I mean do you like to kill things."

Sadie's eyes squinted, her amorous feelings starting to fade away as the feeling of being worried and creeped out replaced them. "No."

"That's too bad, but you look like a smart girl with lots of potential and the ability to learn quickly. Tell me, Sadie, would you consider running over me with the van a few times?"

"If you die, you'll just get all fiery again and be okay?" she asked.

"Yes," he answered.

"And the fire won't hurt me?"

"Not if you're careful."

"Okay, I guess," she said, the disappointment clear on her face that she wouldn't be getting naked, but her eyes shone, still more than a little curious about the turn in events.

The Phoenixian smiled and took her arm in his. "This could be the beginning of a beautiful friendship. Tell, me how do you feel about constructive criticism?"

BE CAREFUL
A tale of Jinn & Tonic

"Hello Edgar," said the blonde woman in the leopard fur, diamonds, and stretchy pants as she looked down her nose at the others waiting in line for hot dogs. Melinda tried to make it as clear as possible to anyone watching that this particular curbside eatery cart was far beneath her.

The hotdog vendor's face turned dark crimson and his jaw muscles visibly tightened.

"Hello, Melynda, you thieving, adulterous bitch," Edgar said. "Go away."

Melynda's smirk revealed much about her character. "Glad to see that you've come up in the world."

"Exactly. I'm not with you anymore," Edgar said.

"This is the infamous ex-Mrs. Tonic?" came a voice from inside the bun warmer. "I'm disappointed. I expected horns or at least a crooked nose and some boils."

"Hey, you're talking about the woman I love," said a well-muscled man standing behind her.

"There's no accounting for taste," Edgar said.

"That's how I've always explained our partnership," came the voice from the bun warmer.

"Tommy, not now," Edgar said. "Scram!"

"Edgar, after all we've meant to each other, you can't mean that," said Tommy's disembodied voice. "I mean where will I go, what will I do?"

"Frankly Tommy, right now I don't give a damn," Edgar said. "And you know I meant them."

"Oh, that's okay then," the jinn replied from inside the bun warmer. "But with the food inspector as my witness, I swear I will never go hungry again. Although with this slop you serve, it's a tough call. I mean, squirrel chili? Ready? Is that the best we could manage?"

"At these prices? People should be happy it's not rat chili like our competitors," Edgar said.

"There's more meat on a rat, so we'd get more mileage out of one, but I guess you're right. People are funny about eating vermin. Maybe we should try to start a citywide open season on rats. It'd be fun and a win-win situation. All those guns on the street could be put to good use. And in this economy, the city gets the money for the hunting permits and people get fresh meat, not to manage the satisfaction of hunting and killing their own food. Plus, it would take the stigma off a perfectly good food source and there would be less vermin running around the sewers and subways," Tommy's voice said.

"There are more than enough vermin right here for my tastes," Edgar said. The crowd in line was laughing at what they thought was street theater and it made the former Mrs. Tonic very upset.

"Trevor, are you going to let him talk about me that way?" Melynda whined, putting her hand on her forehead like she was having a bout of old-fashioned vapors.

"Hell, no, baby," Trevor said, taking off his coat and rolling up his shirt sleeves.

"What's the big deal?" came Tommy's voice from the bun warmer. "From what I hear that's how everyone talks about her. The story I heard is she was doing the gardener, postman, cable guy, and a guy impersonating a Jehovah Witness who just wanted in on the action. You were the guy she ended up with because you weren't embarrassed to be seen with her in public and were the least afraid of vernal disease."

"Edgar, I'm warning you. Don't talk about Melynda like that," Trevor said. "And I was her mailman and personal trainer. Unlike some people, I have ambitions and delivering mail paid the bills while I worked on building my workout empire."

Edgar laughed at the muscle man. "Empire huh? That must not mean the same thing it used to. And I'll call a treacherous slut a treacherous slut, but it's not me saying it. It's my partner."

"What partner? It's just you pretending to be a ventriloquist," Trevor said.

Edgar rolled his eyes. "Why does everyone think that?"

"Well, your lips don't move when I speak. And because, unlike me, most people can't fit in a bun warmer, even after a diet," Tommy said.

"Speaking of diets, Melynda, you've really plumped up." The ex-Mrs. Tonic gasped in mock horror. "Stretch pants are not a good look for you."

"I'll have you know that these are designer jeggings," Melynda scolded.

"You always were a sucker if someone told you something was designer. I figure that part of the reason you went for Trevor is because his last name was Valente," Edgar said. "Pity about you tubbing out, but maybe you can hire a personal trainer to help you work off those pounds. It's a shame you don't know any good ones."

"Hey, what do you think I am?" Trevor said.

"I'm afraid I can't say with ladies present," Edgar said.

"Thank you," Melynda said, primping herself up.

"Oh no, not you. I meant them," Edgar said, pointing with his chin to a pair of obvious cross-dressers standing in line behind his ex.

"Thank you," they purred in unison.

"My pleasure, ladies. What can I get you?" Edgar said to the cross-dressers.

"Wait a second. We were here first," Melynda said.

"Right, like I'm going to sell you two anything after what you did," Edgar.

"You have to. It's the law," Trevor said.

"So, you're a lawyer now, Trevor? You couldn't pass an open book trainer test, so you had to make up your own certification," Edgar said.

"I hear he couldn't figure out how the book opened," Tommy said.

"Watch it. And I'll have you know there are many people who have signed up for Valente certification," Trevor said.

"You, your mother, and your slut hardly count as many," Edgar said.

"Actually, maybe he's learning impaired. He might count one, two, many," Tommy said.

"And he was dumb enough to quit his job at the post office for it."

"That's it. We're throwing down," Trevor said, rushing Edgar with his fists up in front of him.

Edgar threw a knish up in front of Trevor who reflexively reached up to catch it. Edgar stepped in and slugged him right in the breadbasket and the large trainer doubled over in pain.

"That wasn't fair," Trevor gasped.

"And the two of you stealing eleven million dollars from me was?" Edgar said. "Get out of here."

The transvestites each ordered 2 dogs with everything and a soda. Edgar turned to make their order and Trevor attacked him from behind, grabbing the back of Edgar's collar and shoving his head toward the hot water that contained the hot dogs.

Caught off guard, Edgar barely got his arms up in time to stop his face from being burned. Worse, Trevor had the muscle and the leverage.

"Tommy, a little help here please," Edgar shouted.

"Your wish is my yadda, yadda," Tommy said.

A hand materialized out of the steam and grabbed Trevor by the front of his shirt. The hand was followed by an arm in a pin-striped suit. The rest of the suit with the jinn inside followed and backed Trevor away from the cart. He then looked around. Sweat started to bead on his forehead and he casually stepped so his back was against the cart.

"Touch my friend again and you'll wish you were never born," Tommy said, trying to make like the hot dog cart wasn't having the same effect on him as a safety blanket on a toddler. "Hey Edgar, see what I did there?"

"Hilarious Tommy," Edgar said.

"And?"

"And thanks," Edgar said. Trevor shoved Edgar. Tommy and Edgar both grabbed hold of either of the muscleman's shoulders and pushed him back so now all three men were standing in the middle of the sidewalk. Tommy's eyes darted around, looking at the cart and the buildings and his grip loosened. "I think the cops want to talk to the two of you about your theft. Maybe we should deliver you ourselves."

Tommy was suddenly three shades paler. "Hey Edgar, about that…"

Edgar looked over and realized his friend was having a panic attack from being out in the open. He put a hand on the jinn's shoulder. "Go on, Tommy. I got this."

"Thanks, buddy." There was no smoke. Tommy simply disappeared from the street back into the safety of his bun warmer.

"Now to get the cops for you two," Edgar said, pulling out his cell phone.

"No can do, sweetie. The statute of limitations ran out last week, so we're back in the country," Melynda said.

"What do they carve that statute out of?" Tommy said. "Is it near the statute section? It's not gonna replace the Statue of Liberty, is it?"

"Either way, we'll see about that," Edgar said, flipping the phone open.

"Put it away, Edgar. They have us. They have outsmarted us. We never had a chance. Best just to let them go," Tommy said.

"What are you talking about?" Edgar said.

"And what does it matter to you? After all, you have your own genie, so anything you wish for is yours," Tommy said.

"You hate being called a genie."

Tommy's head flashed above the cart and winked at Edgar.

Edgar finally caught on. "Fine. You win. Just leave me now to my happiness."

"Wait a second. You have a genie? I get half of anything that was yours."

"We're divorced. You don't get half of bupkus."

"I never signed any papers," Melynda said.

"The hell you didn't. You left them waiting for me when you left," Edgar said.

"But I never mentioned anything about a genie in there. Half of him is mine," Melynda said.

"Doesn't apply. I got him after you spilt with Captain Musclehead here," Edgar said.

"I want him," Melynda said.

"You can't have him," Edgar said.

"Edgar, you don't have to put up with this. You can just wish them away," Tommy said.

"I can? I mean, I can. I wish the two of you were out of my city," Edgar said.

An instant later, the pair vanished.

"Tommy, you giving out wishes now? You haven't had to do that since Bulfinche Moran freed you from your bottle," Edgar said.

"I figured you deserved some payback. They ran a con on you're and took everything you had. It's time we returned the favor," Tommy said.

Edgar smiled. "I like it. Especially since when we're done, we can turn them over to the cops. A lot of good people lost their jobs because of these losers. And the idiots don't realize that the statute of limitations stopped running when the DA filed charges against them."

They turned to the applause of the two transvestites. "Your performance art is always great."

"I'm not a performance artist. I'm a hot dog vendor, Trixie," Edgar said.

"And I really love how you always stay in character, but this time you pulled out all the stops. I simply adored those special effects. I couldn't even see the light source for the hologram. Simply amazing. I have a friend who sets up off-Broadway plays. He'd be able to help you get a bond and you can move up in the world."

"Thanks, Trixie, but I tried that. Too much stress. I'm poorer but happier now," Edgar said.

"Art for art's sake. I applaud you. Keep up the great work," the transvestite said.

Edgar took care of feeding the crowd that had gathered, then turned to his bun warmer. "So, where'd you send them?"

"To Jersey. Well, technically, right above the Jersey side of the Hudson. Close enough that they were able to swim to shore," Tommy said.

"Too bad," Edgar said. "What's the plan?"

After the sun had gone away for the night and the dinner rush was over, Edgar packed up his cart and pushed it inside the garage attached to Bulfinche's Pub, the bar he worked outside of and where he rented a space to store the cart.

He held out a bottle in front of his bun warmer. "You sure about this? I know how you hate open spaces."

"The better part of a century in a bottle tends to make one a little agoraphobic," Tommy replied. They both knew he was more than a little afraid of being outside. It was practically crippling.

Tommy transferred himself into the bottle.

"Paddy–" The leprechaun owner of Bulfinche's Pub. "– drilled a bunch of micro-holes in the bottle. Too small to see, but enough that they can't trap you in there," Edgar said.

The pair walked outside and headed toward the subway stop blocks away.

"Are you sure they are despicable enough to try to steal me from you?" Tommy said.

"Pretty sure," Edgar said and held up the empty whiskey bottle so he could use the glass like a mirror to see behind him. Sure enough, Melynda and Trevor were trailing them. "And for once, Melynda didn't disappoint."

"Edgar, he's got a lead pipe. I don't want you getting hurt," Tommy said.

"I appreciate that, so let's make this easy on them," Edgar said, putting the bottle down on the sidewalk as he bent over to tie his shoe.

Trevor raced up behind him, pushed him over and scooped up the bottle before running away.

Melynda ran by and flipped Edgar the bird. He laughed once the pair disappeared around the corner.

"I can't believe Edgar had a genie," Melynda said, locking the door of their hotel room.

"I can't believe we went through eleven million dollars and that we're broke now," Trevor said.

"If you hadn't invested all our money so badly, we wouldn't be," Melynda said. "I mean, the sock juicer?"

"It's a logical way to get back the electrolytes you lose while working out. It should have been a huge hit. Besides, it was my idea to come back to see what else we could get out of Edgar," Trevor said. "And look how good that turned out."

"How does this thing work?" Melynda said.

"I think you have to rub it," Trevor said.

Melynda took her hand and wrapped it around the neck of the

bottle, moving it up and down.

"Oh, that's good. Rub it faster," came the voice from inside the bottle. Melynda obliged. "Faster. Harder. Oh, that's it. Don't stop." The voice began to moan, then scream until, finally, steam exploded out of the top of the bottle.

Tommy appeared in front of them in his pin-striped suit and spats and slowly backed into a corner before he could let himself talk. "Oh, that was fantastic. Anyone ever tell you that you have great hands?"

Melynda smiled and daintily moved her hands under the light. "Actually, I did consider becoming a hand model once."

"I can see why. You've had a lot of practice doing that. I can tell," Tommy said, winking at Melynda.

Trevor stepped in front of his woman. "Hey, enough of this. Don't we get three wishes?"

Tommy rubbed his chin. "I suppose. But it's three wishes collectively, not each. I'll give you each one, but you'll have to agree on the third."

The couple looked at each other like they won the jackpot.

"Me first. I wish…" Trevor said.

"Shh!" Tommy said, putting his index finger over his mouth. "I decide when the wishing happens, steroid breath."

"Says who? We have the bottle, so you have to listen to us. We're your masters," Trevor said.

Now that had been true for Tommy at one point, but no longer. "Masters? Maybe you haven't heard, but this is the United States of America. You never heard of the thirteenth amendment?"

"That the one you use when you don't want to testify?" Trevor said.

"No, it the one that gives you free speech," Melynda said.

"Actually, it's the one that outlawed slavery," Tommy said.

"But you're a genie," Trevor said.

"What? You think you're better than me cause I'm a genie? You a racist, bub?" Tommy said.

"I'm no racist. Some of my best friends are, um, genies," Trevor said.

"Oh, you've dealt with genies before. Great. So you know that I'm the one in the driver's seat then. No wishes unless I say so," Tommy said.

Trevor held up his hands and moved them in little circles as if trying to get Tommy to move along. The jinn just stood and stared.

"So?" Trevor said.

"No, I have to say it, not you. To tell the truth, I'm just not feeling it. I got to tell you, it gets real lonely there in that bottle and I think it needs some more rubbing before I'm ready for wishing. You up for it?"

"Sure," Melynda said, giggling.

"Now wait a second. You were making all sorts of weird noises when she was rubbing the bottle. What exactly does the rubbing do?" Trevor said.

"Oh, it's no big deal. Nothing to concern yourself with. Now, if you wouldn't mind, I'd like to be alone with her when she's doing the rubbing. Nothing personal, you're just kind of ruining the mood for me, so amscray," Tommy said.

"Now wait a second. Where am I supposed to go?" Trevor said.

"There's a bathroom right there," Tommy said. "Go or no wishes for you."

Trevor grumbled but went.

"Now, Melynda, the last time was good, but I want this time to be great. Do you think you could help me out by making some noises of your own?" Tommy said.

"What kind of noises?" she said.

Tommy wiggled his eyebrows. "Don't play coy with me. You know what noises I mean."

Melynda giggled. "I guess I do."

"Okay, let me get back in the bottle. Okay, let's get the rubbing started. Good, now the noises. Maybe jump up and down a bit? Great. Louder."

Then Tommy joined in and kept the noises going until he heard Trevor's hand hit and go through the sheetrock wall in the bathroom.

"Okay, that was great. Hey, Trevor, you can come out now," Tommy said and Trevor did, cradling his injured extremity. "Hey, what happened to your hand?"

"Nothing," he grumbled. "Do we get our wishes now?"

"Sure," Tommy said. "Would you like to go first?"

"Yes. I wish I was rich and stayed rich always," he said.

Tommy snapped his fingers. "Done."

"Really? I'm really rich?"

"Yes, you're Rich," Tommy said.

"Prove it," he said.

"Open your wallet and look inside," Tommy said.

The personal trainer took out his wallet and pulled out some bills. "This is the same amount of money I started out with."

"Money? You didn't say you wanted money. You said you wanted to be Rich and you are," Tommy said.

"What are you talking about?" he said.

"Look at your driver's license," Tommy said.

He did. "Wait a second. It says my name is Rich Valente. But my name's Trevor."

"Not anymore. Now and forever, you are Rich," Tommy said, pulling a lipstick out of Melynda's purse. "Here, write your name on the mirror with this and watch what happens."

He took the lipstick and wrote Trevor on the glass, but the red streaks reformed into the word *Rich*.

"This is stupid. I want another wish," the newly named Rich said.

"Sorry. No," Tommy said.

"Why not?"

"Because you didn't phrase it in the form of a question," Tommy said.

"Really?"

"Nope. I said you got one and one is all you get. Now, it's Melynda's turn. What do you wish for?" Tommy said.

Melynda looked at Tommy, then at Rich. "It's personal. Could he wait in the bathroom again?"

"Rich, off into the potty with you," Tommy said. Rich reluctantly went.

"Okay. Here we go. I love sex. I can never get enough, but sometimes men turn me down. They are not interested, married, or even gay. I want to be able to have sex with any cute guy I want," Melynda said.

"I understand. Now, you see what happened to Rich there. Wishes have to be worded carefully. Now if you just wish for sex, it might be mediocre or even bad, so you should have the wish be as descriptive as you want," Tommy said.

"I want it good. I want it hard," Melynda said.

"That's it. So, what's your wish?"

"I wish every cute guy I see would ride me like a stallion," Melynda said.

Tommy twirled his hand in her general direction. "Granted."

"Really?" she said.

"Absolutely," Tommy said. "I'll prove it. Rich, will you come out here?"

The man did and suddenly was overcome. He walked toward Melynda who bent down on all fours and he climbed on her back like she was a horse. Melynda in turn, her limbs and back strengthened by the wishing magic, ran over the room, bucking like a bronco.

"How do I make this stop?" she screamed.

"You have to throw your rider off," Tommy said, opening the door. The pair rode out into the hallway, racing up and down the carpeted floors. Tommy hit her bottom as she trotted by, making her rear up, but Rich wasn't so easily thrown. It took the better part of three minutes before he fell off.

"This isn't what I wished for," Melynda said.

Tommy shrugged his shoulders but stayed pressed against the corridor wall. "Actually, it is."

"But I…" Melynda stopped and looked at a bellhop she thought was hot. An instant later she was back on all fours with the hotel employee riding her like it was the rodeo.

"Wow, he's good. Much better than you, Rich. He's not even dropping that ice bucket," Tommy said.

When Melynda's rider was finally thrown free, she rushed into the hotel room and slammed the door behind her. Tommy and Rich opened it and followed her in.

"How come you're not riding me?" Melynda asked.

"Because I'm a jinn. I mean genie," Tommy said. "I'm exempt. All right you two, crunch time. Only one wish left and you have to both agree on it," Tommy said.

"We have to wish to undo our wishes," Melynda said.

"No way. My wish is stupid, but I'm not wasting another wish to undo it," Rich said.

"What about me?" Melynda said. "I have to go through life with men climbing on my back for pony rides?"

"Not my problem. What did you wish for anyway?" Rich said.

Melynda blushed. "Never mind. What are we going to do about the third wish?"

"How about a Lamborghini? That one couldn't get misinterpreted," Rich said.

"I'm not wasting it on a car. Figure out something that will be good for us and cancel out my problem," Melynda said. "We need something great."

"That's for sure. We certainly didn't deserve this nonsense," Rich said.

"That's it! Let's wish that we get what we truly deserve," Melynda said.

"Baby, you're a genius," Rich said. "Genie, we wish that we get what we truly deserve."

"And you agree to this wish, Melynda?" Tommy said.

"I do," she said.

"You too, Rich?"

"I do," he said.

"Then by the power invested in me by the lamp union, I pronounce your wish granted," Tommy said.

Which is when the sprinklers when off, only over the pair's heads. And there was a knock at the hotel room door.

Melynda opened it to see Edgar, who it turns out she still thought was cute.

"Oh no," she said as she dropped to all fours and Edgar climbed on her back. The pair rode down the hall.

"Tommy, I have no idea what is happening, but so far I like it," Edgar said, then added a yee-haw.

Rich stepped out to try to pull Edgar off his girlfriend, but she spun suddenly, slamming Edgar's fist into Rich's face three times. The first blackened his eye. The second broke his nose while the third knocked out some teeth.

"You got them to wish for this?" Edgar said.

"It's all in the interpretation," Tommy said.

"Get off of me!" Melynda screamed.

"Is this harming her?" Edgar said.

"Nope. The magic protects her from hurting herself," Tommy said.

"Then I'm staying on, baby," Edgar said. "Think I could ride her back to Bulfinche's Pub to show the gang?"

"You could get her there, but would you really want to go inside?" Tommy said. They both knew that magic, curses, and the like didn't work inside that particular bar, which meant Melynda would return to normal for the time she was there.

"Good point," Edgar said. "Maybe once around the park then."

"I wouldn't stay on long. The cops are on the way here to arrest them. Luckily, females and homely men only. Don't need anything thrown out of court because the arresting officer took the suspect for a ride."

"We can't be arrested. The statute of limitations was up months ago," Rich said.

"Actually, they filed charges against you while you were out of the country. That stops the clock, so you can be arrested and put away once you return," Edgar said.

"I'm getting out of here," Rich said, running toward the elevator.

"You can't leave me like this," Melynda screamed.

"Watch me," Rich said. The elevator stopped working the instant he pressed the down bottom. "Screw this. Stairs are a great cardio."

As he went to open the stairwell door, it beat him to it, smashing him right in the face and knocking him out. A pair of female detectives stepped out of the stairwell holding pictures and arrest warrants. Rich matched the picture, so they rolled him over and cuffed him. Edgar let himself be thrown off so he didn't have to answer any awkward questions about exactly what he was doing.

Melynda had just managed to stand when the detectives cuffed her hands behind her back. "Melynda Tonic, you are under arrest for embezzlement, theft..." They read off a long list of charges.

Meanwhile, Edgar held out the bottle and Tommy vanished inside of it and started to walk away.

"You Edgar Tonic?" asked one of the lady detectives.

"Yep."

"Thanks for the tip," she said.

"My pleasure. She ripped me off and I lost everything I had. Had to close up shop and lay off a bunch of good people because of what they did," Edgar said.

"Wait, it's not my fault. Edgar has a genie in that bottle that changed Trevor's name to Rich and is making cute guys ride me," Melynda said.

"Sound like you've had a little too much of what was in that bottle," one of the female detectives said.

"I don't know. Being able to get every cute guy interested in me might be nice," said the other, rousing Rich.

"I have one piece of advice-be careful what you wish for," Edgar said, smiling as they took his ex-wife and her trainer into the elevator and off to jail.

Terrorbelle

*Half-ogre & half-pixie, this former
Daemor moved to New York to work for
Nemesis & Co. to continue her fight against injustice.*

UGLY AS A PICTURE

Author's note: This story takes place before the events of Fairy Rides The Lightning.

Why do guys always pick the worst possible time to call? Not that I'm exactly inundated with guys calling me, but this one was an honest to goodness movie star and darn cute to boot.

"Hey, Joe."

"Hi, Terrorbelle."

"What's up?" I said while firing shots at a C-Rex that was rampaging outside a school in Tenafly, New Jersey during a football game.

"Were those gunshots? Did I call it a bad time?"

"No, it's not a bad time," I lied and fired again.

"Belle, are you actually taking a call during a battle?" Nemesis shouted at me as she tried to shoot the C-Rex's kneecap out.

"No," I lied again.

"I can see you on the phone, Belle," Nemesis said.

"Well, kind of," I admitted.

"I can't believe you. Right now, you're on my time so hang up the phone and get to work before this giant, bovine, lizard beast that the pimple-faced mage unleashed kills somebody," Nemesis said.

"Okay boss," I said. "Joe, can you call me back?"

"How long?"

"A half-hour." Then the C-Rex's tail hit me and threw me 25 feet into the field. "Maybe I should call you."

What's a C-Rex? Believe me, it's a good question because before today it thing didn't exist and hopefully would cease existing shortly. We were facing down Milt Dietrich, a teenager and a geney. Not a jinn, who lives in a bottle and grants wishes, but one that can change the genetic makeup of living things.

In this guy's case, he was able to combine the genetics from two different being and make something new out of it. Milt somehow managed to get a hold of some T-Rex DNA. And using his magic combined it with a bunch of cows from a slaughterhouse to give the C-Rex enough mass that he was over two stories tall. His basic body shape was that of a T-Rex with a few differences. For one thing, his arms were longer and had hooves, its skin tone was that of a Jersey cow with white fur with black spots. The beast's head looked like you slapped the mouth of the T-Rex on the head of a bull, complete with horns. The tail was that of a T-Rex but it had that little furry thing on the end like a cow does.

Oh, it also had udders.

Instead of using his powers to work with a zoo or biological lab or even enter the school science fair, Milt was disrupting a high school football game. His reason? Because a cheerleader had turned him down when he asked her to a dance and her football player boyfriend beat him up.

Now we had to stop it from killing any high school kids or their families in the stands. On the plus side, most of the people had at least some common sense and were running away.

Unfortunately, when he saw what we were doing to his creation, Milt ran off. Every time we hurt the C-Rex, its wound healed almost instantly. Since mystic hybrids don't necessarily have a healing factor of their own, we figured Milt hadn't gone far and was using his magic to mend its wounds.

I was also kind of annoyed because, despite being the only one on the team with wings, I was stuck fighting on the ground. Rudy, the Valkyrie daughter of the god Thor, was writing Morningdour, a winged horse whose color matched her red hair.

Rudy was firing from above while Nemesis and I fired from ground level. Ganieda, who is Merlin's twin sister, was floating on her flying carpet examining the beast for weaknesses.

"Shooting this thing isn't working. We need to switch tactics," Nemesis shouted. "Gani, have you figured out how to stop the thing yet?"

"I'm working on it," the white-haired mage replied.

"Well, work faster. How much longer do you think you're going to need?"

"I have no idea. I've never had the chance to examine dinosaur DNA before. Inspiration could hit me in thirty seconds or take me hours."

There was a screech of tires and a loud metal crash. In their haste to escape from the monster, a school bus and a car collided. Neither would give the other the right of way and they went boom. Even better, it happened right in the middle of the only exit that didn't involve driving over the football field.

The crash attracted the C-Rex's attention and it charged toward the parking lot. Rudy and Morningdour dive-bombed his horned head a few times to distract him, so of course, the bovine dinosaur tried to eat them both.

Unfortunately, they only slowed the giant creature. Because of the crash, nobody else was getting out of the lot. I put my gun back in its holster and ran towards the school proper.

I've fought a couple dragons in my time and alongside another and was trying to come up with something that might work on the C-Rex. It worked and I finally had an idea.

When I got inside the school, I found a large group that hadn't run into the parking lot. They were at the windows and recording the creature on their phones. I'd seen it happen before. They'd post it online and people would think it was a hoax, claiming it was CGI or some such. People are just not willing to believe the things that are highly unusual.

"Tell me there's a fire hose in here," I said to a bunch of high schoolers.

"Why? Are you going to squirt that thing with water? What good will that do?" said a teen girl who I ignored.

A nerdy kid with glasses he pointed down the corridor. "There's one over there."

I ran as fast as I can. A girl who looked like she was about seven years old followed me. I opened the metal and glass door and started pulling the length of hose out.

"Hi. My name's Alexandra."

"I'm Terrorbelle."

"Your wings are pretty," the girl said. I had gotten rid of the long coat I normally wear to cover them. Even though I can't fly, my wings are razor-sharp and can be used as weapons in a fight. Case in point, I got to the end of the hose and use my upper right wing to slice through the end of it.

"Thank you."

"I like your hair. Did your mommy let you dye it pink?"

I tied a knot in the end of the hose with the nozzle. "Actually, my hair is pink naturally."

"That's so cool. I was trying to get my mom to let me dye my hair pink but she won't let me."

"Listening to what your mom says is very important. It's her job to take care of you, so if she doesn't want you to dye your hair, you shouldn't. However, when you're older and if you still want to, you can always do it then."

"Are you going to use that against the cowasaur?"

"Actually, we're calling it a C-Rex. And I'm going to try," I said.

"Are you going to kill it?"

"Maybe. We have to make sure doesn't hurt anybody."

The girl nodded as if she understood exactly the reason for that. "Well, be careful, Terrorbelle."

"Thanks, Alexandra. You too."

I hustled back outside. The C-Rex had reached the parking lot and was trampling through cars like Godzilla on a bad day. Its tail swiped and threw a car back towards me. I dove out of the way. I may be strong enough to bench press a car but if I tried to catch one I'd be crushed.

People had given up trying to get out with their cars and were running. One of Rudy's explosive rounds took off the creature's horn. Within seconds, it started to grow back.

The beast wasn't too far ahead of the bleachers on the edge of the football field, so I sprinted to the top, taking the bleacher steps three at a time. I built speed so when I got to the top I leapt over the rail and into the air and let my wings kick in. There's not enough magic on Earth for me to fly, but I can glide and hover enough to leap higher than the bovine dinosaur. As I started my descent, I threw my makeshift firehose lasso around the creature's neck and used my wings to slow my fall. I swung underneath the creature then I pulled hard once I landed. The C-Rex tilted over to the side which is when the boss hit its knee like a linebacker and the thing came down. I wrapped the hose a couple times around the thing's jaws and tied a knot.

Next, I ran towards right arm hoof and wrapped the hose around it and tied a knot then repeated it on the left.

The C-Rex tried to get up, so Nemesis grabbed a hold of the horn that was nearest to the ground and pushed down.

The airborne member of Nemesis & Co. hovered above the supine bovine dinosaur, which turned out to be a bad idea. Feeling trapped, the C-Rex lashed out in a new way and all four of its udders blasted streams of milk that would have put a working fire hose to shame. Rudy and Morningdour hit the ground and Gani and her flying carpet went butt over boobs twisting into a car.

The winged horse nodded that she was okay and a milk-soaked Rudy rushed the creature's tail and grabbed hold. Unfortunately, the Valkyrie didn't have enough traction, maybe due to her dripping milk everywhere and the tail swung side to side with her hanging on like a water-skier.

While the C-Rex was focused on them, I managed to tie it's legs together and then went down to where Rudy was still getting a ride on the tail. I grabbed hold of the tail from the other side and together we slowed it enough for us to tie it with the remainder of the hose.

Gani stomped over, her typically high-end white outfit also dripping with milk, and cast a spell over the whole hose, making it strong enough to hold the beast.

The C-Rex was hogtied and the people safe.

"You guys need me to go get you some cookies to go with that milk?" I said.

They each made a face at me.

"What are we going to do with it now?" I said.

"We could have a barbecue and feed lots of people with the leftovers," Rudy said.

"I bet your dad would be able to make it something delicious out of it," I said. Her father Thor was quite possibly the best cook I'd ever had the fortune of eating with.

"We could keep her as a mascot," Gani said.

Nemesis scowled. "If we're going to have a mascot it'll be a griffin or nothing. We could just put it out of its misery."

"I don't know about that, boss." Rudy walked up to the creature's head and looked into its sad eyes. It'd stopped struggling. "She seems somehow different. And scared."

"That would be because the one who created and controlled it isn't doing it any longer," Gani said.

"Can't you track the kid?" Nemesis said.

"Sure, but unless we get some of his genetics, I have to figure out a power signature from his magic and track him down by that. As to what we should really do with the C-Rex, how about we call the DMA and dump disposal of the creature in their laps?"

The boss shrugged then pulled out her phone and called the director of the Department of Mystic Affairs, Uncle Sam himself.

"Sam, it's Nemesis. I've got something you're going to love. Just send a couple of agents and an animal containment unit." Nemesis gave him the rundown. "No, I'm not kidding. A cow with a T Rex. The thing is about two stories tall. Yeah, it seemed dangerous a little bit ago but calmed down a lot since its maker stopped trying to make it attack and kill people." She listened for a second. "Great. We'll see them soon."

It wasn't too long before the DMA agent showed up.

"A pleasure to see you again, Agent Hightower." Hightower was a jinn or what most people would call a genie. They're indentured to whoever holds their lamp or bottle. It seems DMA Assistant Director Winston got a hold of Hightower's bottle a while back and basically gave Hightower her freedom and she's been working as a DMA agent ever since. "You're flying solo? I thought the DMA made you guys work in pairs."

Hightower smiled and I heard a voice behind me.

"They do."

I turned to see a blonde woman who I hadn't noticed there before. "A pleasure to meet you, Agent…."

The woman rolled her eyes and smiled but it seemed out of habit rather than from any real joy.

"Donna Winks. But we've met before. About five times."

"I don't think so. I have an excellent memory."

"That's what they all say. I was cursed so no one remembers me."

"That's terrible. I bet Gani could help with that."

"And that's the fourth time you suggested that. She's tried twice and failed both times. Not that I didn't appreciate the effort. We'll take this creature off your hands. We have a preserve for beasts like this."

My phone rang I looked down at the caller ID and it was Joe calling back.

I looked up having the feeling I'd been talking to someone but there wasn't anybody there. "Hightower, you got this?"

It was odd that Sam sent her out into the field on her own.

"We've got it," Hightower said.

"We? You got a pixie in your pocket?"

Hightower pointed to a woman standing there that I hadn't noticed before.

"Nice to meet you, Agent…"

The woman rolled her eyes. "Just take your phone call."

I stepped away and answer.

"Hi, Joe. Thanks for calling me back."

"No problem T-Belle. Did you slay your Dragon?"

"It wasn't a Dragon. It was a C-Rex."

"A dinosaur?"

"Part dinosaur, part cow."

"A cowasaur? Are there a lot of those?"

"As far as I know this is the only one. And we're calling it a C-Rex. To what do I owe the pleasure?"

"Can't an internationally renowned actor call up a beautiful woman for no reason?"

"I suppose but you've got a worried tone in your voice so I figured you had something on your mind."

"I know you help people out of jams and a friend of mine is in a bad one."

I almost agreed without knowing what I was agreeing to. Even though I liked Joe, I'd long ago learned that that would be a stupid move. Unless he was somebody I trusted totally like Nemesis or Murphy.

"Your friend having trouble with monsters or the mystic?"

"Not the kind you mean. The person giving him trouble is human but that doesn't make him any less of a monster."

"Tell me what's going on so I can figure out if it's something I can help with."

"My friend Roger recently signed a deal to star in a TV show. But it's with a network that's obsessed with squeaky-clean family images."

"And your friend is not so squeaky clean?" I said.

"Roger's a good guy but he separated from his wife three years ago but wanted to keep it quiet because her uncle is a well-connected movie producer and he hoped that might help him get work so they never filed for divorce. When he found out he might be up for this series he finally pushed a divorce because California is a community property state. He didn't want his ex to have a claim on his money from this show. He's been dating another woman for the last six months. Without checking with him, the studio played up his relationship to his former wife's uncle in their press releases.

"There were rumors right away that he was cheating on his wife so this one paparazzi managed to get pictures of him and his girlfriend in the pool house at a party. Because he's not a big deal yet, the photographer couldn't get much for the photos so this scumbag decides to cut Roger a deal. He won't sell the X-rated photos and in exchange, Roger makes him his personal manager and gets twenty percent of all his future earnings."

"Sounds to me like he's better off just coming clean to the show people," I said.

"I suggested that too but the studio actually put in an archaic morals clause so in theory, they could fire him for dating a woman who's not his wife. The scumbag could prove that the photos were taken the day before he filed for divorce. It gives the studio an excuse to fire him at any time including during salary negotiations if the show becomes a hit."

"What you want me to do?".

"I thought maybe you could talk with a guy or maybe figure out a way to get the pictures."

I think I was insulted. "You know I'm not exactly a leg breaker, right? You can't make a threat if you're not willing to follow through." I certainly wasn't willing to break somebody's legs because someone was worried about losing a job. "Plus, this isn't like the days were there were only photos and negatives. If this guy has any brains at all he's uploaded pictures and videos to multiple clouds so there's no way to get rid of the pictures. I'd say your friend better talk to the studio about the situation and issue a press release announcing his divorce and sometime later put out a second announcing his relationship with his girlfriend."

"You're not wrong as far as my friend goes but I heard some things about this photographer so I did a little checking. Apparently, he's personal manager for no less than two dozen celebrities of varying degrees. There are lots of rumors that he got them to sign with him the same way he's threatening Roger."

"So, you want me to stop this guy from blackmailing people?"

"Yes. You're the only person I know who might be able to do it. Well, there's this one hitman I met once while researching a part but I don't want to go that route. Will you do it?"

I sighed. "I'd have to check with my boss to see if I get the time off."

"Just call in sick."

"Not a good idea. Last time I tried that, she didn't buy it. Nemesis came to my apartment and kicked in my door."

"You got a tough boss."

"You have no idea. Hold on."

I hit mute and walked over to Nemesis

"Boss, can I get the next few days off?"

"Why?"

"A friend of mine in California has a friend who is having trouble with a serial blackmailer. He wanted me to see if I could do anything to help matters."

Nemesis raised an eyebrow. "Who's this friend?"

Rudy jumped up and down like a school kid who wanted to answer a question. "I bet I know. It's Joe Hunk, isn't it?"

I nodded.

Nemesis frowned. "You're giving up on Murphy?"

I could feel my cheeks start to flush. "Yes… No… I don't know." Murphy is one of my best friends and I've had a crush on him since the day we met. Problem is, he still hung up on his dead wife. He's risked his life to protect me and even save my life. He's the one I call when I have nightmares. But we've never been out on a date or anything like that, despite my not so subtle suggestions. "There's no one I'd rather be involved with than Murphy, but I can't wait around for him forever."

Nemesis said "Hmm, I suppose. Then again, there are people who are worth waiting for."

Nemesis didn't warm up easily to people or have many close friends, but she considered the bartender one. Murphy has that effect on people.

"So, can I get the time?"

"I can spare you for three days. Less if we find this geney Milt."

"Thanks, boss."

I stepped away and turned the mute button off. "Joe, I got three days."

"You really think you can stop a blackmailer in three days?"

"I'm hoping it won't take that long."

"That be wonderful. That means we could spend the rest of that time together."

I could feel my cheeks reddening.

"If you can get to JFK I'll have a private jet waiting for you and you could probably be here in a few hours."

I chuckled. "I don't think I need to wait that long. Hold on again." I hit mute one more time. "Gani, you have any doors in LA?"

"A few. Grauman's Chinese Theater is probably the easiest to not get noticed using."

"Thanks." I took the mute off. "How soon can you get to Grauman's Chinese Theater?"

"Maybe half an hour."

"Good. I'll be there and waiting."

"How?"

I smiled. "Don't worry about it. See you in thirty."

A DMA crew had arrived to transport the C-Rex. Agent Hightower seemed to have everything well in hand. Still weird that she was flying solo. I went over and picked up my yellow trench coat from where I'd dropped and walked toward the school with the rest of the team.

Gani found a wall on the school and drew a mystic sigil on it and then touched it. An elevator door appeared then opened. The four of us, plus Morningdour, got on and Gani hit the office button. A few seconds later the elevator opened onto the offices of Nemesis &Co.

Rudy and her winged horse got off first. "Have fun, Terrorbelle. But not too much fun." The pair went into the break room were Rudy poured herself and the horse cups of coffee.

"Rudy, wring out your sleeve if you need milk," I said. Rudy rolled her eyes and Morningdour whinnied.

"Remember, Belle, three days. We find this Milt and I'll need you back sooner. Who knows what he'll make next. I'm sure there are more types of DNA wherever he got the T-Rex sample. We'll start tracing those possibilities."

"I understand and appreciate it."

"Be careful, Belle." Nemesis walked out toward her office. Gani hit the close door button and swiped the wall to reveal a new rack of buttons each time. She found one with Grauman's Chinese Theater handwritten on a piece of white tape and hit it. A moment later it opened in a hallway in the famous theater.

I got out and Gani followed me.

"I'm good, Gani. I got twenty-five minutes to kill. I figure I'll look at some of the handprints in the cement."

"I know but I want to meet this Joe fellow. Check him out and make sure he knows enough not to hurt you."

"Gani, he's human. I'll also several times stronger."

"I wasn't talking about physically."

"You don't have to do that." She was acting like a protective mother. Part of me was embarrassed but a bigger part of me appreciated it.

"Don't have to. Want to."

We spent several minutes checking out old movie stars handprints. I found the Marx Brothers handprints and took a picture. I sent it to Murphy. We're both huge fans.

Gani smiled but her eyes looked sad. "Dagonet performed with them a few times in Vaudeville." Dagonet was better known as the Infinite Jester and was both a jester and knight in Camelot. He was also Gani's on-again, off-again romance for over a thousand years. They loved each other dearly but couldn't make it work long term.

"I wish I could've seen that."

"I snuck in once. Dagonet was made for Vaudeville."

"Too bad none of that got captured on film," I said."

"True, but even back then Dagonet was smart enough to know that if he became famous, years later people would be asking why he was so young or why the person he was pretending to be looked *exactly* like an old movie star. Although he was in *Pardon Us*, a Laurel and Hardy movie."

"I bet he stole the show." Dagonet was a natural born ham.

"Not really. He was only on-screen a few times probably for less than a minute total. He and Negral played extras in a prison. They were on the run from something chasing them and needed to pick up some money. Dagonet knew some people and got them the job. Although I will say it's quite telling that while you're waiting for a date with another man, you're thinking about Murphy and sending him pictures."

"It's not like that…" But I stopped talking as I spied Joe in sunglasses and a baseball cap coming over toward us. He gave me a hug. I hugged back, careful not to crash him.

"Joe, this is my friend and coworker, Gani."

Joe extended his hand. "Pleasure to meet you.

Gani frowned and raised her eyebrows but took the hand and then touched the back of it with her finger. There was a small pop of air rushing in to fill the space where his body had been. In its place, there was a frog who was now in Gani's palm.

"It's nice to meet you as well, Joe. I just wanted to let you know that I'm very fond of Terrorbelle and would be *very* upset if anyone should ever hurt one who is so near and dear to my heart. We understand each other?"

The frog in her hand was trembling but managed to nod his amphibian head up and down. "Very good."

Gani handed me the frog, spun and walked away.

"Wait a second. Aren't you going to turn back?"

"I need to change clothes. You know the drill. The spell is a classic. The bit about it having to be true love or princesses is bunk. Any old friend will do. Ta-ta."

I walked inside the ladies' room which was empty and kissed the frog on top of his head. A moment later, Joe was sitting in my palm. Even as strong as I am that much weight appearing that suddenly toppled me forward and I landed with one hand under his butt and the rest of me on top of Joe.

"Now it's a party," Joe said smiling.

Just then an older woman walked into the bathroom, gave an exasperated little yell then turned and stormed out like she was offended. Luckily, she didn't seem to recognize Joe. He was back as he had been, including the baseball hat and sunglasses.

I untangled myself and stood up and then offered a hand and pulled him up.

"Sorry about Gani. She's a little protective."

"It must actually be nice to have somebody who cares about you that much, although I can't say I'm too fond about having been turned into a frog. But as long as I'm back to normal, no harm, no foul. Besides, maybe I can use it sometime for a role down the road. Although why did she smell like sour milk?"

I smiled. Usually, it would have been me covered in milk. "It's a long story."

"Great, you can tell me on the way and I'll tell you more about the blackmailer. By the way, how did you get here so quickly?"

"I took an elevator."

"But elevators go up and down not cross country."

I chuckled. "Obviously you don't know about as much about elevators as you think you do."

"My car is this way."

Of course, Joe had a Bugatti, a ridiculously expensive sports car.

I wanted to drive but I let Joe. Heaven forbid I dented or wrecked it. I doubt I could afford the repairs.

"What do we do first? Intimidate the guy?" Joe cringed when I crossed my arms and frowned. "I'm not saying we hurt him or anything. Maybe just scare him a little bit so he stops."

I shook my head. "There are times something like that works but only when the person you're intimidating won't go to the cops and squeal on you. This guy has access to national media and could make a big stink." Besides, in New York, everybody from the mayor down to the cops is already intimidated by Nemesis. In LA, that would take a lot of extra work and I'm not sure she'd be willing to do it.

And going that route isn't exactly something I would want to explain to the boss.

"Then what's the plan?"

"Go talk to your friend and anybody else he's done this to and see what we learn."

I was just tickled that I wasn't going to have to be bait for once.

We went out to lunch at some fancy LA restaurant where a meal cost as much as I made in a day. I looked at the menu and must've made a face.

"Don't worry, T-Belle. You are here as my guest. I've got all your meals and lodging covered."

"Lodging too? Wow. What hotel will I be staying at? Motel Seven or something in Beverly Hills?" I said with a mischievous grin.

Joe grimaced like a kid caught with his hand or another part in the cookie jar. "Actually, I was thinking you would stay with me."

"Have a lot of guest rooms, do you?"

Joe kind of shrugged his shoulders. "I do but I wanted you to know that you don't have to stay there if you don't want to. There are other options available to you." The last line his face got it's a ridiculously confident expression and a smile that was part of the reason he got twenty million a picture. "My room, for instance."

"Joe that's very sweet of you but I couldn't kick you out of your own room and make you sleep in your guestroom. That just wouldn't be right."

Joe blinked and took a deep breath. He seemed really confused by how dense I was being. Poor guy didn't realize I was messing with him.

"No, I wouldn't be sleeping in the guest room." The look he gave me would have made women watching a movie swoon.

"But I doubt your couch would be very comfortable. That wouldn't be very nice of me."

Joe reached out and took my hand in his. "Terrorbelle, I was hoping we could stay in my room together."

"Oh, you have two beds?"

"No. We'd both be in my bed."

Took him long enough to get to the point. "Joe you're a nice guy. And good-looking too."

That was an understatement, I'd seen folks using glamour who weren't as good-looking as he was.

"I like you. A lot. But we've only been on a couple of dates and I certainly don't know you well enough to spend the night in your room. I don't know about the women you usually date but for me, sex is a *big* deal. I need to more than like somebody. If that's a problem, I'm happy to book myself at a hotel. I can ask Gani to bring my motorcycle here and handle this all on my own."

"No, no, no. It's not a requirement or deal breaker. I just hoping. You're like nobody else I've ever met and I want to get to know you a lot better."

"That sounds great but I just wanted you to know where I stood."

"Thank you for setting me straight. I hope you don't think less of me," Joe said.

"I don't. You're a guy, but you respected what I said and didn't try to push anything. Which is good for your sake because I have a tendency to push back and quite frankly I could take you without breaking a sweat."

"Of that, I have no doubt." Joe looked at the door. "Here's Roger now."

Joe made introductions and his friend joined us at the table.

"I appreciate you coming out all this way to help, Terrorbelle, but Joe told me what you recommended and I'm not really sure what you can do. I've already come clean with the studio and just hoping for the best."

"Joe mentioned that this Justin Papara had a lot of clients all of which he got by blackmail. I like to see if we can't put a stop to that and put him out of business."

"That would be wonderful but I don't think you'll find a lot of help. People in this business being blackmailed are letting themselves be blackmailed for a reason. For them to help with the police investigation means that they'd have to release the secrets they're willing to pay to hide. I just don't see that happening."

"Maybe, but if we can prove something serious enough, one person might be all it takes.

"At this point, I'd be willing to do it but I don't have any recordings or texts so it's my word against his. Someone going overboard in trying to convince an actor to be him isn't going carry a lot of jail time in LA."

"I'll take any information you have on Papara including any offices he might have."

We had an amazing meal and Roger left.

Joe rubbed his palms together. "What's our next step?"

"We need more information. I think it's time for me to go and see for me to go visit Mr. Papara and see if he can make me a star."

We visited another friend of Joe's and I get some headshots done quickly. Although they weren't so much headshots as head and boob shots. The photographer felt I should play to my assets and I am rather well-endowed to the point where I'm certain I'd be crippled with back pain if I were human.

I got to wear some gogreous outfits and the photographer did things with lighting and makeup where even I thought I looked pretty.

The trick was doing it so my wings didn't show up. The photographer simply digitally erased them. I wore a sleeveless billowing dress I could hide the wings under and made an appointment to meet with Justin Papara.

I called and sent over my headshots. Less than an hour later I had an appointment.

Justin Papara came out into the waiting room all smiles. Maybe not all smiles. He also had a bit of a belly and a rather well-made hairpiece

He held his hands out and took my right in both his as I stood up. His eyes never left my cleavage.

"What a pleasure to meet you, Belle. Come into my office so we can chat." He put one hand on the small of my back low enough so that his pinky was on my butt. Normally I would've hurt him for that but I was playing a part. It wouldn't do good to break character. Or his pinky.

"Today's been a great day already. Do you know who I met in the lobby of this building?" I said.

"No. Who?"

I pulled out my cell phone and opened to a picture. "Joe Hunk. He even let me take a selfie with him." This was all part of the plan, so I showed him the picture.

Papara raised an eyebrow and smiled. "I'm not surprised. Papara Management deals with a lot of the rich and famous. In fact, we helped make a lot of them rich and famous."

"So, Joe Hunk is a client of yours?"

"No, not as such but there's been some talks. Things both sides are considering so you never know what will happen. But enough about movie stars. I'm here to talk about you and your career. I'm thinking we start with some photos."

"But I already have shots from one of the best in Hollywood. You think I need new ones?"

"I wasn't thinking about headshots. I was thinking something a bit more to get you a little more media attention. I can get you placed in some men's magazines and generate some buzz."

"Are you talking nudes?"

"I am, but tastefully done. Nothing too graphic. It's a proven way for a woman to get ahead in Hollywood."

Not from what Joe's told me. Although it works on occasion, most of the time it's just a way for a woman to make some money until she gets a break. She rarely gets a break because of the pictures. But if I did it, he would have something to blackmail me with if I did actually become rich or famous

"Belle, we also should talk about the hair. Pink is a little too out there for the mainstream. I think we should make you a blonde, maybe a redhead. I mean it shouldn't be that big a deal since you've already dyed your hair."

I didn't bother to explain to him that the pink was my natural hair color.

The receptionist's voice came over the intercom. "Mr. Papara…"

"Ms. Parks, I'm in a meeting and not to be disturbed."

He leered at me when he said that. Maybe he thought it was sexy instead of creepy.

"Sir, you're going to want to come out here."

"Ms. Parks, is it worth your job?"

"If I didn't make you come out here, you'd fire me."

Both his eyebrows shot up. "Excuse me a minute, Belle. Apparently, a matter of some importance requires my immediate attention. I'll be back momentarily."

Papara went out the door and shut it behind him. I got up and put what looked like a memory stick into the USB port of his laptop and what looked like a wireless charger minus the wire in the cell phone he left on his desk. About three seconds after I inserted both of them, they seem to melt right into the equipment.

That went smoothly. Now to eavesdrop on how my distraction was working in his waiting room.

"Mr. Hannk, what a pleasure." Hannk was Joe's real name but the media gave him the nickname Hunk and it stuck. "Welcome to Papara Management. What can we do for you today? Looking for new management?"

I heard Joe chuckle. "No, nothing like that. I was in the building today because somebody in one of the other offices won a contest to have lunch with me and brought me in to meet the rest of their friends at work. On my way out, I bumped into an unusual woman with pink hair who was very voluptuous and muscular. She really stuck with me and I noticed her coming in here. We took a selfie together and I sent it to the casting director for a new movie I'm doing. We have a part for her that I think would be perfect. It's a major supporting role with billing in the credits for a female action hero. I think it's something she could pull off. Is see your client?"

"Why, yes she is," Papara lied.

"Excellent. I'd like to set up something between her and the casting director. Between you and me, if she can act at all, she'll get this part based on my recommendation alone. Would you mind letting me talk to her so I can give her the casting director's information?" Joe said.

"Sadly, she's in a meeting now with another casting director and I would hate to interrupt that and ruin her chance for that part. A starring role actually, but I doubt the movie has the budget that yours will. How about you give me the information and I'll set things up."

"I have a better idea. Give me your card and I'll pass it on to the casting director so she can set something up directly with you."

"Sounds great." I surmise that Papara must have given Joe his card because they said goodbye and I heard the outer door open and close.

Papara came back in.

"Actually, my dear, I think we might be able to postpone the photo shoot for a little bit. Something has come up that would be perfect for you and I think I might be able to finagle you a shot. It's a major motion picture. Normally they wouldn't be talking to just anybody but I got enough juice in this town to get you an audition. But for me to do that, I'm going to need a contract signed by you."

Papara opened the top drawer of a filing cabinet and pulled out a pair of stapled documents, put them on his desk and flipped to the last page.

"So, all you have to do is sign right there and you'll be a client of Papara Management and I'll start working immediately on your behalf.

I picked one up and starting leafing through it.

"You don't have to read that. It's pretty standard for the industry."

"You get thirty-five percent of all my earnings? That seems awfully high. And that carries over even when you're no longer my manager? I'm not sure I'm comfortable with that." I put the contract down. "If you don't mind, I'd like to have my uncle take a look at it."

"Is he in the business?"

"Not exactly. He's a partner in a law firm and makes a ridiculous amount of money. I couldn't even afford his rate of seven hundred an hour but luckily I'm his favorite niece," I lied.

Papara bit his bottom lip. "I see." He scooped up both contracts and tossed them in a desk drawer, then went back over the file cabinet. He opened the second drawer and pulled out two different contracts.

"You know I have such confidence in you that I'm willing to give you an amazing deal. I will manage you for only twenty percent and just for the time I'm your manager. Give this contract to your uncle and let's see if we can hammer something out within the next day or two because I'm not sure how long this opportunity will be good for."

"Thank you, Mr. Papara," I said.

"Please, my clients are like family and once you sign, you will be family. Call me Justin. And actually, my afternoon just freed up. I'd be able to take those photos right now."

"That's something I'd have to think about. My uncle is a busy man. I like to get this to him as soon as possible to make sure he can read them over quickly."

Papara nodded. "That's a good idea. But let your uncle know he can call me directly if he wants to hash out any details."

I walked out of there with the urge to go disinfect my hand.

"You were able to bug his office?" Joe asked.

"Not exactly, but yes."

Gani is a genius and gets bored easily. A while back she came up with ways to combine magic and programming to get information off computers, clouds, and phones. Basically, I entered her spell through the ports of his laptop and his computer. I had a corresponding app on my phone that let me go through what he had on the hard drive as well as listen to anything happening in the vicinity of either, which included phone calls.

"I found at least twenty-seven people he's blackmailing." Like I suspected he was keeping the photos and video on a cloud. The spell signed in using his own passwords that he was kind enough to save on his devices.

"Can't you delete them?"

"I could but that would alert him that something was up. We don't want that. Not yet. You want to take a look at the names?"

Joe frowned. "All of them are successful enough that they would be rather reluctant to come forward to put him in jail."

Gani's app beeped. "Wait. He's calling someone."

I hit a button on my phone so we could listen in.

"Isn't this technically illegal?"

"There is no technically about it but we're not planning to use any of this in court. Or get caught. Now shush and listen."

"Hi, Tiffany. Justin Papara. I just heard about you landing the part as the host on a brand-new kids show. I can't tell you how happy I am for you."

"Thanks, Justin. You know I've been trying for five years. Looks like I'll finally be able to give up waitressing."

"That's great. I was just calling to let you know I got a deal for those photographs we did years ago. Quite a coincidence??"

"I bet it was anything but," Joe said. I nodded and put my finger on my lips for him to be quiet.

"Justin, you can't do that. It would torpedo my big chance. This gig is good for a million dollars a year for me. Those photographs get out, parents' groups will protest and they'll fire me. I'll be screwed. You don't have my permission. I revoke it."

"Actually, you can't do that. You signed a contract giving me all rights to those photographs. I own them, not you, and I can do whatever I want with them."

"Justin, please don't do anything with them. Have a heart. If you do that you'll ruin my life and everything I've been working for."

"That would be a real shame. However, there are two things that might be able to persuade me to keep those photos where no one will ever see them."

"And what would that be?" Tiffany's voice was filled with a mix of anger and sobs.

"First you sign with me to be your manager at twenty percent of your earnings."

"But I already fired you as my manager because you didn't do anything for me. Twenty percent of my earnings for doing nothing is an awful lot."

"But I would be doing something – not ruining your career. And eighty percent of your earnings is a lot better than not having them at all, don't you think?"

Tiffany sniffed. "Fine, you're my manager. What else? More money?"

"No money at all. You know I always found you attractive…"

"No. Absolutely not. I turned you down when you took those photos and I'm turning you down now. I'm in a committed relationship. With a *woman*."

"Perfect. You can bring her too if you like. Or not tell her. It's not like you'd be cheating on her with another woman, only a man. I'm afraid this part is non-negotiable. Once a month for the duration of your show."

"But I don't want to have sex with you."

"However, I want to have sex with you so I guess you'll just have to decide which is more important. Being a star for the little kiddies and joining me once a month or seeing how many more years you can handle being a waitress."

Tiffany was outright sobbing now. "I need some time to think about it."

"Of course. Take all the time you need. I'll call you back in an hour to set something up for tonight."

"You bastard."

"Well, that much is true. Mom was a bit of a slut and I never knew my dad. See you later, sweetie."

Five hours later, Justin Papara showed up at Tiffany's apartment door bearing gifts. He didn't go with the traditional flowers or candy. He had a bottle of tequila and a bag from a lingerie store.

He had to the ring the bell four times before Tiffany opened the door. Her hair was a mess, she was wearing no makeup and a ratty T-shirt with just as ratty sweatpants.

"Oh, how sweet. You dolled yourself up for me. I don't care what you wear because you look just as good naked. Although you're gonna start out wearing this." Papara pulled a French maid's outfit and threw it at her.

Tiffany held it up like it was the most disgusting thing she'd ever touched. "There's not a whole lot of material to this."

"That's the whole point."

"No. I don't want to do this. I don't want to have sex with you."

Papara shrugged his shoulders. "That's your right. No one is forcing you to."

"And what happens if I don't have sex with you?" Tiffany asked.

"I sell those naked pictures of you to the highest bidder and you more than likely will get fired from your job hosting a kiddy show."

"And if I do have sex with you?"

"No one sees the pictures."

"How about we just have sex one time and you give me all digital copies of the pictures?"

"Why would I do something stupid like that? Then you won't pay me the twenty percent of your pay to be your manager and you won't have sex with me once a month."

"That is the very definition of forcing me to have sex with you."

"There's no gun or knife to your throat. You can say no."

"But then my dreams die."

"A sad story but most dreams do die. So, are you going to dress up in that outfit or do I have to go look for buyers for those pictures?"

Papara stopping sounding so cocky when he heard the applause. He literally growled as he turned to face me, sitting in the corner and clapping my hands.

"That was that was really good. Tiffany, you were wonderful. I really felt your performance. Totally fantastic. Justin, you, on the other hand, were a little bit over the top with the maniacal, blackmailing rapist vibe. Think we could do it once more with feeling?"

"Belle? What the hell are you doing here?" Papara had a look on his face that looked like he was trying to have a bowel movement then it turned into a lear and a grin. "Oh my. Belle is the woman you are in a relationship with. This is too good. Both of you can have sex with me or else I'll ruin your career and your lover's."

"I don't think you understand. We're ruining your career. We recorded everything that's happened here."

"Wait a second. You don't want to do that. I'm a wealthy man. I can make both of *you* wealthy too. I'll give you half a million…" I rolled my eyes. "… each if you don't turn this stuff over to the cops. Hell, I'll even destroy all copies of Tiffany's photos. And I'll get you a starring part in the next Joe Hunk movie."

"But you'd still be in business to hurt other people. I'm not so wild about that. I'll make you deal. You give each of us that half-million, destroy Tiffany's fake pictures, and you sign this contract," I said holding out three identical pieces of paper.

"What's this?" Papara said.

"You don't have to read that. It's pretty standard for the industry. It just says that you're folding Papara Management services and releasing all of your clients from their contracts."

"I'd won't do that. That's my main source of income."

"True, but that money won't do you much good in the penitentiary now will it? I think there's a few hundred dollars limit on what you can spend in the commissary. And once this comes out your business is going to fold anyway and all your clients will have no choice but to pull out from you."

"So, if I sign this neither one of you will show this video to the cops or any law enforcement or news service?" Papara said.

"It says that right there in the contract. Neither one of us will do any of that."

Papara was still waffling. "I could beat both of you up and destroy the recording."

I stepped forward and grinned. "I'd love to see you try."

Papara stopped pretending to be a tough guy and stared at the papers.

"Or we could just call 911, say exactly what happened on the recording and get it on the Internet within the hour. If that goes public how many other blackmails could you be charged with?" I said.

"Fine," Papara growled. I handed him a pen. I signed all three so Tiffany and I each got a copy too.

"Now you delete all her pictures."

"I don't have them on my phone."

"On a server? Or cloud?"

"Both actually."

We watched over his shoulders as he went to the cloud I already knew about and signed into a server that I didn't. Now the spell left me a backdoor into both so I could delete the rest of his blackmail material.

"Now I can just open up a new company. I bet you all my old clients will be fine with it. Pleasure doing business with you ladies."

Papara walked to the front door and opened it, where he was greeted by a detective and two uniformed officers.

"You're under arrest," said the detective who turned Papara around, handcuffed him then read him his rights.

Apparently, he didn't want to listen to the right to be silent part.

"You lying bit…" He had some unkind words for us. "You said you wouldn't give the cops anything. I will sue both of you. I got the contract to prove it."

"We didn't give it to the cops. However, a friend of ours was actually running the recording remotely. The contract didn't cover what *he* did with it."

Joe had enough pull to arrange for the cops to be part of the sting and to wait until we were done. He only gave them video of the blackmail part, not the contract part.

The cops dragged Papara away as he screaming promised to all of us.

"I don't know how I can thank you both. This really would've ruined my life," Tiffany said.

"It was all Joe's idea," I said.

"But it was all T-Belle's work."

"Do you think you might consider being a guest on my show?"

"No thanks. I'm not really into the showbiz thing," I said.

Tiffany looked at me confused.

"I think she meant me," Joe said seriously.

Which I knew. Murphy would have gotten the joke. "Oh."

"I'll consider it." He handed her a business card. "Have your people call my agent with a proposal. I'll get back to you either way."

When we left the apartment, the detective was waiting for us.

"Mr. Hannk, it was incredible that you were able to do all this. With your permission, I'd like to contact the media and hold a press conference announcing how you took down this blackmail ring. It will be great publicity for you and for the department."

"Thank you, detective. I can always use good publicity. T-Belle, what you think?"

"I'm not in it for publicity. Don't involve me."

Joe nodded. "Doing the right thing just because it's right. I like it. Detective, please keep my name out of it. You can have all the credit."

The detective frowned. I was guessing a press conference next to an A-list movie star would've actually done more for his career than getting the credit for one case would.

"Are we taking the stairs down?" Joe said.

"Stairs, elevator, rappel down the outside of the building. Whichever you want to do," I said.

Joe looked intrigued by the idea of going down the outside of the building. "Rappelling sounds like fun but I didn't really bring any equipment."

"I don't need any."

"How how about we do the stairs?"

"Sure."

No sooner had the stairwell door close behind us then Joe turned and opened his arms like he was going to embrace me.

"May I?"

"You may. Just be careful with your hands."

Joe seemed insulted. "I wasn't going to be fresh and grope you."

"I meant don't touch my wings. You'll cut yourself."

"Oh."

Joe wrapped his arms around me carefully and I did the same. We were the same height. I dipped him down but it seemed to worry him or maybe his masculinity so I brought him back up. Murphy never had problems with that.

Joe leaned in to kiss me. Part of me was thinking of Murphy and wanted to pull away but part of me wanted to kiss those perfect lips. Before I could see which part was going to win, my phone sounded a klaxon alarm and we let go of each other.

"What the heck is that?" Joe said.

"Work."

I answered the phone. This is T-Belle."

"We've got a lead on the geney. He's let loose a giant goat raptor and a pigeon pterodactyl. We have to stop them. Gani will pick you up as soon as you can put the runes on a wall for the elevator," Nemesis said.

"Boss, any chance this could wait about ten minutes? Maybe five?" I said.

"*Now*, Belle," Nemesis said in a tone that was not to be argued. Then the boss hung up.

I sighed then took a piece of chalk out of my pocket and started drawing a special sigil on the wall and then pressed the center of it. The wall started to glow with the outline of an elevator door.

"Sorry, Joe I have to go. Duty calls."

"What? Right now? But you haven't used up all your time."

The elevator door opened with a ding and Gani stepped out and grabbed me by the shoulder.

"Actually, she did. Say goodbye, Joe."

"Bye, Joe," I said as Gani pulled me into the elevator and hit a button. I waved as the doors closed and my first chance in forever at romantic kiss disappeared with it.

Lasa have guarded mankind's final resting places through the ages. The half-human Moni strives to live up to her legacy and punish those who would disturb her dead as a

Graveyard Angel

MOTHERS AND ROBBERS

Some people hear that I protect graves and they automatically assume there's a huge ick factor involved, plus everything I do happens at night. It's simply not true. A lot of what I do as a lasa takes place during the day. A lot of what I do isn't that exciting either, although that doesn't make it any less important.

As far as my personal life goes, my keeping track of things is a shambles. But when it comes to my duties as a graveyard angel it's like I have some inner personal assistant always reminding me of important dates and times. Take, for example, Mabel Flanagan. She's going to be turning eighty next week and today is the day she and her husband would've celebrated their sixtieth anniversary, but Michael Flanagan died almost 6 years ago and was buried in Calvary Cemetery in Queens, New York.

Mabel visits Michael's grave often, but she always comes to take care of it on his birthday, the anniversary of the day he died, and on their wedding anniversary.

Calvary Cemetery is huge. It used to be under my mother's protection but now it's under mine. It's a big place and like pretty much everything is these days has been hit with its share of budget cuts. However, the staff – from the gravediggers to the groundskeepers – all take special pride in their job and keep the place in good shape. I tend to take notice of people with special devotions to a grave. Now I know that in reality, the devotion is to the person who is in the grave, but in my line of work, it's a subtle distinction.

Calvary is near where I grew up in Sunnyside. In fact, Mabel still lives in the same neighborhood. She's known me since before I had wings.

She heard the subtle flapping of my ebony wings and looked up as I came to land beside her.

Mabel smiled and took my hand in both of hers. "Moni, it's so good to see you. Thank you for coming."

"It's my pleasure. I hope you haven't been waiting long." While the lasa magic may be like an internal alarm clock, it doesn't give me a whole lot of advance notice if I fogret, say if I've been out clubbing and slept in like I did this morning. I was 10 minutes late and I knew Mabel had been at least 10 minutes early.

"Not long at all my dear. It looks good doesn't it?"

I looked down at the grave. "It does." The grass was bright green, and there was a fresh bouquet of flowers on Mr. Flanagan's grave. The grave next to it looked just as good, with a matching bouquet on it.

The marker read:

Melissa Flanagan
Beloved daughter.
Taken far too soon.

Their daughter had only lived for six months and they were never able to have any other children so they were especially attentive to all the other kids in the neighborhood, myself and my brother included. Melissa's was the first grave duty my mother ever took me on. I was eight at the time and years away from my wings sprouting. Dad had lain Melissa out at his funeral home. My dad was normally the consummate professional, showing sympathy without ever breaking down himself. During the hours of Melissa's wake, my dad actually had to subtly walk off a few times and I saw him taking a handkerchief out and blotting away tears.

I had known Melissa, at least as much as an eight-year-old can know a baby. I'd seen her on a few occasions and had made her smile. Even at that young age, it seemed especially wrong for a baby to have died.

For years before I got any supernatural abilities, my mother continued to take me down and I took care of the grave as best as I could.

I placed a single white rose on each grave. Mrs. Flanagan scrunched up her face, took my hand again and patted it.

"You're such a good girl." Then Mrs. Flanagan reached into her oversized purse and pulled out a plastic container and handed it to me. "I made you some cookies."

I popped open the top and took a big sniff. "Snickerdoodles. My favorite."

"I know."

Mrs. Flanagan brought two stones with her and placed one on top of each of the grave markers. They weren't Jewish, but after the movie Schindler's list, a lot of people started adopting the custom of leaving a stone on top of the grave to show that it been visited. There were seven there now. The cemeteries staff cleared off the flowers once a week but left the stones. I put one on each of the graves as well.

"Hello, Michael. Hello, baby girl. It's been a busy few months." Mrs. Flanagan proceeded to give to give her departed husband and daughter an update on the neighborhood, friends, and relations. I did my best to fade into the background. Our section of Calvary wasn't very crowded, which wasn't unusual. Cemeteries tended to get very crowded on sentimental holidays like Mother's and Father's Day or Veterans Day. There were only two other people near us.

It took a while but Mrs. Flanagan was finally done with her updates. "Take care, Michael and Melissa. I love you both and miss you. I guess I'll see you soon, but not too soon I hope." We turned and walked away.

"Can I give you left home?" I said.

Mrs. Flanagan made a face like I've asked her to eat a bug. "Oh, heavens no. A woman my age doesn't need to be flying around with you. Besides, I'm wearing a dress. It wouldn't be very ladylike." She looked down at the skirt I was wearing. "As a matter fact it doesn't seem very ladylike for you either."

I laughed. "Don't worry about my modesty, Mrs. Flanagan. I always wear biker shorts underneath my skirts." And when on duty

I used a shroud which made me the next best thing to invisible.

"Well, I suppose that's okay then. At least I won't have to have a chat with your mother about your immodesty."

As an adult, I can appreciate how sweet Mrs. Flanagan is but as a kid, I had a bit of a different opinion. A few times she caught me doing stuff that she didn't think I should be involved in and made sure my mother knew about it before I got home.

Now I know she was just looking out for my best interest. A lot of people complained that New York City is too big and that small towns are much better for getting to know people. Those people haven't lived in my old neighborhood. The one block area where I grew up was a lot like a small town. Everyone knew everyone and as a kid, if you stepped out of line, your parents knew about it before you got home.

A lot of my magic works without conscious thought. Even though I wasn't looking, I suddenly knew that a grave was being robbed. It was Melissa's. I'd turned around quickly and Mrs. Flanagan's eyes followed mine. A young boy about ten years old had picked up the bouquet of flowers Mrs. Flanagan had left on her daughter's grave and stuck them casually under his coat.

A normal person would've probably yelled and told the boy to stop. No one has mistaken me for normal in years. I flapped my dark wings and flew up, then dive-bombed the kid, swooping in and lifting him off the ground. We did a loop and a twist then landed back in front of Mrs. Flanagan.

"How dare you steal from a grave," I yelled. The kid was freaked out by what just happened and was on the ground putting his hands and the bouquet of flowers in front of him as a shield to protect himself from me.

"Moni, you're scaring the boy," Mrs. Flanagan said.

"No one steals in one of my graveyards," I said.

Mrs. Flanagan made a *tsk* noise at me and reached her hand out to help the kid up. "He doesn't seem like a bad boy."

"He just stole flowers you bought for your daughter's grave. When I was a kid and you thought you saw me taking someone's paper off their porch, you called and told my dad. I'm seeing a double standard here."

"But I made a mistake, didn't I? You had bought an extra paper and were bringing it home because it had an ad for your father's funeral home in it. With age comes wisdom and a little more forgiveness. I was wrong about you and I think you might be wrong about this boy."

I sighed and rolled my eyes.

"What's your name, young man?" Mrs. Flanagan said.

"Dennis."

"Why are you taking flowers that don't belong to you?" Mrs. Flanagan said.

Dennis' head pivoted back and forth between me and Mrs. Flanagan. From the expressions on his face, he apparently thought she was a good cop and I was a bad one.

"I know it's wrong to take things, but today's my mom's birthday and I didn't have any money to get her anything so I took the flowers."

"Giving a mother flowers on her birthday is a good thing for a son to do, but I'm sure your mother wouldn't want you to steal something for her, now would she?" Mrs. Flanagan asked.

Dennis hung his head and looked but he was trying to bore holes into the tops of his sneakers. "No ma'am, she wouldn't. I'm sorry. I'll put the flowers back."

"See, Moni, Dennis is a good boy at heart."

Mrs. Flanagan held out her hand and Dennis put the purloined flowers into it. She reached into the center of the bouquet and pulled out a single red rose, then handed the rest of the flowers back to the boy.

Dennis wrinkled his brow and looked at the flowers and then back at Mrs. Flanagan. "But I thought you told me giving her stolen flowers would be wrong."

"It would be, but those aren't stolen anymore. I'll put this red rose on Melissa's grave. The rest you give to your mother with my compliments. It's good for you to take care of your mother."

There were tears in Dennis's eyes. "Thank you very much."

Mrs. Flanagan put her hand on his head and messed his hair. "You just make sure this is a good birthday for her, you here? You be a good boy for her and do everything she tells you."

Dennis gave her sort of a half nod, wiped his eyes then looked at me.

I sighed. Not that I had any sort of legal jurisdiction, but any claim I had to the crime of bouquet stealing was ended when Mrs. Flanagan gave them to Dennis. "Go on and get out of here before I change my mind."

Just then a hatchback pulled up and stopped at the roadway nearest us.

"That's my ride." Mrs. Flanagan handed me the rose. "Moni, would you be a dear and go put this on Melissa's grave for me, please? My knees have been acting up and I'd like to get home and put some rub on them. Would you mind?"

"Not at all. You take care of yourself."

"You too, young lady. Give your parents and your brother my best."

She got in the passenger door. I waved to her friend Mrs. Harmon and the two drove off. I flew to Melissa Flanagan's grave and placed the red rose next to the white one. I turned to fly home to Manhattan when my Lasa sense started tingling again. Dennis hadn't left the graveyard. I flew over to see what was going on, thinking maybe the kid pulled a fast one on us and was going to lift flowers from other graves, maybe to sell them to people on the street.

I landed behind him. He was kneeling in front of a tombstone that he had placed the flowers on. It read:

Daisy Addison
Beloved daughter, wife, and mother.

I pulled my shroud around me so I couldn't be seen or heard.

"Happy birthday, mom. A nice lady gave me these flowers to give to you. I love you and I miss you very much

I removed my shroud, feeling lower than a piece of crap. I knelt down beside Dennis and put my hand on his shoulder. He startled and twitched but didn't move away.

"So, this is your mom's home?" He nodded once and wiped his left eye with his fingers. "You miss her a lot?" He nodded again. "I bet she misses you too."

"Do you really think so?"

It was my turn to nod. It was true that many of the dead miss the living, especially parents with young children. "My job is to take care of graves. If you like, I can help you take care of your mom's grave. You can even tell me all about her," I said.

"That would be nice, but you've got to tell me what's the deal with those wings."

"Dennis, you've got yourself a deal."

PATRICK THOMAS is the award-winning author of 40 books including the beloved fantasy humor Murphy's Lore series, which includes *Tales From Bulfinche's Pub, Fools' Day, Through The Drinking Glass, Shadow Of The Wolf, Redemption Road, Bartender Of The Gods, Nightcaps, Empty Graves, The Mug Life* — as well as the future space adventures S*tartenders* and *Constellation Prize.*

The Murphy's Lore After Hours spin-offs star the half pixie/ogre Terrorbelle (*Fairy With A Gun, Fairy Rides The Lightning,* and *Terrorbelle The Unconquered);* the former demon-possessed serial killer Agent Karver of the Department of Mystic Affairs *(Dead To Rites, Rites of Passage);* the cursed magi Hex *(By Darkness Cursed and By Invocation Only);* Vince Argus, the Soul For Hire *(Greatest Hits);* and Negral, a forgotten Sumerian god who works as Hell's Detective (*Lore & Dysorder, Bullets & Brimstone,* and the graphic novel *The Moon Maniac* with Blair Webb).

His Mystic Investigators paranormal mystery series includes *Shadows & Brimstone* (omnibus of *Bullets & Brimstone* and *From The Shadows* with John French), *Once Upon In Crime* (omnibus of *Once More Upon A Time* and *Parners In Crime* with Diane Raetz) *Mystic Investigators, Mean Streets,* and the upcoming *Fear To Tread. Assassins' Ball* is his first traditional mystery, co-written with John French. He co-edited *New Blood, Hear Them Roar, Camelot 13* and was an editor for the magazines *Fantastic Stories of the Imagination* and *Pirate Writings.*

His other works include the steampunk *As The Gears Turn* and the space epic *Exile & Entrance.*

Patrick's darkly humorous advice column Dear Cthulhu has been running since 2005 and includes the collections *Have A Dark Day, Good Advice For Bad People, Cthulhu Knows Best, Cthulhu Happens, Cthulhu Explains It All* and *What Would Cthulhu Do?* The Dear Cthulhu advice empire has expanded from magazines and books to radio as Dear Cthulhu now broadcasts monthly on the show *Destinies: The Voice of Science Fiction* which is hosted by Dr. Howard Margolin.

His short stories have been featured in over sixty anthologies and more than forty-five print magazines.

A number of his books were part of the props department of the CSI television show and *Nightcaps* was even thrown at a suspect's head. His urban fantasy Fairy With A Gun had been optioned for film and TV by Laurence Fishburne's Cinema Gypsy Productions. Top Men Productions has turned his Soul For Hire Story, *Act of Contrition*, into a short film.

He also writes books for kids as **Patrick T. Fibbs** including the *Undead Kid Diaries: Over My Dead Body,* the *Babe B. Bear Mysteries: Bad Hair Day* and the picture book *5 Silly Monsters Jumping On The Zed: A Ughabooz book* (all with artist Shawn Evans).

Please drop by www.patthomas.net or follow him at I_PatrickThomas at Twitter or www.facebook.com/PatrickThomasAuthor to learn more.

Help is only
a Rainbow Away...

"Mix Gaiman's American Gods and Robinson's Callahan's Crosstime Saloon on Prachett's Discworld and you get an idea of Thomas' Murphy's Lore." -David Sherman, author STARFIST and Demontech

"ENTERTAINING, INVENTIVE AND DELIGHTFULLY CREEPY." -JONATHAN MABERRY, New York Times and Bram Stoker Award Winning Author

"SLICK... ENTERTAININ Paul Di Filippo, ASIMOV'S

"HUMOR, OUTRAGEOUS ADVENTURES, & SOM CLEVER PLOT TWISTS." -Don D'Ammassa, SCIEN FICTION CHRONICLE

PATRICK THOMAS

"Patrick Thomas is... so believable it's unbelievable."
-Ida Vega-Landow, The Journal of the Lincoln Heights Literary Society

DEAD TO RITES
Patrick Thomas
C.J. Henderson

rites of passage
John L. French
Patrick Thomas

When Darkness Falls
The Department of
Mystic Affairs
Picks up the pieces

From The Murphy's Lore Universe of
PATRICK THOMAS
www.patthomas.net

Find us on Facebook!

Even the things that go Bump in the night
will learn that you DON'T mess with...
Terrorbelle

Fairy Rides the Lightning
Terrorbelle
from the pages of Murphy's Lore
PATRICK THOMAS

Fairy With A Gun
from the pages of Murphy's Lore
PATRICK THOMAS

More

"Thomas certainly brings the goods to the table
when it comes to writing urban fiction...I promise, you will love...
Terrorbelle: Fairy With a Gun. Who doesn't love a well-stacked,
ass-kicking, gun-toting, woman with bullet-proof, razor-sharp win
that investigates all manner of supernatural spookiness? I know
and Thomas's humor shows through in every tale. Jim Butcher an
Laurell K Hamilton have nothing on Thomas." The Raven's Barro

From The Murphy's Lore Universe of
PATRICK THOMAS
Find us on Facebook!

Terror the Unconq
PATRICK THO

Shape up...
You only get
ONE Warning

Invocation
Only Hex Factor
PATRICK THOMAS

By Darkness Cursed
Hex marks the spot
PATRICK THOMAS

Hell's Detective

No One Is Above The Lo
Even In

LORE & DYSORDER
PATRICK THOMAS

SHADOWS IN FLAMESTONE
PATRICK THOMAS
JOHN L. FRENCH

CASE OF THE MOON MANIAC

"Dark... and charming."
- Ellen Datlow,
The Best Horror of the Year Vol. 4

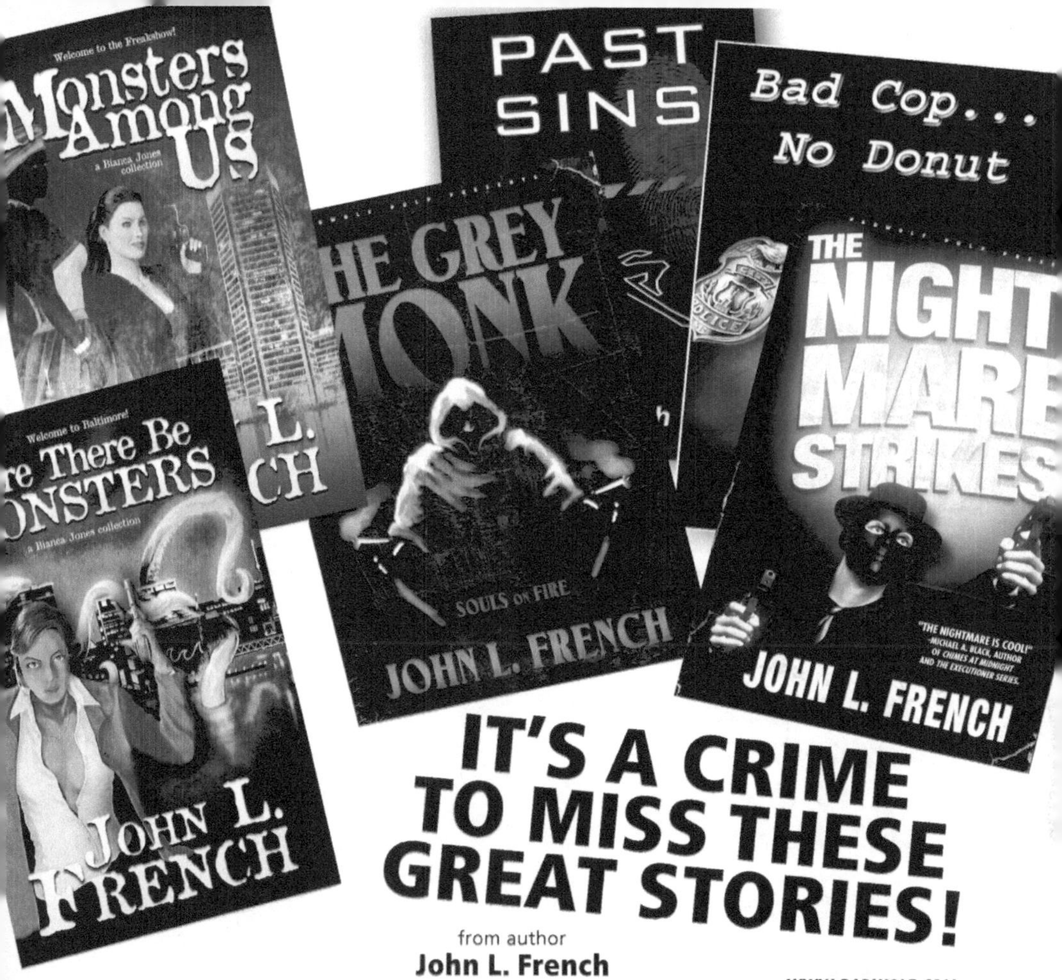

A detective's work is never done
And don't call him Baby Bear...

NO TEACHERS.
NO PARENTS
SCHOOL IS OUT....
OF THIS WORLD

15th Aniversary
Omnibus of
Books 1-6

The zombie
apocalypse
is over...

Now even undead kids have
to go to school

5 SILLY
MONSTERS
JUMPING ON
THE ZED

a picture book
for kids

www.talehaven.com

DOWN THESE MEANS STREETS
of Magic & Monsters walk the

MYSTIC INVESTIGATORS

www.ingramcontent.com/pod-product-compliance
Lightning Source LLC
Chambersburg PA
CBHW050357190726
48284CB00007BB/2322